————STAG————

ALSO BY DANE BAHR

The Houseboat

STAG

A NOVEL

DANE BAHR

COUNTERPOINT
CALIFORNIA

Stag

This is a work of fiction. All of the characters, organizations, and events portrayed in this novel are either products of the author's imagination or are used fictitiously.

First Counterpoint edition: 2024

Library of Congress Cataloging-in-Publication Data
Names: Bahr, Dane, author.
Title: Stag : a novel / Dane Bahr.
Description: First Counterpoint edition. | San Francisco, California : Counterpoint, 2024.
Identifiers: LCCN 2023041774 | ISBN 9781640096226 (hardcover) | ISBN 9781640096233 (ebook)
Subjects: LCGFT: Thrillers (Fiction) | Psychological fiction. | Novels.
Classification: LCC PS3602.A465 S73 2024 | DDC 813/.6—dc23/eng/20231002
LC record available at https://lccn.loc.gov/2023041774

Jacket design by Nicole Caputo
Jacket illustration © Brooke Figer
Book design by Laura Berry

COUNTERPOINT
Los Angeles and San Francisco, CA
www.counterpointpress.com

Printed in the United States of America

1 3 5 7 9 10 8 6 4 2

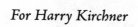

For Harry Kirchner

In loving memory of Marilynn Mancini

Mostly it is loss which teaches us about the worth of things.

—ARTHUR SCHOPENHAUER

──────STAG──────

PROLOGUE

(1989)

THE ONLY LIGHT WAS FROM AN OLD LAMP, AND THE GIRL watched them pace about in it. Lank figures the color of wax. The girl had been given a mixture of heroin and ketamine. Her clouded eyes rolling in their sockets. She lay on a spongy twin mattress on the floor and gripped the sheets as best she could. She had been dressed in a threadbare cotton shift that covered her body like skin about to be shed. The rain lashed on the wilted tar paper roof of the shack and where the roof was coming undone, plastic tarps, shredded to the point of strands of hair, attempted to restrain the water. The floors of the place were soaked. Outside, the mud, cut by tires, was deep as canyons. A black stain climbed the crumbling siding like ivy.

The shack was deep within the woods and just back from the banks of a river that ran wide and swift and milky from the mountains to the east. All manner of trash was snared in the thorns of blackberry. Shipping containers and rusted-out carcasses of cars and disfigured machinery lay hidden in the vines or half-sunk in the earth. Forgotten about and discarded just like the people who lived there.

The shack had no furniture. Only a couple metal folding chairs pilfered from the dump. Those in the living room lay stoned on pallets of moldy blankets and damp pillows. Some used needles. A blackened pipe. A couple of spoons. The kitchen was used not for food but cooking the trash and then cutting it at a round table under a single fluorescent bulb.

In her haze the girl watched them pace. Two of them. A man and a woman she knew very little about. Just two dopers the girl had been running with.

They were muttering to themselves. The girl thought she heard the woman say,

He should be here by now.

Fuck, the man said. This is all fucked.

They were harried looking in that wan light. The man kept pacing and picking at his face.

Where the fuck is he! the man shouted.

The girl slipped further and it could have been a minute or it could have been an hour when she saw a third come through the bedroom door. First as the shadow of a man and then as a silhouette against the malarial light. A towering figure filling the tiny room. His head seemingly reaching the ceiling. His movements were steady. He spoke in a low deep voice. The woman said,

We gave her the juice just like you said.

He came over to the mattress and squatted beside her and brushed away the dark hair from her forehead. Then he went to the corner of the room and knelt with the leather gladstone he'd come in with and took out a camera and a tripod and set them up. The camera's red light began to blink. Then he went back to the mattress with a length of rope.

So you got it for us? the woman asked.

Her hands were shaking. The man had not stopped picking his face.

Shh, the big man said.

He tied the girl's wrists together and then to an exposed stud so that her arms lay out above her. Again he brushed his hand over her forehead. He went back to the gladstone and from it produced a garish mask with antlers and a long, curved knife. The handle was made from some kind of bone. Polished stones inlaid in the grip.

What's the knife for? the woman asked.

Stop asking questions, the big man said.

He put on the mask and stood facing the girl. The horrible sight of him terrified her and she expelled a drugged gasp and hauled against the stud she was bound to, and when she did, moving away as much as she could, he saw a dark stain of urine on the mattress. He knelt and touched the spot with the back of his fingers. It was cold.

How long has she been like this, the big man said.

They didn't answer him.

He stood from the mattress.

I need to clean her, he said.

He removed the mask and laid it on the gladstone and left the room and stepped outside into the wet dark. He went to his car and opened the trunk. He removed a towel and went down to the river. The surface was boiling under the rain. At the shoreline he dipped the towel in the cold water, wetting half of it. Then he stood and looked up at the rain.

Back at his car he opened the trunk again. There was a duffel bag. Some jumper cables. A jerry can of gasoline. A brick of packed white powder and a pistol. The pistol he put in the waistband at the small of his back. He lifted a halo made of feathers and sticks. He carried this along with the wet towel into the shack. He stopped at the front door and looked inside. He didn't remember leaving it open. He turned back, out into the rain and the dark, but there was nothing to be seen out there. He went in and closed the door behind him.

Inside an acid haze lingered like fog. He walked toward the

bedroom, stepping over the clamor of figures strewn about the floor. The bedroom was empty. The rope tied to the stud was frayed where it had been cut, and the girl was gone. The big man stood there looking down at the mattress. Holding the halo at his side. Then he looked at the camera. The red light was still blinking.

The man and woman stumbled back into the room.

Where did the girl go? the big man asked.

She was just here, the woman said.

Yes. And now she is gone.

Did you see her go? the man asked.

Is that your question to me? the big man asked.

Where's the wash, man? the man said. His tone was desperate.

The wash?

The stuff, man. The shit. You bring it or not?

You let her get away.

We had a deal, the woman said.

You are not very smart, the big man said. Are you?

Please, the woman said. Please.

She fell to her knees and began clawing at the big man's belt. He grabbed her by the shoulders and stood her up.

We had a deal, Noon. The girl for the wash.

You let her get away.

Noon took a step back and regarded them. Then he went to the corner of the room and lifted the tripod and rearranged the camera. He looked through the viewfinder and focused the lens on the man and the woman. When he was satisfied, he stepped from behind the camera.

Take off your clothes.

What? the man said.

Take off your clothes.

Just do what he says, the woman said.

They undressed with reluctance and stood there swaying in their stupor like dead alder trees.

Get on the bed, Noon said.

He pointed at the woman.

I want you to have sex with him.

What? the man said.

The words seemed to cauterize something within him and he blinked with a sense of dire clarity.

The two of you are going to have sex, Noon said.

Just do what he says, the woman said.

The man lay down and the woman got on top of him. She began to move. She began to make sounds for some kind of effect.

Noon stepped forward a little. Cautious not to be in the shot. He said, Is he inside of you?

The woman shook her head.

Then keep going, Noon said. He went back to the camera. We are not going to fake this. He looked through the viewfinder. Said, This is the most honest thing you will ever do. This will live on forever.

A moment longer he asked her the same question.

This time she nodded and he pulled the pistol from his waistband and shot them each in the head. She collapsed onto his slatted chest and they lay there as if sleeping with the blood soaking into the mattress. He put on the antlered mask and walked over to them. Then he turned back to the camera. Said, Cut. He turned off the camera and put it and the tripod under one arm and lifted the gladstone and walked out of the room.

In the living room the others were passed out. He regarded them for a moment. He clicked his tongue in disapproval. He trained the gun at one of them but let it fall to his side. Instead, he stepped out of the shack and went to his car. He took out the can of gasoline from his trunk and went back to the shack and emptied it on the siding. Then he set the camera up again and pressed record and lit a match. He stood back as the heat grew.

PART 1

Yeh head out for the day; yeh stop someone for speedin. Yeh might think yeh know what yer pullin over but that ain't always so. I agreed to a job out in Casper Wyomin for a spell. No more than a couple months. July and August. It was Sara's idea. Thought it would be good to have a little change of scenery. This was back in sixty-three. After the whole Sellers scare. That was the first time I ever left sheriffin in Oscar, second time was when I retired. Anyway, one afternoon out in Wyomin I get a call out from dispatch. It was a Wednesday I remember. Some breakdown called in out on Glennferry Ranch Road. Some cowpuncher saw it from his horse. Took him almost three hours to ride back. Wasn't in no hurry. Didn't think too much of it. Why would he? Not unusual. Glennferry's a private road and it was trespassin for sure, but it ain't nothing to rush home and call the law about. Maybe just some kids out there kissin or somethin.

So I'm watchin this herd of antelope out grazin and the radio squelches and dispatch lets me know. Alright, I say. Took me almost a hour to get there. Wyomin is a big empty place and gettin anywhere in it takes a bit of patience.

Comin down the road I see it, the car that was called in. It wasn't runnin. I flash my lights to make sure they seen me. I hate to make the jump on anyone. That's how an otherwise peaceful day can turn out very different. So I flash my lights and pull over and get out of the truck and put my hat on and approach the car. At first it looks like two people just sittin there. But it wasn't. The side window of the driver's side is blown out and the glass all over the road is red and slick lookin. I look in on them and the guy's sittin there with half his head slumped against the door and the other half is god knows where. He still had the gun in his hand. The woman in the passenger seat had her throat cut and she was bled out down the front. He even shot the dog in the back seat. I turned away and threw up my breakfast and my lunch. Gathered myself together and wiped my mouth and then threw up again.

I called it in, though I don't remember doin so, and waited in the truck till someone came. Eerie. Just sat there watchin this car with those people in it. Found out later they ruled it a homicide suicide. As for the why? Who knows and I didn't care to. I put in my two weeks and me and Sara was out of there back to Iowa. My point in tellin all this is that there are some things you can't unsee.

1

(1989)

FROM AN UNSETTLED SKY THE FIRST SNOW OF THE SEASON
was falling. Amos Fielding was sitting in his office with his hands
laced behind his head staring at a framed photograph of his late
wife, Sara. It was mid-October and all the leaves had long since
fallen and been swept away by the north wind. His office was
entirely empty save for a box or two of photographs and placards
that had hung so long the walls were stained with the outlines
of each. The boxes were stacked near the door where Betsy, his
longtime secretary, was crying. Between sobs she said,

Where yeh going again?

Washington, Fielding said.

The capital?

Other direction.

Don't it rain there all the time?

I don't know.

It's a long way for a *I don't know*, she said.

Yeah, Fielding said. Long way.

He kept his eyes on the photograph.

Just cause Sara ain't around don't mean yeh get to fly off the
handle and move halfway round the world. You're almost sev-
enty for godsake.

Seventy-three.

You're provin my point.

Bought a small horse ranch, he said. Fully furnished. Got a whole Western motif. Paid in cash. Cheap land out there. Big back deck that looks the Cascade mountains square in the eye.

Goin a have any neighbors out where yeh going?

Nope. Just me and the horses. Suppose I ought to get a dog. Dogs like horses, don't they?

Betsy shrugged her shoulders.

Well, Fielding said, I'll get one anyway.

He could see she was hurting.

Don't take it in vain, Bets, he said.

What's that supposed to mean? *Don't take it in vain?*

I don't know. Thought it sounded good.

With all the *I don't know*s you're filled with, yeh should be able to cobble something together.

Yeh know John Wayne had a place out there. A place on the . . . the . . . Hell, what do they call it?

He looked at a magazine opened on his desk. Tapped the photo with his finger.

Juan de Fuca, he said.

Juan de what?

If yeh didn't know better you'd think it was a place filled with senoritas and margaritas.

Yeh *don't* know better.

Betsy shifted on her feet.

Yeh don't even like horses, she said.

Neither did John Wayne.

So that's it? Betsy said. That's why you're going? Cause John Wayne lived out there?

Yeh know the reason.

No I don't. None of us do. No one in this town does.

I'm goin because every damn little thing reminds me that Sara ain't here.

And how about that? Betsy said. She nodded at a box of old police records, testimonies and photographs of particularly heinous crimes collected over the decades. She said: Yeh wouldn't happen to be runnin away from that too?

Maybe, he said.

Maybe?

Yeah maybe. Maybe it's a way to forget it. To reconcile somethin. Keep it as a reminder of things I never want to see again.

Isn't there anything we can do to change yer mind?

I reckon not.

Yeh always been bullheaded.

Yeah.

When yeh hittin the road?

Fielding looked at his watch. He compared it to the time on the wall clock. He took his feet off his desk. He tucked the photograph of Sara under his arm.

Right now, he said.

He put on his hat and walked to the door and took up the last two boxes and leaned down to kiss Betsy on the cheek and then walked out of the Allamakee County courthouse for the final time.

2

THREE WEEKS TO THE DAY FIELDING WAS UNPACKING THE final box in his bedroom. A few things of Sara's he decided to hold on to. A lock of hair tied with a pale blue ribbon. Her wedding ring. A bottle of perfume. He laid them out on the bed and crossed his arms and compared them to the austere Western tones he had surrounded himself with and he wondered what the hell he was even doing out here. In this place so far from Iowa.

Nearing the end of October and he still hadn't caught sight of the mountains. Day after day they were tucked away, folded up in the oily clouds. Betsy was right, he said out loud, it does rain all the time.

His routine was simple and unencumbered. He cooked meals and washed the dishes. He started a fire and drank a little whiskey. Sometimes he read, sometimes he watched television. He got a heeler, named it Tito. At night when the rain was pounding down and the fire was warm the dog would curl into him. And every day in the last desperate moments of light Fielding would put on his hat and waxed coat and go out and see to the horses.

He had two. One was a stocky pack mule, the other an Appaloosa with a chestnut blanket and good blood. He gave the handle of Buckshot to the mule and Snake, lovingly, to the Appaloosa. Snake's proud bloodline didn't mean much to Fielding when he purchased him, but the horse's dalmatian pattern on its croup and quarters did and that, along with the striped hooves, was one of the prettiest things Fielding had ever seen.

He would wake early and pull his pants from the trunk at the foot of the bed and a snap shirt from the closet and go out to the living room and turn on a lamp and dress by the faint warmth of the stove and go into the kitchen and microwave a day-old cup of coffee. While the coffee spun on its mindless carousel he would regard his own face in the plastic window and wonder about the old man looking back. He would open the microwave door a few seconds before the timer went off out of habit because Sara had hated the sound of the beeping. Then he would put on his coat and his hat and take his coffee into the rain, covering it with one hand until he reached the barn, and switch on the lights to find Snake and Buckshot staring at him.

Under the electric light Fielding would pitchfork hay onto the floor of the stable as Snake watched with eyes so dark they seemed all pupil. Eyes so deep and pure Fielding saw his reflection in them. So pure he saw himself looking out from within.

Through the open bay doors to the west, where the sky was still full of night, the rain would fall with drops big as marbles. The yellow light of the barn would spill out into the darkness and catch the rain and hold it in place.

There was a tack room in the barn but he didn't really know what tack was other than it was associated with horses. In the tack room was a nice saddle with the leather horn so worn and smooth it could reflect the stars. There was ornate tooling in the seat and fenders and the silver of the conchos were dull with age and going black in places. Fielding had a vague idea of how the saddle might fit on the Appaloosa but knew that once it was laid over the animal's back and the billet strap cinched it would look like a pearl in the ear of a good-looking woman.

Once all his morning chores were out of the way he'd let the horses out to pasture to stretch their legs. Walking back to the house he'd turn and see Snake following him at a distance through the grass. Fielding would click his tongue and Snake would start into a trot and once he caught Fielding, he would shake his head and Fielding would rub the spot between his eyes.

Gonna catch yer death standin in the rain, Fielding would say, and he didn't know if he was speaking to himself or to the horse.

3

LATE OCTOBER AND A BIG STORM WAS BLOWING. FIELDING had a fire going in the stove and was drinking rye out of a glass that once held jelly. A detail that Sara would have admonished him for. He held up the jar. The pebbled image of the fire through the glass rippled. He thought about getting up to pour the rye into a better glass but then resigned himself to stay put.

The wind shuttered against the house. The heeler was curled near the stove and he rose his head at the sound. Then he stood and circled around three or four times and then lay back down and fell asleep. The fire behind the stove glass tumbled oddly as the wind fought the draft in the flue.

Fielding went to the window and looked at the big fir trees swaying up there in the sky. Cupped his hand at his face and watched for a while. He couldn't believe they kept standing. The rain was falling sideways. It came at the windows as if from a hose.

All this bad weather made him think about the horses and he worried about them, so he finished his rye and put another chunk of cedar in the stove and went to the mudroom and snapped on the light and found his rubber boots and pulled them on and wrapped himself in his slicker and squared off his hat and looked back into the warm room. Looked at the heeler, said, Tito, don't let that fire go out.

Outside his boots sank in the wet ground. He had to look down and hold his hat and turn sideways to the wind. The wind high in the trees sounded like a marauding beast, bellowing with an incredible kind of anger.

At the barn he went in through the man door and snapped on the light. The horses raised up. Despite what was happening outside, the barn was quiet. The rain on the roof was almost peaceful.

Boys, Fielding said. Helluva storm.

He took off his hat and slung it down by his leg and shucked off the water. Then he put it back on. He scooped a couple handfuls of oats into a tin pale and went to Snake's stall. The Appaloosa moved forward with Fielding's approach. Buckshot was looking on, blinking with big jealous eyes.

Don't worry, Buck, Fielding said, plenty for yeh too.

He put the oats in the palm of his hand and offered it to the horse. His lips moved like someone slipping on ice.

Jest wanted to come check on yeh is all, he said.

He felt something at his ankle through the boot. He looked down and the barn cat had found him and was looking for attention.

Hello, cat, Fielding said.

The cat made a gentle little sound and arched its back and put its tail in the air. Fielding reached down to pet it but when he did, the thing darted off into the shadows and Fielding didn't see it again.

Fielding gave another handful of oats to Snake and then he gave a handful to Buckshot. He stayed with them a little while longer. Petting them sometimes between the eyes.

Okay, fellers, he said. That's all. Sleep tight.

Fielding clicked off the light and in the relative quiet he could hear the horses breathing in the darkness.

He made his way back to the house and took off his boots in the mudroom and hung his slicker on one of the hooks and hung his hat over it. The room was warm and dry and the cedarwood was popping in the stove. The dog was snoring.

He poured himself another finger's worth of rye and went to the television and turned it on. He turned the knob until he found the news. Then he sat down in his chair and pulled the reclining lever.

The weatherman was talking about the storm. Talking about low pressure and isobars and rainfall amounts. Said, If you can avoid travel tonight I would recommend it. This one's a doozy, folks.

Fielding said, No kiddin.

The news anchor came on with the night's main story.

Halloween horror story, he said. The body of a young woman, identified as Amy Barnhardt, was found in the hills early this morning by a hunter and his son. The scene eerily similar to the one years ago when the remains of a young woman were discovered by local Fish and Wildlife officer, Dee Batey. Marnie has more with this bizarre story.

The screen cut to a reporter standing in the rain. Dark hair, dark eyes. She was holding an umbrella. A man beside her. Trees behind them, covered in moss.

Yes, hi, Peter, she said. She looked at the camera. I'm with Jim Delaney, the man who, with his son, came across the horrifying scene this morning while hunting up around Canyon Creek. Mr Delaney, what exactly did you see?

The man went into the morbid details. Stammering and stumbling and trying in vain to remember what was real and what was not. He had a hard time looking at the camera or at her. Visibly shaken. Almost in shock.

She signed off and Fielding watched a little longer. They

showed a shot of the scene: the crude altar the woman had been laid upon, the stone cairns, the burned-down candles, the gruesome ornaments of feathers and bones hung in the trees. Fielding went to the television and turned it off. He gazed out the window into the howling darkness.

In the corner of the room was the box of old police records. He turned and eyed it with suspicion. He had sealed it with packing tape so he'd never have to open it again. But he knew. He knew every detail of every word of testimony. A lifetime's worth. Some of the records had photographs to accompany the testimony. Just a snapshot of the body at a horrible angle. But Fielding had been there and seen it all and talked to the victims' mothers and fathers and husbands and wives. He never spoke to the children, figured it wasn't his place. But they still looked at him, and that was just one of the many things he was trying hard to leave behind.

He looked back at the dead screen of the television. The wind slashed at the windows. He put another log on the fire because it suddenly felt very cold, and he stood next to the stove and tried to feel the fire's heat.

4

THE SUN SLOWLY ROSE OVER SEATTLE. THERE WERE SHOALS
of pink clouds in the sky and all that pink was stamped in the
glass of the skyscrapers. In an upper floor of the government
building, Philip Wilson stood at a large table with his shirt-
sleeves rolled to his elbows, leaning on his fingertips, poring over
a few dozen eight-by-eleven black and whites scattered over the
polished metal. His black tie was in a loose Windsor and the
tips were tucked in between the buttons of his shirt. The cup of
coffee from the night before sat untouched.

The photographs were morbid. Scenes of violence. Expired
lives. Figures of grim fate. Poses supplicant to madness and lu-
nacy. All of the bodies were naked and all of them female. Some
appeared merely sleeping, almost peaceful. Some crumbling
with decay. Wilson had studied these photographs so many
times that when he closed his eyes he saw the gray limbs, the silent lips, the dead hands and feet as clearly as if he were standing
over the bodies.

He had categorized them based on motives and timelines
and had them numbered in different folders with the victim's
name below. The manila folder he examined now had the number three written on it. In capital letters: BARNHARDT. The

door to the office opened and then closed but Wilson did not look up.

Sleep at your desk again? the voice said.

Hmm? Wilson said, his eyes focused on the photographs.

You look like shit.

Wilson saw the captain standing there with a cup of coffee in each hand. The captain handed one to Wilson but Wilson motioned with his chin to the cup already on the table.

Suit yourself, the captain said.

Wilson was thirty years old and tenacious. Even at that hour, despite what the captain said, all he would have to do was tighten his tie and he'd be ready for dinner. He didn't drink and he didn't smoke. Wasn't married and didn't date. He was eager to make a name for himself and volunteered for the most violent crimes as if to prove he could handle it. *Stomach it*: that's what the other agents would say. But not Wilson. He didn't like to dilute language.

The captain reached out and turned the folder on the table and read the name.

Barnhardt, he said. That the girl found up in Whatcom County?

Yes sir.

How long you been looking at these pictures?

I don't know, sir.

Go home.

I'm fine, sir.

I'm not suggesting, Agent Wilson. Go home. That's an order.

Outside the building the clouds had moved in and the sky was gray. The tops of the buildings were lost in the mist and the wind was coming in off the sound. An hour later he was sitting in his bare studio apartment in his one chair staring at the wall. The room had nothing in it and every wall save one was empty. The wall Wilson was staring at, however, was covered in clippings and photographs. There were articles and testimonials and pictures of the victims before their demise and pictures of the victims' friends. There were names and places written on a chalkboard. There were pictures of suspects thumbtacked into the drywall and a little note by each detailing their background and their crimes.

He sat for a long time with his hands in his lap. Just looking at the wall. There was an answer in there but it wasn't giving itself up. His fingers drummed against his forearm. His lips muttered mutely over and over: Barnhardt, Barnhardt, Barnhardt.

When his watch read 12:09 a.m., he went to the kitchen and put a TV dinner in the microwave and watched it cook under the yellow light. When it beeped he took it out and ripped away the plastic wrap and took up a fork and standing in the kitchen he ate whatever mash it was. It was too hot but he didn't seem to notice. His eyes never left the wall of evidence. When he was done he drank a glass of water and threw the plastic tray in the trash and washed the fork and water glass and stood them on a hand towel near the sink. He went into the bathroom and brushed his teeth. While he was brushing he leaned out to look at the wall as if to make sure it was still there. When he was done he rinsed and spit and then pissed and then turned off the bathroom light and looked at the wall a final time. He turned off the light in the living room and got undressed and lay down in his bed and pulled the blanket over his chest and looked up at the ceiling and listened to the rain falling against the window until he fell asleep.

5

FIELDING WAS SHOVELING SHIT FROM THE STALLS WITH A
wide flat shovel and pitching the stuff into a wheelbarrow. His
horses in other stalls watched him from over the boards. When
that was done he eyed Snake and said,

What say yeh? Go fer a ride?

He moved Snake into the open and got down the blanket
and saddle. The blanket was white and red with black chevrons
and the red was faded with years.

He lay it over Snake's back and then lifted the saddle. Snake
stepped uneasily.

Whoa, Fielding said.

He passed the latigo under Snake's barrel and cinched it to
the billet. He stood back and let Snake get the feel for it. Snake
watched him through the blond hair of his mane.

Alright? Fielding said. Goin a put this on yeh now.

Fielding slid the bosal over the horse's muzzle and tightened
the hackamore and draped the rope back over Snake's head and
dallied it on the horn. Snake snorted at him.

What's that about? Fielding said.

He said, Yeh know what's goin a happen.

Said, You wouldn't toss a old man, would yeh?

Fielding led the horse into the field, stepping at the horse's

pace, a little unsure and not wanting to force anything. I'm probably doin this wrong, he said to himself.

Out in the open grass he looked at the horse. There was no
wind and the sky was overcast and the air was cool. The ground
was soggy and made a lot of noise. He heard the chittering of a
bird and he looked up to where a kestrel had taken perch on a
wire going to the barn. Tiny little thing. Even in the pallid light
its pastel feathers were colorful. It cocked its small head down
and waited for something.

Fielding said, Okay, Snake. I'm goin a climb up now.

Fielding gripped the horn and put his boot into the stirrup
and swung his leg over and sat the horse holding the braided
rope of the hackamore. Felt pretty proud of himself.

Go for a walk now? he said.

He nudged the horse on with the heels of his boots but Snake
did not move. Fielding tried it again. This time a little harder and
at that Snake bent around and nipped him in the shin.

Damn, Snake, Fielding said. Yeh goin a be a rascal about this?

He clicked his tongue and said giddy up because it sounded
like the right thing to say and in an instant the Appaloosa was
pounding over the wet earth with the water shooting out from
under the hooves like bird shot. Eyes big as dinner plates and his
knuckles on the hackamore rope gone white as ivory. He called
out to the horse to halt but the Appaloosa was in full gallop.
Fielding gripped the horn. Hundred yards from the barn and
Snake came to a sudden stop by digging his dalmatian hooves
into the ground and in a cartoonish fashion sent Fielding cart-
wheeling into the wet grass.

Fielding lay there for a moment wondering how much of him
was broken. The water soaked through the back of his coat and
jeans. He had lost his hat a ways back. And as if in jest Snake
stepped over and with his damp nose nudged Fielding in the ribs.

Little devil, he said. Yeh meant to do that.

He rose stiffly. From heel to collar his backside had been painted in mud. The horse stepped closer and put its face into Fielding's chest, looking to get pet.

Yeh little devil, he said again.

He took up the rope and started back to the barn, leading the horse. Along the way he found his hat upended in the grass and he dipped to pick it up and wiped the mud from the crown and slung it against his thigh and then put it on. He looked to the dark mountains to the east where wisps of low clouds like parched cheesecloth were tumbling through the high valleys in the cold wind. It felt like it might snow. In the settling dark the doves were coming out to call to one another. The horse was breathing and Fielding's boots sucked in the mud but all else was silent. The light coming from the open barn looked like a refuge.

A mist began to fall and Fielding walked the Appaloosa into the barn. He finished feeding the horses and cleaned up and then left the barn during a break in the rain and looked west over the flat country where the sun was sinking below the plum cloud bank. Fielding had to squint and fashion his hand in a visor to block the light. For ten minutes the sun remained in that void between cloud and horizon, quaking like a mirage. And then the sun sank and darkness came again.

6

THE NEXT MORNING FIELDING AWOKE EARLY AND MADE HIS
coffee and shaved and then went to the barn and fed and talked
to the horses. By the time all of that had been taken care of it
was still early. He'd found a café in town and decided to get some
breakfast.

It was a place called Ted's Country Café but it wasn't in the
country and there was no one named Ted. There was a linoleum
counter and the smoking section was near the back. He always
took a table by the window. The waitress always called him
honey or sweetie or dear. She had long legs and wore cowboy
boots and Wrangler jeans and she had a reputation that could
only be described as flirtatious.

It was still dark when Fielding showed up. He ordered eggs
over easy and wheat toast with black coffee. The waitress pointed
her pencil at him.

You're the one who bought the old Harris place out past
Twelve Mile ain't you?

Maybe.

Got horses? Or are you just one a them hobby ranchers?

Two horses, Fielding said. One's a mule.

Two horses and a mule?

The one is a mule.

So just *a* horse, she said.

Mule ain't a horse?

A mule's a mule, she said. Just like a dog's a dog and cat's a cat.

And a bird is a bird, Fielding said.

Now you got it.

She smiled at him and he smiled right back.

And I'm a Cheryl, she said.

I know, Fielding said.

So what are you?

Old enough to be yer granddad, that's what I am.

She laughed at that and hit him in the arm with her order pad.

An order was called from the kitchen and she winked at him and turned heel.

Fielding picked up his paper and popped it but before he could read anything he heard someone say:

You the one from back east?

Fielding looked over the top of his paper. There was a uniformed man sitting not far from Fielding's table. Fielding said, If yeh consider Iowa back east.

I suppose everything is east of here, the man said.

Amos Fielding, Fielding said.

Dee, the man said. Dee Batey.

Dee Batey? That sounds made-up.

I guess it is a little. Someone had to make it up.

Based on the uniform the man was wearing Fielding asked if he was a game warden.

Fish and Wildlife, Batey said.

Don't call it a game warden no more?

I don't know.

Fair enough.

You want a little company, Batey said. See you in here most days. Don't want to intrude on your routine none.

That'd be fine, Fielding said. Got all kinds of new routines these days.

Batey stood and took his saucer and coffee and paper and went to the table. He set the coffee and paper down and then they shook hands. Cheryl brought the pot of coffee and refilled their mugs.

Thank you, darling, Batey said.

You know animals, don't you, Dee, Cheryl said.

Batey tapped the insignia on his chest.

Is a mule a horse? she asked.

A mule's a mule, he said.

Thanks, Dee, she said. She winked at Fielding again. Your eggs are almost ready.

They both watched her walk back to the kitchen.

Yeh think she had to practice that walk? Fielding said.

Practice got nothing to do with it.

I think she might like me, Fielding said.

Hate to steal your wind, partner, but she likes everyone.

Too young for me anyway, I suppose, Fielding said. Wouldn't even know where to start. Must have one understandin husband.

Hell no, Batey said. Jealous as a penguin.

What's that?

Jealous as a penguin? Bird that can't fly.

That a Fish and Wildlife thing?

I don't know. Just come up with some things sometimes and hope one or two will stick.

Fielding sipped his coffee. Batey pointed at it.

Will never go below half, he said.

Sign of a good place, Fielding said.

Sure is.

Your name rings a bell.

What kind of bell?

Then it occurred to Fielding who this man was. Fielding snapped his fingers.

You're that warden who found that body up in the mountains. All them years back. Heard it on the news the other night.

Yes, Batey said. He looked down at the table and combed his black hair over with his fingers. That was unlucky.

Heard they found another.

Also unlucky.

They sat there nodding at each other. They sat there for a while. They drank their coffee. There was music playing in the café. It sounded like it was coming from the ceiling. Batey pointed a finger upward.

You like this, he asked. Grunge music, they're calling it. The kids love it.

It's all I hear these days, Fielding said. This or that Madonna lady.

You don't like Madonna?

Fielding shrugged. Kind of spooky, if yeh ask me. Kind a like a siren.

Like the one with a light?

Like in the sea, Fielding said. Them pretty girls that would call sailors into the rocks. That's what she reminds me of. She'll call yeh in with that pretty voice and that pretty face and then she'll eat yeh alive.

I can see that, Batey said. What kind of music do you like?

Older stuff, I suppose. I ain't too good on names anymore.

Uh-huh, Batey said. What kind of cheese do you like?

Cheese?

Yeah.

What kind of question is that?

Just a question.

Fielding thought. Orange, I guess.

Orange?

I guess.

Uh-huh.

Uh-huh, what?

Orange cheese, old music, and you take your coffee black. You're a simple man, Mr Fielding. And I mean that in a good way. Everyone these days is trying too hard to be complicated. Everyone's a goddamn artist.

Yeh got kids, Fielding asked, nodding at Batey's wedding ring.

Yes sir. Eighteen and twenty. Both girls. Both out of the house.

Must be quiet.

Deathly. But it has its moments of solace. How about you? Any kids out there?

Not that I know of.

You got a missus tending the new homestead?

No sir, Fielding said. I'm what yeh call a widower.

Oh, Batey said. Shit. I'm sorry.

Nah. We had a good run.

It was almost 8:00 a.m. and still dark and all the trucks passing the café had their lights on and through the streaked glass you could hear the tires zipping on the wet asphalt and when there was no traffic the rain could be heard on the café's windows and sometimes, faintly, on the hood of Batey's Bronco parked just beyond the glass.

Sun ever come out around here? Fielding asked.

Oh sure, Batey said. There's a week or two in July when you can almost get a sunburn. What did you do back in Iowa?

Sheriff, Fielding said. Small town of Oscar.

Sounds made-up.

Like your name.

Batey smiled.

Must have been quiet, Batey said. For a lawman, so to speak.

It had its moments.

World's gone crazy, Batey said.

It's always been crazy. It's jest new flavors.

Yeah, Batey said. New flavors.

Yeh always been Fish and Wildlife?

No sir. DEA. A few lifetimes ago.

DEA, Fielding said. Bet yeh saw a few things.

A few don't even scratch the paint. I got stories that'll curl your toenails.

Well, Fielding said, we'll always have somethin to talk about, I suppose.

Not sure if any of that needs to be said ever again.

Fielding just nodded.

The front page of the paper had a picture of Amy Barnhardt on it. Senior photo. Little caption of achievements. The accompanying article had a few vague details. Both men looked down at it. Batey shook his head.

They're saying drugs are playing a big part in all this, he said. Autopsies coming back with all kinds of nonsense loaded into these girls. Cocktails of shit that could knock out a Clydesdale. Pardon my French.

I suspect we'll start seein more suits and ties round here.

I suspect you're right. Batey sipped his coffee. Maybe you can lend a hand in all of it?

In all of what?

An old lawman might come in handy around here.

Count me out, Fielding said. That life's behind me.

Nothing's ever behind us, Batey said. As long as we can still remember it, it's there.

Yeh read Schopenhauer?

Schopen-what?

Arthur Schopenhauer, Fielding said. He said life swings backward and forward between pain and boredom. When we're in pain we want the numbness of boredom and when we're bored we want to feel somethin else.

Sounds bleak, Batey said.

Yeh've never lived through a Midwest winter I take it. Anyway, Fielding said, I'm tryin a keep that pendulum right down the middle. No pain, no boredom.

Sounds nice.

Sounds is one thing. Doin is another.

I take it back, Batey said.

Take what back?

That stuff about you being a simple man.

Ah, don't let it fool yeh, Fielding said. I'm as simple as they come.

7

IT HAD SNOWED DURING THE NIGHT AND DAWN BROKE COLD
and clear and the stars were paling against the growing light until there was only a single faint star left. Fielding watched it till
it too was gone. Then he led Snake unsaddled from the barn
and out the gate and down the drive toward the county road
where the snow was untouched. It was a heavy, wet kind of snow.
Full of water. Wherever Fielding stepped he made a little puddle. Snake's breath smoked from his nostrils like exhaust from a
machine. At the road they proceeded, Fielding leading the horse
by the reins, the wet snow coming up to Fielding's ankles and the
horse tossing his head in the cold air.

The road was empty. He saw no one. There were only the
marks of one vehicle. Coming or going, Fielding could not tell.
The mountains rose up in the east. It was the first time he had
seen them. He paused at the sight of them and said, My god. *My
god* for their absolute beauty and *My god* for the absurdity that
he had not seen them until this moment. He counted out the
days he had been there. He had lost track. He stood and stared
east. The mountains towered. That there could be such landscape seemed inconceivable. The tallest and most prominent
stood white and impenetrable. The whole range seemed to have
a destructive quality that he could not reconcile.

How bout that, he said to Snake.

He said, I've never really seen mountains before.

Said: Do they all look like this? Huh, horse?

Snake nickered and tugged back on the rope.

Alright, Fielding said.

They kept on. Fielding was leading the horse with his head turned toward the mountains and he talked to Snake like Snake was capable of comprehending. Alone as he was, he was walking down the middle of the road. The muffled noise of a truck over the snow shook him from his daydream and he turned and saw the brown paint of a Fish and Wildlife vehicle. Fielding moved to the side and the truck slowed as it came upon Fielding. Fielding turned his head and squinted at the Bronco, and recognizing the face through the glass Fielding shook his head. When Batey leaned over and rolled down the passenger window Fielding said, Not a word.

What are you doing? Batey said.

I'm walkin my horse.

You're supposed to ride him.

He doesn't like it.

Doesn't like it?

Doesn't like it.

He tell you that?

He's a horse, Dee. Doesn't speak English.

If you aren't going to ride him then why do you have a horse?

Fielding stopped. He looked at Batey.

There something I can help yeh with?

Nah, Batey said. Just out driving around. Burning up some gas. How about that, eh?

He nodded at the mountains. The sun was hitting them and turned the snow pink.

Never seen em before, Fielding said.

I grew up here and I never get tired of it.

Somethin special. Feels like a storybook kind a thing.

I hate to be the one to break it to you partner, but you're living in a storybook kind of place.

There was a moment of silence. Only the horse breathing in the cold air.

Stopped by your place, Batey finally said.

Wasn't there was I?

Glad I ran into you.

Why's that?

Wife wanted me to get you over for supper.

Tonight?

Any night.

Alright.

Fielding started walking again. Batey let out the brake. Started shaking his head.

You really aren't going to ride him, are you?

Ain't up to me, Fielding said.

Alright then, Batey said.

Okay.

I'm getting on then. Talk later.

Fielding lifted a hand as Batey drove off. He looked back at the mountains. The sun had climbed higher and the mountains were no longer pink but stark white against the blue sky. He turned to Snake. He said, Ride yeh? Heck of a thought.

8

THAT AFTERNOON THE PHONE RANG. FIELDING ROSE UP FROM the sofa and went to the kitchen. Said, Hello.

Amos?

Who's this?

Dee.

Twice in one day?

Figured you might like a beer after walking that Appaloosa of yours.

Wore me out.

How's an hour sound?

It was a little tavern Batey had suggested on the phone. The Logger Inn. A place with neon signs and small windows and trucks parked out front. A rustic kind of place. Taciturn men and peanut shells on the floor.

Fielding showed up ten minutes early. He saw Batey's Bronco already there. When he walked through the front door the wood floor was dark with water and there was country music playing on the jukebox. All the men at the bar turned as one like some theater prop, but seeing Fielding and making their judgments turned back again. There was a couple of deer heads mounted on the wall. A mountain lion sprung in some perpetual attack.

Fielding heard a whistle and found Batey sitting alone in a booth at the rear of the bar.

Get you one, Batey said. Got a tab going.

Fielding went to the bar and leaned on the old wood and a middle-aged woman with platinum-blond hair and a lot of cleavage asked what he was having.

What's he havin? Fielding asked, nodding at Batey.

Ginger ale.

Ginger ale?

What're you having?

Beer, I suppose.

Rainier?

What're my choices?

Rainier.

Okay, Fielding said. Twist my arm.

She held the glass under the tap and drew off a pint and slid it to him.

Fielding thought that was a good trick and said:

Yeh ever spill one?

No, the woman said plainly.

Fielding nodded but she had already turned. Fielding took his beer and went back to the booth.

Mr Fielding, Batey said. Batey held out a hand to the bench across the table.

Fielding sat down and took a drink off the beer.

Thanks for the call, Batey said.

Yeh called me, Fielding said.

Well, Batey said, Cora was getting tired of me anyway. One of her shows was on. Probably for the best.

Which one's got her locked up?

Dynasty, I think, Batey said. Or maybe *Dallas*. Yeah. *Dallas*. I don't mind *Dallas*.

No?

Nah. Me and Sara used to watch that together every week. That J.R. is a mean sumbitch, ain't he?

I wouldn't know. I hear that song and see those opening scenes of the flyover of all that boring Texas country. Batey shook his head. I hightail it out of there.

It was musicals for me, Fielding said.

Musicals.

Sara loved em.

You don't like music?

I like music. Musicals is different. How they break randomly into song. Ruins the story for me.

I'll have to watch one sometime.

Fielding looked around at the place.

Got a good feel in here, Fielding said.

You get the occasional college kid every now and then, Batey said. When they want to feel authentic and tell their friends they went to a *dive bar*. But they're few and far between.

Yeh ever miss being young?

Occasionally, Batey said. You?

No, Fielding said. I like knowin what I like.

Batey held his glass to toast that sentiment.

So, Fielding said, what does a Fish and Wildlife officer do out here on the edge of the earth when he's not watchin *Dallas* and rubbin his wife's feet?

Ha, Batey said. Don't let her hear you say that. Put ideas into her head. Batey sipped the ginger ale. What do I do, he said. What do I do. I guess I tinker around in the barn. Change a light bulb. Fix a leaky faucet.

Jack of all trades, Fielding said.

Cora wishes, Batey said. He snapped his fingers. You know what I do? Just got really into it.

What's that?

I tie flies.

Flies?

Fly-fishing. You know. Batey made a casting motion. Dry flies and nymphs. Blue-winged olives. Elk-hair caddis. Bead head prince.

Woolly bugger, Fielding said.

You fish?

Sure.

We ought to go. There's some great holes on the Nooksack. The big salmon runs. You ever spey cast?

No sir.

I'll teach you. Easy. Throwing big streamers. Big streamers for big fish.

I've seen pictures, Fielding said.

Pictures ain't nothing. When you see it for yourself. Live in the flesh. All that big water and all the eagles, a bear or two. Mountains all around.

Sounds like a heart-stopper.

You bring the coffee, I'll bring the gear.

That sounds like a deal.

Deal it is.

Both men drank at the same time. They were both quiet. Fielding wondered about the ginger ale but knew better than to ask. Finally Batey said: You going to eat?

Nah. Had a bite before I came. Try not to drink on an empty stomach. Learned my lesson.

I hear that, Batey said. He shook his ginger ale and gave Fielding a look.

But, he said, you do get hungry, they make the best cheeseburger. Scout's honor.

Yeh been to Missoula? Fielding asked.

Montana, sure.

Place there. The Missoula Club. Nothin but fluorescent lights. A big flag reading: Montana Till I Die. About a quarter inch a grease on all the liquor bottles. But I tell yeh what, yeh won't find a better hamburger. Cheap too.

Cheap, Batey said. That's key. I was down in Seattle last year. Ordered a hamburger in this sparkly little place. Looked at the menu to see how much I was in for. Damn near seven dollars. Can you believe that? I said no way. Waiter brought it to the table and I told him to take it right back. Of course it embarrassed the hell out of Cora. But seven dollars is seven dollars. And no hamburger in the world is worth seven dollars.

Fielding nodded. Goddamn inflation.

Goddamn inflation is right.

There was a small silence between them again. Waylon Jennings on the jukebox. A couple of men in Carhartt jackets walked past the booth and said Batey's name. Batey nodded. Then Batey asked a question Fielding felt he'd been wondering about.

So tell me, he said. How does a guy like you, forty-odd years as sheriff, just up and quit and move three thousand miles away? And don't tell me it's just because you miss your wife.

Fielding squinted at him. Then he took a drink off his beer.

Horses, Fielding said. Always wanted to be a cowboy. Like John Wayne.

John Wayne hated horses.

Fielding smiled.

Hell, he said, I don't know myself sometimes. Probably the same reason yeh ain't DEA no more.

But I'm still a little bit the law, Batey said. When you're the law, and I mean L-A-W, that's in your blood. You just up and quit. Cold turkey. So what was it? Certain incident?

Incident?

What got you spooked?

Fielding took a long sip of beer. He looked up at the mountain lion snarling down at them.

See that cougar? Fielding said. They made him out to look like the bad guy, didn't they? But he ain't bad. Someone shot him and then someone else stuffed him and arranged his teeth and claws and eyes like that, and when we look at him we're supposed to see an enemy. Somethin we can't trust. But that cougar wasn't doin nothin wrong. Poor guy probably out mindin his own business and then got treed by some hounds and a man with a gun shot up at the tree and that cougar just fell out of it. And now here it is, collecting dust. I look at that cougar and it's not fear I feel. I only have pity for it. Compassion. Because that's what cougars do. They eat other animals so they don't starve. And all the things we find frightenin about them are simply their tools so they can eat. So to answer your question: How does someone like me just up and quit? They do it because they have seen too many awful things done to other people. Not out of survival or sustenance, but for sport. Malice and anger. I had to quit because I couldn't face the survivors. The wives and husbands. The kids. The next of kin and offer my condolences anymore. Words didn't mean anythin to them at that point. Words couldn't bring em back.

Fielding looked at his beer. Swirled it a little. Took a sip.

I came out here, he said, so I would never have to tell anyone I was sorry for their loss ever again. Because all the things yeh want to forget are usually the worst things. And those things seem to last forever.

When Fielding got home that night he found Tito asleep on the floor near the woodstove. There was a low pulse of ember yet and Fielding opened the stove and fed in a chunk of cedar and closed the door and sat down on the sofa and watched the fire take. Tito lifted his head. He climbed up beside Fielding and lay his head in his lap. They sat like that for a long time. Fielding looked at the box of police records in the corner of the room. A box full of ruined lives no one had any answers to.

9

LINED UP ALONG THE SIDEWALK RUBY AND THE OTHERS WAITED
in various states of composure for the doors of the shelter to
open. A wide awning offered them a small respite from the rain.
The street gutters ran with dirty water. A man wearing three
pairs of pants and a tank top stomped in the middle of the wet
street shouting some gibberish. His hair was matted into three
or four dreadlocks and bleached the color of stained teeth. Ruby
sat huddled against the wall with her knees pulled up and her elbows resting on her knees and her head buried in her arms. She
might have been asleep. The others in line paid the crazyman no
mind and didn't look at him when he ventured in from the road
to yip at anyone foolish enough to give him attention.

Ruby sat there unmoving. The crazyman came in from the
rain and began to shout at the others. They all pretended not
to hear him. As if he weren't even real. He skipped down the
sidewalk like a fairy-tale character and something about the desperate girl must have appealed to him and he stopped in front
of her and put his hands on his knees and bent over and spoke
softly in some cryptic tongue. Then he squatted on his hams and
asked the same incoherent question and when Ruby looked up
the crazyman must have seen something in her bloodred eyes

because his own eyes flared and he rocked back on his heels, falling onto the sidewalk and pointing a gnarled finger at her, saying: You! You have been marked! Your soul is blighted by shadows!

Darkness! he screamed. Darkness!

A woman came and kicked at him like one would a feral cat. Git, she said.

The man on all fours now, trying to crawl around the woman and look at the girl again, had fallen back into the chattering of the insane.

Git, I said, the woman said again. She kicked him again and he howled and lifted himself from the concrete and limped-ran into the street and kept on with that loping run till he found an alley and disappeared into it. The few in line that had found an interest in the scene had returned to their malaise and looked straight ahead or down at the ground as though nothing had happened.

Ruby looked at the woman's boots. They were shiny. They went halfway to the woman's knees. They had a squared toe. The kind a biker would wear. The woman knelt and cocked her head at the girl. She reached out and tilted the girl's chin up so she could better see her face. The woman watched her for a long while without saying anything. There was a sound and the doors of the shelter swung open and the destitute line began to move forward like stockyard animals knowing they're about to be fed.

Come on, the woman said. You come with me.

The girl tried to stand but fell back into the concrete. Her legs had given out. There was no strength in them. The woman knelt again and helped her up by holding one of her hands and placing the other around the girl's small waist. Seeing her stand now, the woman took note of the track marks on her arms.

Let's get you inside, the woman said. Get you warmed up.

They stepped slowly with the others and when they got to the doors the woman spoke solemnly to the pastor standing in the entrance. Said, This one needs a bed.

On a bed no wider than a cot the girl lay in a fetal position. The woman sat beside her and tried asking questions but the girl stayed quiet. The woman wondered if the girl was mute. But then she said, Can I get a cup of water?

Of course, the woman said.

She raised her hand and the same pastor came by and asked how he could assist.

Are you hungry? the pastor asked. You must be.

The girl said nothing. Stared straight ahead as if afraid to look at him.

The woman said, Bring something along, won't you, Pastor Lee?

He went away and the woman spoke.

He's a wonderful man. I've never met anyone kinder.

The woman pulled the blanket up around the girl's chin.

She was a woman who had seen hardship but her enameled spirit kept her from quitting. She was small in stature with small hands and small feet and wide hips and large breasts. She had tattoos on each arm that ran down to her small hands and each tattoo stopped just back of the knuckles. A tattoo of a woman being carried away by a giant raven across her chest. She had short black hair that was cut like a boy's and a hoop nose ring. Her name was Dani, she said. She was thirty-two years old.

Are you warm enough? Dani asked.

The girl nodded.

Where are you from? Dani asked.

Where are we now?

Port Cook.

There were enormous windows on all sides of the room and Ruby could see a tall fir tree out one of them and she watched as the wind came in off the water and bent the tree and drove the rain against the window with such force that the glass seemed lacquered with water. The lights flickered in the gust. The girl flinched under the blanket at the sudden hint of darkness and the woman looked down and saw the girl was pinching her eyes shut and she said,

Nothing to be afraid of. Just a little wind.

The pastor returned with the water and a plate of banana bread.

I didn't know if you care for it, the pastor said, but I took the liberty of bringing you butter for the bread.

Dani thanked the pastor and he went away. She helped the girl to drink the water. She broke off a chunk of the bread and offered it but the girl shook her head.

You should eat something, Dani said. It'll help.

Ain't hungry, the girl said.

How long have you been out?

I don't know.

Are you using?

The girl was silent.

When was the last time?

A long pause. Then: A few days.

Who's chasing you?

How do you know I'm being chased?

You have the look.

What kind of look?

Scared.

The girl looked into her lap.

You're safe here, Dani said.

The girl's hands were trembling and Dani reached out and held them.

You're in here, the woman said, and the world's out there.

But you can't use. Can't drink. Can't help you if you want that. Got to make a choice.

The girl nodded.

Dani stood to leave. She said, I'll let you rest. I'm going to check on the others. I'll be back.

But the girl grabbed her leg.

He's coming for me, the girl said.

Who?

Him. He's out there. He's going to find me.

Suddenly Ruby burst into tears. She began to sob uncontrollably. The others in the room ceased what they were doing and all turned their heads as if they were all fastened to the same string.

He's out there, Ruby said. He's hunting me.

The girl began to howl. Dani tried to console her but it did no good. The pastor quickly came and together he and Dani lifted the girl from the bed and ushered her into a private room off the chapel. The room was small and simple. There was a twin bed and a cross nailed to the wall above the bed. There was a bookshelf holding copies of the bible. There was a desk opposite the bed and a single reading lamp and a legal pad that had some of the pastor's scribbling in it. Above that was a small oil painting of Jesus on the cross.

They lay the girl down on the bed and Dani closed the door behind them. The girl was terrified and could not speak. Could only mutter some word in an unintelligible whisper over and over and over again. Her eyes racing like marbles in a gutter. She sucked air between each whisper like a toddler after a tantrum. All Dani could say was, Shhhhhh.

It was hours before the girl could utter a real word. The pastor had gone at Dani's request to get some fresh clothes and some fresh underwear and some gauze for the girl's cut feet. He returned with them along with a basin of water and a hand towel and a bar of soap.

Dani was seated on the bed with the girl. The pastor sat at the desk with his legs crossed. They had had the girl's supper brought in but it went untouched and stood cooling on the bedside table with the steam of the meal twisting up in a thin thread until all of the heat had gone out of it.

What was that name? the pastor finally asked. He asked it carefully. It was like pushing a small boat into the sea after a storm.

Name? the girl said.

I think it was a name, he said. Sounded that way, at least. The word you kept repeating.

Horns, Ruby said.

Horns? the pastor said.

Yeah.

Why horns?

He was wearing horns.

The girl had her head on the pillow. Dani was seated beside her, holding her hand. Dani and the pastor looked at one another.

What kind of horns? the pastor asked.

Twisted kind, the girl said. Like a deer has.

The man was wearing antlers?

Ruby stayed quiet. Then she said, I just saw horns. Just the outline of horns.

You've seen the devil, the pastor finally said.

The girl's lips were starting to ripple and her breath was beginning to jump.

Dani said again, Shhhhhh, and smoothed down the girl's hair. We don't need to talk about that anymore. You're safe here. He's a million miles away.

The girl closed her eyes and when she opened them back up

Dani and the pastor were gone and the clock on the wall near the desk read 8:04 p.m. The sky behind the windowpanes was black. There was rain falling on the glass. That and the ticking of the electric heater were the only sounds. Ruby stood from the bed and went to the door and turned the lock and went back to the bed and sat down and looked at the oil painting of Christ on the wall and then up at the crucifix over the bed. She watched the rain on the glass window. She went to the bookshelf and opened a bible and thumbed through its thin pages and then set it back down again. She undressed in the wan light of the lamp and fully naked it turned her skin orange. She looked down at herself. Full of bruises and smudged with dirt. Her legs full of cuts. Little pin marks in the crook of her elbow where the needle had lanced her. She recognized none of it. Only nineteen but she appeared years older. A lifetime even.

She went to the basin of water and took up the hand towel and soaked it and dabbed it at her skin. She dipped the towel and the water went cloudy. She cleaned herself up as best she could and then put on the fresh underwear and the fresh clothes and then crawled back into the small bed and fell asleep with the light on.

In the middle of the night came the fever and shaking and all the terrible effects of withdrawal. She had sweat through the clothes. The sheet beneath was wet. She trembled under the blankets, balled up like some abandoned newborn. With her eyes pinched shut it all came rushing back. In that strained darkness came the gnashing teeth of the devil who haunted her. The terrible horns rising up into the air and tearing through anything proud enough to stand before them. That mouth full of daggers glinting in the spectral light to unhinge and swallow her alive.

And in the big room where the others slept, over the sounds of snoring and sleep talking, the girl's screams could almost be heard through the walls.

10

IT RAINED FOR DAYS. THE STREETS RAN WITH WATER. ALL THE smaller streams and creeks swelled and all the sedge along their banks were under half a foot of runoff. Not quite a flood but a far cry from dry. Fielding kept the horses in the barn most of the day because he felt bad for them, having to just stand around in all that rain. At twilight one day he let Snake out to pasture and watched as the horse found some spirit and pounded out over the wet grass. The ground bursting under its speckled hooves and the long mane swept back like the tail of a comet. When Snake returned, he was breathing hard with his nostrils big as poker chips. The horse allowed Fielding to pet him between the eyes. And then Fielding led the animal back into the barn.

Earlier that day Batey had called about supper. Said: Cora won't take no for an answer. So at half past six Fielding pulled up to their place. He put the transmission into neutral by swinging the long stick like a railroad lever. He kept the engine running. He leaned forward over the wheel and looked out the windshield. The rain fell steadily. It pattered on the hood, on the roof.

The house was on a ranch of its own. Just shy of two hundred acres. Horse country. There was a barn with stables for thirty or so animals and a covered arena with floodlights. As Fielding drove in he could see the heads of horses above the boards of their stalls. Beyond the arena was a large pasture and beyond that a wall of cedar trees. Even in the darkness the place looked well cared for.

Parked in front of the house, Fielding kept the headlights on for a time and then turned them off and once he did he saw the curtain in the front room pull aside and saw Batey's hand raise in welcome. Fielding returned the gesture and then he cut the engine.

The front door opened as Fielding took the last step. Batey was in a cowboy shirt with pearl snaps. He was wearing a rodeo belt buckle. It caught Fielding's eye.

Should've brought my spurs, Fielding said.

Batey looked down and tilted the buckle upward.

He said, I take her out for special occasions.

Well I hope for yer social life's sake I ain't considered a special occasion.

Come on in, he said. Stand out here long enough it might stop raining on us.

Inside Batey took Fielding's coat and hung it on the wall. Fielding took off his hat and Batey took that too. Fielding smoothed down the hair at the back of his head and looked around at the home and he took a certain amount of comfort in its simplicity. The decorum was quaint and western looking. There were rugs on the hardwood. There was a woodstove burning in the main room and the air was warm and dry. There were framed photographs on the wall of two girls at various stages of life. Fielding had his hands in his hip pockets and leaned in to look at the pictures. The girls were riding horses in most of them.

Yer girls? Fielding asked.

Sure are, Batey said. That's Lola there. And that one's Emmy Lou.

Sunny names, Fielding said.

Ironically named for their stormy dispositions, Batey said with a wink.

Fielding smiled at that.

I'm just kidding, Batey said. Cora would tan my hide if she heard me say a thing like that.

Who's the elder? Fielding asked.

Lola, Batey said. Two years. Premed. Emmy's studying law. Both at Bowdoin. Can't say Cora cares for them to be so far away.

A doctor and a lawyer, Fielding said. No belt buckles for them.

Oh, they got em, Batey said. Good riders both. Barrel riding. Mama don't let yer babies grow up to be cowboys. Or cowgirls.

Ain't that the truth. Come on. Sit by the fire.

A woman came from the kitchen. She had an apron wrapped at her waist. Behind the apron Fielding saw she wore a pale yellow dress that fit her nicely all over. She was wiping her hands on a rag. She was tall and beautiful and her hair was still thick and black. Her skin was the color of cedar and she had a long neck and big dark eyes that Fielding couldn't quite look directly into.

This is my wife, Cora, Batey said.

She came proudly into the room as if leading an army.

Coraline, she interjected. In case your sentiments reside in more well-rooted ways.

Fielding looked at Batey.

I think she just called me old, he said.

Her face blushed.

Don't worry, mam, Fielding said. I am old. And I like Coraline. I like that just fine.

She did not take his hand which he offered but embraced him like a longtime friend not seen for quite some time.

Taken you long enough to get over here, she said.

Has it? Fielding said. He looked at Batey. Fielding was genuinely confused by that statement. He felt he'd only just met Batey himself.

Well, you're here now, she said. Dee, won't you get him a drink?

What do you take, Mr Fielding? Batey asked.

What are yeh havin?

This here's a club soda with lime.

How about somethin with a little more kick.

Get him a bourbon, Dee, Coraline said.

One, Batey said, holding a finger out sideways and then his middle to accompany the first. Or two?

That one, Fielding said, pointing at Batey's two fingers.

Well, come on now, Coraline said. Sit, sit.

Fielding sat on the sofa near the stove and put his hands on his knees like a teenager waiting for his date to come down the stairs. The leather under his legs squeaked. It had a rich smell. It smelled like the woodstove and the woodstove reminded him of Christmas Eve.

That's the hot seat there, Coraline said.

I like it, Fielding said. Can't seem to get warm enough out here.

Then you sit as long as you'd like, she said. I got something cooking that I need to see to. Make yourself comfy.

And then she went away. And for a moment he was left alone in the room. It was quiet save for the wood popping. The house smelled nice and for the first time in a long time he felt at ease. Behind the stove there were ancient pieces of horse tack hanging like art. There were paintings of horses on the walls and paintings of men and women riding those horses. There was a braided coil hung up that Fielding assumed was once used for roping.

There were some Navajo blankets and jars of feathers from different kinds of birds and a neat stack of elk sheds on a wall table. Above that was an antler display with a dream catcher hanging from one of the points. Fielding was looking up at it when Batey came back into the room.

Like her? Batey asked.

Her? Fielding said.

Batey was holding a glass in each hand. He pointed to the elk rack on the wall.

My first, he said. Got it when I was sixteen. Out in eastern Washington. Shot it and the dude took off on me. Couldn't believe it. I'd been watching the herd all day. Took the shot two hours before sundown. Stupid.

Batey crossed the room and handed one of the drinks to Fielding. Then he went to the other sofa and sat down and took a drink and crossed his legs.

That little devil took off on me. O-F-F. Full-on sprint. I tracked him to a fence line of this ranch out there. This was fall, when they were driving the cattle down out of the mountains. Sure enough the track runs right into the drive. Cows everywhere. No sign of it. No blood. Nothing. The cows are getting all edgy and I'm right there in the middle of it. Then I hear this whistle and this old cowboy comes riding up on me. I mean it was right out of a movie. He's all silhouetted with the sunset behind him. His skin looks like leather. So here's me, this sixteen-year-old punk kid with a big-caliber rifle on his shoulder in the middle of this cattle drive in the middle of nowhere. I don't know how much you know about cowboys but they don't take kindly to strangers with big guns walking around their herd. Anyway, so he comes up on me. He's got this rifle laid across his lap. Got his thumb on the hammer. Rides up and stops and looks down at me. And I mean I'm frozen. Not a muscle. He says: Long way from the schoolyard ain't you, son? I say, I'm tracking an elk I shot. An elk, he says. Yessir, I say. An elk, he says again. No way he believes me. Not a chance. And you know why? Because no one's dumb enough to shoot an elk at sunset, that's why. I started to stammer a bit. Searching for an explanation. Just then I look down and there's the blood. I pointed to it and said, There! My voice squeaking like a little girl. This old cowboy leans over and looks down and nods and says: Well, I appreciate you not givin up on it, but my name's Bill Slack and you're disrupting my cattle drive. Next time I'd suggest aimin. And then he sort of smiled and winked at me. And just like that he rides off. I'm telling you, just like a movie.

You find it? Fielding asked. The elk.

Wouldn't have those antlers if I didn't, Batey said. Took me most of the night. It was a smart animal. Knew what it was doing. There were patches of snow where I'd catch the blood then it'd go cold. I'd have to go back and set my hat down where I last saw the blood and then start walking circles around it. He was zigzagging all over. When I finally caught up to him he was in a bed of willows. He just stood up and stared at me. He knew the fight was over. I shot him again and he bled out right there. Middle of the night. I dressed him, quartered him, packed it all out. Got back to the truck at eight o'clock in the morning. Twenty-five hours in all. Then I see something hanging on the antenna. I go around and find it's a dream catcher and it's got a note attached to it.

Get some sleep, kid. You earned it. Signed Bill Slack.

Batey sat back and took a drink and looked up and admired the trophy. He had a look of exhaustion on his face. As if the retelling were arduous. As if he'd just tracked that elk all over again.

That's a heck of a story, Fielding said.

One of the happiest days of my life, Batey said. Marrying

Cora, birth of my daughters, and that day with that elk. He raised his glass. Best days, he said.

Batey took another drink. He looked as proud as if the story reminded him of youth and what youth feels like and the things a young man can do and get away with. Things that seem limitless and untouchable. Things an older man wouldn't dare.

The two men looked at one another as if agreeing upon things that didn't even need to be said.

Coraline came into the room and shook them out of it.

Is he telling you his elk story? she said.

Yes mam. Heck of a story.

That story is shaped like a bell, she said.

A bell?

It starts off down here, she said, then gets more exciting and Dee with it, till finally it peaks and Dee's a young man again and then it falls off and he realizes those days are gone. Look at him. He's feeling nostalgic.

Nothing wrong with nostalgia, honey, Batey said. If it wasn't for nostalgia, we'd forget about everything.

She turned to Fielding.

Are you a hunter, Mr Fielding?

No mam, I am not, he said. And we better get into the habit of Amos. Only time it's Mr Fielding is when I'm in trouble.

Very well, she said. Amos. Has a horse ranch. Not a hunter. What else is there?

She looked at his wedding band.

Is there a Missus Amos that we are leaving out tonight?

Missus Amos passed away a little while back, he said. He looked at the ring. Habit, I suppose.

I'm sorry, Coraline said. I shouldn't have made a joke.

That's fine, Fielding said. Yeh didn't know. I don't take yeh for a cruel woman.

Any children?

No mam. Would've been nice though. I will say that.

They sat a moment in silence, not saying anything but listening to the fire in the stove. Coraline was wearing a bracelet with turquoise in it and the blue of the polished stone was bright against her dark skin. The dress had no sleeves and the skin of her arms was as smooth as the turquoise. He knew she wasn't but she could have passed for thirty-five. Maybe even thirty. Her arms were lean and she had the strong hands of a woman familiar with horses. In fact, it was her hands that gave her away. Maybe even tacked on a couple of years.

Even though he knew the answer, Fielding said: Yeh ride horses too? Seems everyone but me rides horses out here.

Yes, she said. Barrel riding. I was on the circuit for a while. Some good money in it. If you win.

Did yeh win? Fielding asked.

Most of the time, yes. Most of the time I won.

To Batey, Fielding said: Is that how the two a yeh met? Barrel riding?

Men don't barrel ride, Batey said.

So how'd yeh meet her?

You want to tell it? Batey asked his wife.

No, she said. I'd hate to interrupt you.

It was down by the river, Batey said. One summer day. I was sleeping with my hat over my eyes. Had my horse tied off to a cottonwood. I hear this noise and I wake up to find her sitting on her horse bareback. She's in these short shorts, long legs that looked like they could wrap around that pony twice. Boom. That was it. Struck with the lightning bolt, as they say. Cupid's arrow.

I was twenty, Coraline said. Dee was twenty-two.

Twenty, Fielding said. He shook his head. Goldang.

Goldang is right, Batey said.

I'll have to sit with that for a while, Fielding said.

So you bought the old Harris place, Coraline said, changing the subject from her nice legs. You must like horses too.

Yes, Fielding said. But they scare the hell out of me. Pardon my French.

No pardon needed, Coraline said. They can be a scary fucking animal. Do you ride often?

No, Fielding said. But I take Snake for walks every day.

Walks?

Yeah. I walk him.

Batey said, Remember I told you I found him walking that Appaloosa down the road.

That's cute, Coraline said.

I think he appreciates it, Fielding said.

Appreciates it how? Coraline asked.

Not bein ridin. All that weight. I know I'd appreciate it.

But you're not a horse, Coraline said.

We got a understandin.

And what's that?

He won't buck me if I don't ride him.

Well, Coraline said, you know what they say: When you fall off the horse . . .

What about bucked off the horse? Fielding asked. They got any wisdom for that little chestnut?

I'm going to teach you to ride, Coraline said.

Fielding looked at Batey.

Batey shrugged. Don't look at me.

What do you say? Coraline asked.

I'm a bit of an old dog.

That woman could teach a blind pig to ride, Batey said.

Well that's good, Fielding said. Cause that's what we're workin with here. A blind old pig.

Tell you what, Coraline said, when you're not working on this case I'll come over and we'll ride around a bit.

Case? Fielding said.

Aren't you involved with this body being found?

No mam, Fielding said. I'm retired.

Dee said it was pretty horrific what they're saying in the papers.

And I ain't carin to see it myself. There's some things in this world yeh can't unsee.

Suppose that leaves more time to learn to ride then.

Now yer speakin my language.

Once you learn you'll find great happiness in it, Coraline said.

Fielding smiled sardonically and laughed through his nose.

What's so funny? Coraline asked.

Nothin, Fielding said. Happiness, I guess. Happiness is what's funny.

I'm guessing not the *ha ha* kind of funny.

No mam. It's a finite thing, happiness. It's fickle and it changes shapes. Heck, it's a little like the sun out here: when it shines yeh got a take note because it ain't goin a last and soon it'll start rainin again.

That's a very cloudy outlook, Coraline said.

It's a cloudy world.

You have those horses, Coraline said. That nice place in the country. Must count for something?

Oh sure, Fielding said. The other night I put Snake and Buck out and right as I did this gorgeous sunset hit. Wham. And with the horses standin there. It was somethin.

There you go, Coraline said.

Yeah, Fielding said, but then it was gone. And then it just got dark.

Batey just sat there watching him. Not saying anything. Just watching.

Every night, Coraline said. It always gets dark. Helps us sleep better.

That's a nice way of lookin at it.

Couldn't appreciate the sun if you never saw the moon, she said.

And if my feet could fit a railroad track, I guess I'd been a train.

Is that poetry?

My point in all this is, he said, in all my years sheriffin yeh accrue things. Things yeh want to hold on to and things yeh want to forget. Sometimes the things yeh want to forget outweigh the ones yeh want to hold on to. Life is a long and cold winter but sometimes the sun comes out and when it does yeh got to be ready to open yer eyes and embrace it cause it ain't stickin around.

Later that night after they'd eaten and after Fielding had gone home and the kitchen was cleaned and all the dishes put away and they were getting ready for bed, Batey said to Coraline:

You think he really believes all that? All that stuff about life being a long cold winter?

I think he's lived longer than us.

You think it's that simple?

Nothing is ever that simple. Nothing worth living for anyway.

11

THE SHELTER WAS EMPTY DURING LUNCH. RUBY HAD BEEN there for almost a week. Dani came and sat with her. She had a slice of pie in each hand. She set one in front of the girl and then set the other across from her and sat down. She said, You mind if I sit?

No, the girl said. Her voice was soft. Almost a whisper.

No, you don't want me to sit? Dani asked. She said it in a playful sort of way. A way that made Ruby smile a bit.

There it is, Dani said. I knew there was a smile in there. It's a nice one too.

Dani sat down.

How are you liking it here? she asked.

Ruby shrugged.

Sure, Dani said. What a dumb thing to ask. It's a shelter, not a Howard Johnson.

Ruby smiled thinly with her lips together. Her shoulders were slumped. Her hands in her lap.

It's chocolate cream, Dani said, pointing at the pie. You like chocolate cream?

I don't know, Ruby said. I've never had it before.

Never?

No.

Well, Dani said. I think you'll like it.

Dani cut a bite with her fork and leaned across the table.

Here, she said. Try it.

Ruby reached for the fork and took the bite. She chewed and nodded.

You like it? Dani asked.

Ruby nodded again.

Good, Dani said. You have as much as you want.

Where do you stay at night? Ruby said.

I have an apartment down the street.

How long?

How long what?

How long you been there?

Almost a year. I was in a halfway before that. When I stopped using, I had to prove that I stopped using. That halfway helped.

You live with someone there?

The halfway? Of course.

No. Your apartment. You live there with someone? Your boyfriend or something?

The corner of Dani's mouth lifted.

You trying to find out if I got a sweetheart at home?

No, Ruby said, I was just—

I'm teasing, Dani said. She put her hand on Ruby's. I'll show it to you one day, okay? Have a girl's night. Watch a movie.

Okay, Ruby said.

That night Dani left the shelter thinking Ruby was asleep, but when Ruby heard the door close she opened her eyes and got dressed. She followed Dani at a safe distance so as to not be seen. Ruby kept looking back so she wouldn't forget where she had come from. At a building with the name and year it was built carved into the stone, Ruby watched Dani greet a woman standing near the door. Dani and the woman embraced and kissed and then went in through the doors holding hands. Ruby waited to see if they were going to come out again but they never did.

Ruby was making her way back to the shelter when a car passed. Driving slowly. Ruby couldn't make out the driver but it looked like they were searching for the numbers to the address of a building. The brake lights flared and the car came to a stop in front of her. Ruby kept on and when she passed the car she noticed the passenger window was cracked a bit and a voice said: Maybe you could help me?

Ruby stayed on the sidewalk. Squinted as if to see into the car but it was too dark to see anything.

You live around here? the man said.

No, Ruby said.

You know of any good hotels in the area?

No.

The man didn't say anything. Just his outline against the wet street. The exhaust was smoking up from the car. As it passed the taillights it burned cherry red.

A police cruiser was coming up the block and when it saw the car idling in the street the cruiser flashed its light. Ruby saw the man wave to the cruiser and then put the car into drive.

I better get out of this rain, Ruby said.

Yes, the man said. That's a very good idea. Thank you for your help.

Then he drove off. The cruiser turned and Ruby was left alone on the sidewalk.

The next night Ruby asked, Why are you being so nice to me?

It was raining and the rain was popping on the glass of the girl's room.

Dani was sitting behind her, combing her hair. Dani said: Why am I what?

Why are you being so nice to me?

Dani stopped a moment. Then continued combing. Said, Because the world is cruel and some people don't deserve to be treated the way they have.

Like I've been.

Yes, Dani said. Like you've been.

You make me feel safe.

Good.

Ruby turned around toward Dani and tried to kiss her. Dani leaned away. Ruby tried again and Dani grabbed her shoulders and held her there.

That's not what this is, Dani said.

What're you trying to get out of this then?

Helping you, Dani said. That's what I'm trying to get out of this.

Ruby moved away on the bed.

Ruby looked down into her lap. She started to pick at her nails. Dani reached and quieted her hands.

He's going to find me, Ruby said.

Who?

The one who's chasing me. If I leave here, he'll find me.

Then don't leave. We'll go to the police, okay? File a report.

They're not going to know anything.

That's their job.

Not this, Ruby said. Not about this.

You don't have to be afraid, Dani said. I'll be there with you.

Dani finished combing Ruby's hair and stood from the bed and lifted Ruby's legs onto the mattress and pulled the covers up to Ruby's shoulders. She went to the door and turned and looked at the girl.

That life you lived, Dani said. You never have to go back to that. That all happened to someone else. Okay?

She turned off the light. She said, I'll be just outside if you need me.

Then she closed the door.

About a half block away a car was parked with its engine running and the wipers swishing back and forth in the rain. The driver of the car was sitting behind the wheel with his arm laid over the back of the seat. He watched the shelter, watched the small square of light from Ruby's room snap off and the whole building go dark save for the neon cross glowing on the roof.

Found you, he said.

PART 2

One evenin out there comin up the drive I saw somethin flash. Not like it was movin or alive. Just a flash in the headlights. Caught my eye. I stopped the truck near the stables and backed up and put the truck in neutral and pushed in the brake. I got the flashlight out and shined it into the woods. I've never been afraid of the woods in the dark, but for some reason that night I was. Felt like a child who's afraid of the dark. But I walked into the woods anyway and what had caught my eye was a single wing of an owl. I lifted it and spread the feathers out. Yeh ever see an owl feather? Odd lookin, but very pretty. Very different from other birds. The trailin edge is soft so it doesn't cut the air and make a sound. Silent. But that's what got me. Somethin out there got that owl. Somethin quieter than silence. I held that wing there in the dark woods with the flashlight in my mouth and those feathers spread and I couldn't help but feel helpless. Nothin is above an owl at night. Or so I thought. But there it was, just the wing. Somethin out there got it. Somethin in the dark. Left a single wing as a warnin. Left it there for the rain to fall on. For me to find it.

12

A PHONE CALL CAME EARLY IN THE MORNING, WAKING FIELDING from a dream so vivid it might as well have been real. In the dream he was walking with Sara down the sidewalk of Oscar, Iowa, on a warm evening. Just as the birds were beginning their evening songs. All the storefronts were closing up. They were holding hands. Just walking, not saying a word. The air was sweet smelling and there were children running down the sidewalks. In the dream they were still old but Sara's hand felt young. Felt like the first day he had held it. They walked like that all the way home and then sat together on their porch swing. Still holding hands and still not saying anything. The lightning bugs blinking on and off in the warm air like far-off satellites. They sat there till the stars came out. Finally, Sara said, Nice night. Sure is, he said. Then they went up to bed and together they fell asleep.

The ringing phone tore all that away and Fielding rubbed his eyes and looked at the clock on the bedside table. Saw that it was a little after five. The phone stopped ringing and then it started ringing again. Who the hell, Fielding said. He threw off the blanket and walked to his robe hanging on the door and put it on and walked to the kitchen where the phone was ringing on the wall.

Yes, he said quickly.

Amos.

Yes.

It's Dee.

Why the hell yeh callin me so early?

Is it early?

It's still dark.

It's November. It's always dark.

What the hell yeh want?

I'm headed over.

Over where?

Your place. Get dressed.

Dressed? Hell, I ain't even awake yet.

Then wake up.

I need to wake up before I can wake up.

Need your lawman eye on something.

Think I misheard yeh. Sounded like yeh said lawman.

They found another, Batey said.

Another what?

Body.

What kind a body?

You know.

Not sure I want to see that.

Not sure I do either.

Then don't, Fielding said.

Not sure I have a choice.

We all have choices. Everyone has a choice.

I wish that were true.

It is true. Why yeh goin in the first place? Yeh ain't the police.

They called me up. Maybe because I've seen it before. Want me as a witness or something. I don't know.

Well sounds like yeh got it all taken care of then. I'll just head back to bed.

Be good to have your opinion.

Fielding took the phone from his ear and let it fall to his side. He could hear Batey on the other end. Fielding looked out the window. It was dark and raining.

Yer an idiot, Amos, he said to himself.

He brought the phone back to his ear.

Who you talking to? Batey asked.

No one, Fielding said. Where yeh at?

The station.

How long till yeh get here.

Could be there in twenty.

Then I'll see yeh in twenty, Fielding said. But only to prove it ain't our business anymore. Okay?

Fielding hung up the phone. He went and started some coffee. Heard the heeler behind him and when he turned he saw Tito sitting just within the light with his head cocked, acting like he was about to be fed.

Don't look at me like that, Fielding said.

The dog cocked its head the other way.

Don't yeh know it ain't even day yet.

Thirty minutes later Fielding was riding shotgun in Batey's Bronco. He was holding his mug by the rim so he wouldn't spill on himself.

You know they make mugs with lids these days, Batey said.

I'm startin to regret ever talkin to yeh.

The wipers were working against the rain. The sky was paling to the east, and the flat country to the west was taking shape under the gray light. They were driving west through farmland. Winter cropland with flooded furrows and the remnants of past harvests standing brown and shorn like whiskers.

Where yeh takin me anyway?

The beach.

Fielding looked out the window and tapped on the glass.

Hell of a day for the beach, he said.

It was a long drive. They had to get on the freeway at one point. They drove north. Fielding started seeing signs for border crossings. A place called Blaine. A place called Sumas. It dawned on him that he was nearly in Canada. In that rain and darkness he suddenly felt very far from home.

The freeway ribboned through stands of tall cedars and firs. Trees that knew the world before people did. Old trees that had seen the world change many times and with grace many to come.

They pulled off at an exit and turned west and drove through low country with vines of blackberry and half-dead scrub trees no taller than bicycles. They drove through tidal flats where the mud at low tide had a sheen like oil and thin-legged plovers and herons stepped mechanically among it with their heads bobbing like tin toys, their long faces tilted to see their prey below, to strike as quick as electricity and then step off again in search of more.

Death from above, Fielding said.

What's that?

Nothin.

The road bent at the shoreline of a shallow bay that was protected from the wind. Fielding could see the wind blowing out there. The water was darker where the gusts were hitting the surface. Looked like shifting stains. All the big trees had given up by this point and they were into a coastal landscape of grasses and crippled pine that huddled low and thick against the earth like battered soldiers. The road led out to a spit no wider than a four-lane interstate. Out at the end a harbor of grim fishing boats moored to creosote docks.

But before all that Fielding saw the lights of several patrol cruisers in the accruing dawn and the yellow tape ratcheting in the wind.

Found em, Fielding said.

How's your gag reflex? Batey asked.

Gaggy, Fielding said.

They pulled to the side of the road and one of the officers recognized Batey's Bronco. The officer walked over in his long slicker. Batey rolled down his window.

Morning, the officer said.

Yes it is, Batey said.

The officer leaned to get a better look at Fielding.

You Amos Fielding?

That all depends.

The officer grinned and then nodded.

Pleasure, he said. Marty Rawlings. Deputy.

Well? Batey said.

About like you might think, Rawlings said. Want to take a look?

Rawlings stepped back to allow Batey's door to open. Fielding said, This is goin a be somethin we can't unsee. If yeh catch my drift.

They exited the Bronco and the wind came at them and tried to convince them to turn back. Fielding shut his door and went around the front of the Bronco where the two men were standing and together they crossed the road to a short boardwalk leading to the beach. They stopped at the end of the boardwalk and looked where the yellow tape had been strung up around the body.

The beach was in the lee of the dune where the wind was abated. Fielding looked down at the washed-up eelgrass clumped like discarded whale's baleen. Bleached driftwood tumbled smooth as stone pushed against the high-water mark. Old pieces of construction and rotten pilings with squarehead fasteners rusted into the wood. Twists of rebar tangled like root balls.

Forgotten feathers of dead birds. On the crest of the dune the dune grass and the dogwoods heeled over and the thin stalks of sedge threatened to snap in the wind and the stunted pine grew sideways because it knew no better.

They walked together to where a small crowd of onlookers was gathered. Some with cameras. Some holding bandannas to their noses. The faintest bit of smoke was twisting up from a burned-out pile of wood.

Someone reported it last night, Rawlings said. Saw a fire going.

It was the same as before only now the body was half burned. She had been laid on a bed of driftwood. Her skin was black and pink and yellow and was stretched tight and where it wasn't stretched it was peeling away. There was no hair left. Her lips were gone and her mouth was slightly open as if calling out and her teeth were a brilliant shade of white against the black skin. Batey and Fielding just stood there squinting their eyes. Scattered about were a dozen or so miniature structures. Little cairns arranged with no real discerning sense or order. Each cairn had a number laid out by it for evidence's sake. A halo of barbed wire and vines had been placed on her head.

They ID her yet? Batey asked.

Not definitively, Rawlings said. But they got a guess. Molly Summers. Eighteen-year-old runaway from Lynden. Her grandmother reported her gone three days ago. Seems to fit the profile anyway. Have to confirm off the dental records.

Batey nodded at a young man standing near the scene. He was wearing a long coat and holding an umbrella. Expensive-looking shoes.

Who's that? Batey asked.

Agent up from the bureau, Rawlings said.

Seattle?

Yep.

He got a name?

Wilson, Rawlings said. Sticks to himself. Peterson told me he's part of the special crimes unit.

Special?

Yeah, Rawlings said. The kind of a sexual nature.

I see, Batey said. Well, suppose we go introduce ourselves.

They walked over to where the man was standing. He turned and regarded them with a plain look.

Rawlings started it off. Held out his hand to him.

Deputy Marty Rawlings, he said.

The man shook his hand.

Agent Wilson.

Pleasure, Rawlings said. This is Dee Batey and Amos Fielding.

Wilson shook their hands in turn.

Are you deputies as well? It seems I've met more deputies out here than civilians.

No, Batey said. Fish and Wildlife. Fielding here's retired.

Retired? Wilson said. Retired from what?

Sheriff, Fielding said. Small town back in Iowa.

So a game warden and a retired small-town sheriff. Wilson's lips thinned. What are you two even doing here?

Fielding said, That's a heck of a good question.

Wilson gave Rawlings a look.

Dee here found that woman in the hills all them years back, Rawlings said.

What woman? Wilson said. Lots of women been found up in the hills.

That one in the cave that made that big splash in the news.

Wilson's demeanor changed. As if everything suddenly came into focus.

Oh, he said, *the* Dee Batey. I've studied that case extensively. Still unsolved.

Yes, Batey said.

I would love to pick your brain sometime, Wilson said.

Not much to pick.

I've read your accounts many times, Wilson said. I was always intrigued that he arranged her the way he did after defiling her.

Defilin her? Fielding said.

Yes, Mr Fielding, Wilson said. Congress. Intercourse.

He did that to her, Batey said. After she was dead?

Yes, Mr Batey. Several times. And I suspect the last time he did it he knew it was going to be the last and so he arranged her the way he did. A final goodbye, if you will. A remembrance.

What do yeh mean the last time he did it? Fielding said.

He had returned to her, Wilson said.

Returned? You mean to . . .

Yes, Mr Fielding. Right up to the point of putrefaction.

Putrefaction, Fielding said.

Decomposing, Mr Fielding. The fifth stage in the death process.

Wilson watched them to gauge their reaction. All three of them looked away at that statement.

And I believe, Wilson said, this is what happened here. Also with Amy Barnhardt. I trust you have heard about her. I believe it's the same perpetrator.

But this is a popular beach, Batey said. A woman's body wouldn't just be left here and go unnoticed for three days.

No, Wilson said. She was brought here. As a final resting place. Maybe at one point she expressed something about loving the water. Or maybe he does. But he brought her here, maybe connected with her a final time and then started the fire.

So you think he carried her out here? Fielding said.

Wilson smiled a thin smile and said, I want to show you something.

Between the fire and bank of grass where the beach ended there were dozens of fluorescent markers. The markers highlighted boot prints. The boot prints went out to the fire and came back again. Wilson knelt down to one of them. He pointed things out with his finger.

See how this print is deeper than this one? See how it wavers slightly? How this one here walking away from the fire is even and the pace is regular as if just going for a stroll on the beach?

Let me guess, Batey said. Not just a stroll?

See how the heel is marked on this one? See how it goes deep into the sand? This tells us a lot. Tells us he was carrying something.

Or someone, Rawlings said.

You can follow these prints all the way to the fire. You can see the moment he put her down. His next step is lightened.

Yeh can tell all of that, Fielding said, just from a boot print?

Ask Mr Batey here.

Ask me what?

You're Fish and Wildlife, Wilson said. You must have done a fair amount of tracking in your time.

Sure, Batey said. Fair amount.

And?

And what?

And would you agree that whoever made these prints was carrying something heavy?

Yeah, Batey said. Yeah I would.

But why the fire? Fielding asked.

Wilson shrugged his shoulders.

I don't know, he said. Anger. Regret. Ablution.

Remorse? Rawlings said.

No, Wilson said. Remorse would indicate some kind of empathy. Whoever did this lacks that. Remorse wouldn't even register. Incomprehensible. There is a ritual taking place, however. The cairns. The halo. The crude dolls they're finding in the trees about. What do they mean or symbolize? Again Wilson shrugged. What we do know is that it's typical behavior.

Typical behavior? Fielding asked.

Perpetrators like these have a ritual they perform. It doesn't always have to be elaborate. Perhaps *routine* is a better word. People who do this like their routines. Ritual has the connotation of a cult, and I don't believe any of these were the result of a cult.

Like Manson? Rawlings asked.

Yes, Wilson said. Take Bundy for example. He would bring his victims up into the mountains and visit them several times. He believed a part of his victim's soul was now a part of his. That the two souls were joined forever. No cult there, but it is a ritual. Remember Berkowitz?

That Son of Sam shit? Batey said.

He believed the same thing. Believed that the ground he shot those people on was hallowed. And just like Bundy he'd return to the place to . . . reconnect. If you will.

Did he . . . Rawlings asked timidly.

No, Wilson said. He never engaged in necrophilia but it was of a sexual nature. After he would visit the site he would often go home and masturbate.

Sick shit, Batey said.

Yes, Wilson said. Definitely a disease.

So that's what we have here, Rawlings said. We got another Bundy on our hands? Another Berkowitz?

No, Wilson said. His face darkened. There's something else

going on here. This is something new. These kinds of killers are like artists, they're always trying to invent something new.

New? Fielding said.

Wilson motioned with his hand. Come here.

He walked them to a taped-off area about fifteen feet from the fire. Wilson pointed at the sand.

What does that look like? he asked.

There were three marks in the sand. Evenly spaced. Three points of a triangle.

Looks like three dots, Fielding said.

What would make three dots in the sand? Wilson said. He was asking it almost rhetorically. As if to play this out a little longer.

A tripod would, Batey said.

Yes, it would, Wilson said.

Why would there be a tripod here? Fielding asked. Steady a gun?

Not a gun, Mr Fielding. A camera.

You think this guy was taking pictures? Rawlings said.

No, Wilson said. I think he filmed it. I think he films every one.

13

WILSON ENTERED THE COURTHOUSE THROUGH THE HEAVY WOODEN
doors and went to the directory on the wall and ran his finger
down the list till he found Chief Price and tapped the name.
Price had an office on the fourth floor and rather than the elevator Wilson took the stairs. He wore a gray suit and a black tie
and his white shirt was starched.

He jogged up the steps with one hand holding his clipboard
and the other holding his tie flat. By the time he reached the
fourth floor his breathing hadn't even changed.

Going down the hall he passed other officers. None of them
saying anything to him, just nodding and then going on. There
were secretaries in low heels with reams of paper clutched in
their arms. Legal documents. Stapled affidavits. Some holding
cups of coffee. One woman a little younger than him gave him a
look and when Wilson turned back, she was still smiling.

The door to Price's office was at the end of the hall. His name
was stamped on the pebbled glass in gold leaf like the transom of
a yacht. Wilson looked at his warped reflection in the glass and
pressed his palm into the hair on the top of his head. Satisfied,
he opened the door.

There was an anteroom where Price's secretary's desk was

and when Wilson came through the door she looked up and before she could ask any questions Wilson spoke.

Good afternoon, he said. I'm Agent Philip Wilson from the Seattle bureau. Wondering if I might have a word with Chief Price.

It caught her off guard. She looked down at a ledger and when she did Wilson said,

I don't have an appointment. I hope that is okay.

Well, she said. She stood up in her chair and looked in Price's office. Price was on the phone.

He's on the phone at the moment, she said.

Yes, Wilson said. I can see that. Do you might if I sit?

She held out a hand to one of the chairs by the door. Then she sat back down and just watched him. Wilson looked up and smiled thinly with his lips closed.

Can I get you anything? she asked.

No, thank you, he said.

Coffee?

I've already had my coffee.

Water then?

Wilson inhaled deeply like someone waiting out the questions of a child and then smiled that same thin smile. Said,

No. Thank you.

Okay, she said. She pretended to busy herself with paperwork. She'd glance up from time to time. Then go back to the paperwork.

Fifteen minutes passed and Price hung up the phone.

I believe he's done in there, Wilson said.

He stood.

Thank you, Evelyn . . .

He squinted at the nameplate on the desk.

. . . Olson.

Evelyn went to Price's door and knocked and then opened it and leaned in and said,

Agent Wilson here for you.

Who?

Agent Wilson. From the Seattle bureau.

Why is there someone from the Seattle bureau up here?

I have no idea, sir, she said. Then in a softer voice said, He just showed up. She shrugged her shoulders.

Okay, he said, send him in then.

Wilson stepped into the office with both of his hands on his clipboard and the clipboard turned on its side in front of him. He turned back to Evelyn with an impatient look as though annoyed that the door was still open.

Okay, Evelyn said. You boys let me know if you need anything.

Price nodded at her and Evelyn closed the door.

She's a sweetheart, isn't she? Price said.

Chief Price, Wilson said.

Mr Wilson.

Agent.

Price nodded at him. Okay, he said. Agent. Does Agent Wilson got a first name? We're kind of big into first names around here.

Philip.

Philip Wilson.

Yes sir, Wilson said. But Agent Wilson will be just fine.

Okay. Agent Wilson it is.

Price sat back in his chair. He took off his hat and put it on the corner of his desk and then put his feet up.

So what can I do for you, Agent Wilson?

May I sit?

Be my guest, Price said.

Wilson smiled and sat. He opened a manila folder on his lap. He flattened his tie. He said,

Amy Barnhardt. Molly Summers.

Yes?

What can you tell me about them?

What do you want to know?

I want to know what you know.

You asking if I knew them personally?

Did you know them personally?

Price squinted at him.

I'm sorry, Agent Wilson, Price said. My hearing hasn't been the same since my tour over in Nam, so you'll have to forgive me, but sounds to me like you got yourself an agenda.

No more than anyone else.

Price combed his hair with his fingers. He said, Maybe we got off on the wrong foot.

No, Wilson said. Exactly the right one.

Price nodded and then said, Then let me ask you something.

Please, Wilson said.

I look twelve years old to you?

No sir. You do not. I'd put you at forty-five or so. Why do you ask?

Because it seems like you want to play some kind of game.

Far from it, Wilson said. By definition, games illicit an amount of fun for at least one participating party. And I'm not having fun, Chief Price. Are you? Is this fun for you?

Any hospitality still left in the chief dropped out and he took his feet from the desk and leaned forward on his elbows.

Why don't you cut the shit, Price said. You probably think you're dealing with some hick cop in some hick town in some hick county, but you ain't. And you keep running your mouth like you are I'll run you out myself. I'm busy and this bullshit you're trying to spread is starting to stink.

Interesting metaphor.

You tell me then, Price said. He leaned back in his chair and crossed his arms.

Tell you what? Wilson asked.

Your theory on all this. You seem to have it all figured out.

Do you know what a theory is, Mr Price?

Price didn't answer. He just sucked at his teeth. Trying his best to humor him.

A theory, Wilson said, is a principle intended to explain a fact or an idea. A hypothesis, on the other hand, is a proposed explanation for some phenomenon or another based on limited evidence.

Price only squinted at him.

So what is it, Chief Price? Do I have a theory or a hypothesis?

You got five seconds to ask what you want to ask.

Wilson leafed through some papers in the folder.

Those girls disappeared, Wilson said, looking down.

Five.

Both were found with high levels of ketamine in their systems.

Four.

Both were raped several times postmortem.

Three.

And I don't believe in coincidence.

Two.

Wilson stopped leafing through the papers and set his hands squarely on the folder that was resting on his lap and looked up finally at Price.

And you're the chief of police, he said. And these girls were murdered in your arguably erudite jurisdiction. And you're counting down. Like a game. So?

One, Price said.

Wilson sat forward. There was a miniature replica Gatling

gun askew on Price's desk that Wilson turned so the barrel was pointing straight at Price.

Here's my question, Wilson said. What can you tell me about Amy Barnhardt and Molly Summers?

Price sat back again in his chair. Mimicked the sarcastic smile of Wilson. Propped his boots back on the desk. He laced his fingers together. Rested his hands on his paunch.

It's a goddamn tragedy, Price said. And we're looking into it. Price shrugged his shoulders.

The clock ticked on the wall. The traffic was muffled through the windows. Voices in the hall.

And what have you found, Chief Price? Wilson asked. In all your looking?

Tragedy, Price said again.

Okay, Wilson said. He stood. Thank you for your time.

Price stayed seated.

I hope you'll reach out, Price said, if you happen to dig up anything we missed.

Oh, I will, Chief Price, Wilson said. I look forward to it.

Price stood and shook Wilson's hand and squeezed hard. But Wilson did not blink. Didn't bat an eye. Like he had just bought a used truck from Price. On the glass of the fourth-floor windows the rain began to tap.

You have a good day, Chief Price, Wilson said.

Only good days around here, Price said.

Wilson left Price's office, closing the door slowly, quietly behind him as though an infant were asleep and he was afraid to wake it. But he did so in a strange way, watching Price the whole time, not taking his eyes from him. When the door was closed and the glass separated them Wilson finally gave him that same odd, thin smile. And then he turned and walked out into the hall.

14

OCTOBER. EIGHT YEARS AGO. GOING UP AN OLD LOGGING ROAD out on the Olympic Peninsula that scantly resembled a road at all. Two faint lines between rows of thick moss the color of key lime ran at a steep grade up the mountain. The road was gated and the gate locked and the only reason Batey was headed up was a report that it had been opened.

Batey had already put in a long day. There was bad weather moving in and the last thing he wanted was to make his day any longer. The radio had squelched. He had been thinking about something important and was annoyed that the voice on the other end interrupted that important thought.

Okay, he said. I'll give her a look-see.

He had just turned forty-five years old and with that his first gray hairs had appeared. He considered himself pretty lucky up till then. He was in good shape and had no ailments. He had left the DEA for Fish and Wildlife at just the right time. Right when the world seemed to be going sideways. The morning he found the first gray hair he called in Coraline and she called him her old man and kissed his temple. Dee Batey. The old game warden, she said.

Batey drove south into the mountains. He suspected some hillbilly out poaching. Or some punk kids gone up to drink beer.

There was a fine mist falling but the wind was up and he knew the dark clouds would bring worse.

At the gate he found the lock had been cut. The metal U-bolt lay snipped in the mud. Just beyond the gate there were slicks in the ground where a previous vehicle had lost traction in the mud and Batey thought it best to put the truck in 4Hi before going on.

The road followed a creek and at some places the runoff nearly washed out the road. The old cedars and Douglas firs stood hundreds of feet in the air and wide as his truck. The going was slow and Batey wondered if he was just chasing his tail. Anyone up here, he thought, is long gone by now.

It was getting on three o'clock which meant in about half an hour it would be getting dark and half an hour after that all dark. He didn't mind being out past dark but the weather was worsening and he'd rather be home sooner than later. And he was just about to reconcile that sentiment when he saw the fresh marks of tires where the vehicle had turned around. Batey pulled aside and got out and left the engine running. Higher up now and getting colder and the mist was turning to snow. A flake or two falling alongside the rain like a beautiful face in a crowd.

He stood with his hands hooked in his belt. He looked down and there they were: large boot prints leading off the road, into the caged woods where the floor of the forest was so protected by the canopy it was almost dry.

Goddamnit, he said.

He sucked his teeth. Then he spit.

Shit, he said.

He reached into the cab of the truck and turned off the engine. The open door rang like a small clock. He took up his flashlight as if it might protect him. The dome light was warm looking and the cab was warm and dry and he almost climbed back in.

Forgot about the whole thing. But he couldn't stand poaching and he couldn't live with himself if he pretended he didn't. He took up the flashlight and closed the door and stepped into the ancient forest following what might be something.

For a while the bootpack followed the trail but at some point it veered and Batey found himself bushwhacking through fern and bracken so dense and seemingly untouched it might as well have been virgin.

But it wasn't. Wasn't at all.

Snagged in a tall salal bush was a narrow strip of silk that was white as cow's milk. He knelt and felt it between his fingers. Gave it a sniff. Nothing. Just the scents of cedar and moss and dirt. Kept it though. Tucked it in his pocket. He gazed skyward. It was all but dark. A deep shade of amethyst and coal-colored clouds to the east.

Goddamnit, he said again.

Then something caught his eye. He trained the flashlight upon it. Walked a little closer.

What's this? he said.

He said, What the hell?

What he found was a crude doll made of linen and hay and rough stitching and small button eyes. It was hanging by a thin piece of string from the limb of a tree. He grabbed it. Looked at it like it was some kind of ornament. Some red stitching was done across the neck and the hair fixed on the doll looked to be real. Batey shined the beam of light ahead. Through the thicket the bootpack was not so delicate. More of a trough, like something had been dragged through it. He unsnapped his holster and removed his gun and trained it in the direction of the light beam.

He followed that trough a little farther and the ferns and bracken turned to scree and the bootpack had all but vanished. By now it was full dark and the rain had all turned to snow.

With the trail gone cold and the light long since gone Batey was beginning to question his judgment. More than that he felt he'd gotten himself into something he couldn't back out of, like driving into a blizzard in a bad car. It spooked him.

The only way the bootpack could go from there was up the mountain, and the only thing up the mountain that any bootpack might lead to was a cave no bigger than a shipping container.

Well, Batey said. You've stepped in it now.

For a reason he did not know he climbed the scree, slipping more than once, cutting his palms, scuffing his shin, cursing the rock, the dark, himself. With a line of sweat frosting his brow, he finally reached the mouth of the cave. Brushed himself off and wiped his mouth with the back of his hand. A shot of bats exploded from the entrance of the cave, sending Batey reeling backward to the rocks. Lifting himself a final time he shined the light in the cavernous dark where the only breath of life came as a cold whisper from somewhere deep within where not even the bravest dare go and in that shock of cold he fell back again in a start. The flashlight leapt from his hand. He scrambled to retrieve it. The darkness and silence from within the cave pounded in Batey's ears like kettledrums. Trembling when he ultimately recovered the flashlight, his hat askew. Snow was falling through the beam of light, illuminated for the briefest of moments, and at the end of that light was the body of a young woman, stripped naked, lying stiff and cold on a rock altar. An image of otherwise peaceful repose. Batey went closer. The woman was barely that. More like a child. Maybe between sixteen and nineteen years old. Her throat had been slit and sewn shut again in a nightmarish design using red thread. The stub of a pale candle stood guttered to the rock near her feet. There was the fragrance of lingering woodsmoke and the charred twigs where someone had stayed long enough to make a fire.

He stepped closer. Batey shined the light upon the woman's face. He reached for her foot. Her skin was cold. Her toes were stiff as roots.

He didn't know how long he'd been running. He followed his own path back to the truck. Clamoring and stumbling in the vine like a drunk boar. Moans escaping with his harried breath. All around him snow was falling like ash.

Back at the truck his hands didn't work, as though the joints were seized. Opening the door after some struggle he got on the radio and called out for someone to answer.

15

EIGHT YEARS LATER AND IT WAS STILL HAPPENING. HADN'T stopped. And now Fielding had seen it. Had witnessed it. Was now part of it.

That night he couldn't sleep. Couldn't get the image of the charred girl out of his head. He watched television for a while. When that did nothing he drank half of a fifth of whiskey and when he still couldn't sleep he drank the other half. Even with his eyes open the image preyed on him. He went to the front door and locked it. He locked the back door. He went to his room and laid atop the sheets and looked at the swirling ceiling and listened to the rain. Then he got up again and washed his face in the darkness and went downstairs and started some coffee, knowing what he was about to do.

He went back upstairs to his room and knelt down and reached under the bed and when he felt it he pulled out the small case and set it on the bed and flipped one silver latch then flipped the other and opened the case and looked down at the .45 Ruger. He hadn't looked at it in years. Hadn't even thought about it. But here it was. Like an old acquittance he was afraid of. He had fired it only a handful of times and then only at targets. He didn't care for guns other than for hunting and even then saw them only as a tool like a shovel for digging a hole. And as he looked at the gun, a hole was all he saw. He was climbing down into it again.

Yer a goddamn fool, he said.

Then he lifted the gun out of the case and opened the cylinder and found it empty and closed it again and stuffed the revolver in the small of his back and took out the box of bullets and closed the empty case and slid it back under the bed. He went back down into the kitchen and filled a thermos with coffee and went out to his truck.

The freeway was all but empty at that hour. A semi here and there. A delivery truck. He drove the speed limit, maybe a little under. He had no rush in getting back out there. Any excuse to turn him around he'd take. But there were no excuses and it was easy as an invitation. He followed the same route he and Batey had taken earlier. The rain was still falling but the wind had died. Nothing looked the same in the dark. Nothing ever did. Driving out he knew he was looking at the fishing harbor only because of a red navigational light that lit up and went out every few seconds. Farther out, across the water, a lighthouse was flashing.

At the same place as before, Fielding pulled over and parked the truck on the grass of the shoulder and turned off the engine and sat there looking out the window at the yellow tape blocking the boardwalk. He reached for the thermos and opened it and poured a cup then closed the lid and set it on the seat beside him and blew away the steam from the hot coffee. He looked at the tape again. Nothing moved out there. If it weren't for the newness of the tape and what he had seen earlier it would almost look abandoned. As if the tape were there to keep people off a crumbling structure. And in a way it was. It was all rotten.

Now's the time to leave, he said. Could just drink yer coffee and go home. No one would fault yeh for that.

He did drink his coffee but he didn't go home. He looked at his watch. It read 2:37 a.m. He blinked. His eyes were heavy from all the evening's whiskey. He took a deep breath in and let a deep breath out. Then he clicked on the dome light and reached for the glove box and took out the flashlight and set it on the dash and then took up the box of bullets and broke open the cylinder of the gun and loaded it one bullet at a time then closed the cylinder and set the gun on the dash next to the flashlight. He sat there looking at the gun. What it stood for, what it was capable of. The reason he had brought it in the first place. Then he grabbed the gun and opened it again and dumped the bullets out and put them back in the box and closed the gun and set it in the glove box. Then he grabbed the flashlight and clicked it on and opened the door and stepped out of the truck.

He listened for something to make a noise out there. Twenty-four hours ago some teenager was set on fire in some kind of twisted ritual. Twenty-four hours ago was not the past but the present and to be alone with all those ghosts made him uneasy. He looked past the tape to the boardwalk where it cut through a hedge of dune grass and knotweed. Looked past it to where the boardwalk ended and the sand met the water. He listened. Only the rain on the hood. The rain over the ground. A buoy some-where out in the water with its lonely bell clanging in the swell.

He ducked the tape and walked to the end of the boardwalk. He stood there like someone might on the deck of a ship looking down into a dark ocean. To go any further would be to step from the earth, to set into motion a series of events with irrevocable consequences. To step from this world into another. Into oblivion.

Waves spilled along the shoreline. They tumbled small peb-bles and the pebbles rolled against each other like a heavy sigh. He trained the flashlight downward and he swung it around looking for something. Anything.

Yeh ain't a detective, he said to himself. What're yeh doin out here? Yeh don't even know what yer lookin for.

He walked over the sand toward the site. Wet nests of eel-grass and driftwood. Old shells breaking under his boots. He shined the light at the charred remains. The body had been taken away by the coroner earlier that day. There was a tent set up over it all to protect any evidence from the rain and there was tape around the whole thing.

He walked toward it. It was difficult going. The rock and the sand giving way under his heels. When he got to the tape he stopped. He knelt down to duck it but thought better and stood and shined his light. The crude bed where the young woman had lain was just as he had seen it. He watched it as if something might move. Watched as if something within the taped-off scene might tell him what the world was or would one day be, give any explanation whatsoever, but there was nothing.

He looked at the burned wood and at the small cairns erected over the sand and the flashlight threw the shadows of them out beyond the tent where the shadows of the cairns and the shadow of the burnt pyre were being rained upon. Quite often the white of a breaking wave would rise up and crash on the shore in the yellow light of the beam and wash over the rocks and then go dark. That's where he was looking when he saw something. Marks over the sand. Indentations like boot prints. He went around the tape and shined the light at them. They looked new—not just looked, they were new. The rain hadn't gotten to them the way it had with the others. The boot print a size fourteen or fifteen and made by someone tall. The stride was long. The prints came out of the darkness from down the beach and under the tape to the back of the pyre and stopped there like their maker had forgotten something. Then they turned around and went back the way they had come.

He felt like calling Batey. Get him out here to let him know he wasn't just seeing things. Fielding looked down the beach. Looked behind him. Everything was dark and there wasn't a pay phone for miles. He was alone in this.

He knelt and looked for any discerning quality in the sole of the boot but there was none. Just a flat print. Still kneeling he shined the light in the direction of the retreating prints. The rain falling through the light was caught for a moment and each drop was a perfect sphere. Looking off into the night, Fielding said: Whoever yeh are, yeh ain't no beachcomber out for a midnight stroll.

He thought about what he was going to do. Clicked off the flashlight to judge any light farther down the beach but there was no light. He stood there thinking. Then he clicked the light back on. A pair of burning yellow eyes stared back at him through the rain, startling him to the point that he fumbled the flashlight and dropped it in the sand. He picked it up and leveled it at the eyes again. Only a raccoon and Fielding said, Yeh little bastard.

It did not move.

Git, he said, waving his hands at it.

The animal lumbered off and Fielding was left alone again.

This ain't yer business, Fielding said to himself.

But the image of the burned corpse flashed in his mind again and it was the innocence that had been scourged out, the terror the poor girl must have felt, that made him turn once more to where the boot prints led.

Goddamnit, he said.

He began to follow them.

Had gone nearly a quarter mile when the tracks veered away from the water and up through the dune grass. Fielding stopped. He shined the light behind him to settle the notion that he was being followed. But there was nothing behind him but his own tracks.

He followed the boot prints up through the dune. The grass was tall as his waist. Anything could be hiding in there. Fielding stopped and listened. There was nothing but the rain. There was no wind and no cars out on the road and even the buoy far out in the water had seemed to cease its clanging. There was only the rain in the grass. Fielding kept on.

The trail narrowed and looked rarely used. Looked more like a game trail. But there was no game out here. And that fact brought Fielding no comfort. The trail led into dune grass that grew to Fielding's shoulders and the bushy tufts were heavy with water and leaned in submission.

The tall grass ended abruptly along with the trail. It was like coming to a wall. Fielding stopped and shined his light about. He shined it behind him thinking he had made a wrong turn. The boot prints he'd been tracking simply vanished. In front of him was a thick hedge of salal and scrub pines with tortured limbs. Beyond that was the macadam of the road. He pushed through the hedge with more than a little effort and stepped finally onto the pavement.

Back up the road he could faintly make out the dark shape of his truck. The tent over the crime scene was hidden behind the dune. Standing there in the road he felt like he'd imagined the whole thing, like he had been tracking the boot prints of a phantom. He looked up at the rain breaking away from the dark firmament. It collided with his eyes and made him squint against it. Then he heard the unmistakable sound of a big-block engine starting up and tires trying to grip the wet asphalt and when he turned he saw a car with its lights off peeling toward him and at what seemed the final moment Fielding leapt off the road. He gathered himself up when he heard the car pass and he watched it race off down the spit. About a mile away its headlights came on and then the car disappeared.

16

IT WAS A LITTLE AFTER FOUR IN THE MORNING WHEN FIELDING
got to Batey's house. He had to knock a few times and then ring
the doorbell before the front light came on over the porch. Batey
answered. He was standing in his robe. Eyes not quite open.
What are you doing? Batey said. You have any idea what time
it is?

Early, Fielding said.

Hell, Batey said, it's still late. What are you doing over here?
You drunk?

A little.

Well, go home and sleep it off.

Batey was turning back into the house when Fielding said, I
think I saw him.

Batey stopped. Said, Saw who?

Him.

I ain't in the mood for games.

Him. Whoever it was that burned up that girl.

Where were you?

The beach. Went down there.

Why did you do that?

Don't know. Somethin didn't feel right.

No shit it didn't feel right.

I saw him, Fielding said. I know I did.

Batey looked down at his watch.

You know what time it is?

Early, Fielding said again.

Alright, Batey said. Come on. I'll get some coffee going.

They sat in Batey's kitchen and Fielding told him the story. The full story. Every detail down to the wet dune grass he had to push through. When he was done he just clasped his hands around the coffee mug, looking into it. Looking like a man awaiting a trial.

Now why did I need to know about the grass being so wet?

I don't know, Fielding said.

Batey nodded.

How do you know it was him?

Jest know.

Batey nodded again.

You tell anyone else about it? You go to the police?

No. Jest you for now.

You get a plate or anything?

Little hard to get a plate when the damn car is tryin to run yeh over.

Batey nodded. Yeah, he said. I suppose.

They heard the sound of feet on the stairs.

Uh-oh, Batey said.

Coraline came into the doorway and leaned against the jamb and crossed her arms. Fielding and Batey looked at her like two caught teenagers. Coraline was squinting in the harsh light. Her feet were bare. She stood there in her robe looking a little annoyed.

Batey pointed a finger at Fielding. Said, His fault.

So you're the one who stole my man from my bed, she said.

Sorry, mam, Fielding said. I'll be gettin on.

He went to stand but she stopped him.

Anything that would keep Dee from snuggling into this is probably worthwhile.

She moved into the kitchen.

Let me get some breakfast going for you boys, she said.

That's mighty kind of yeh, Fielding said, but I'll be headed out.

The hell you will, she said. Now sit.

She opened the refrigerator and took out eggs and a package of bacon and butter. She opened the freezer and took out hashbrowns. She took two skillets down from the cupboard. Fielding looked at Batey. Batey just raised his shoulders. She scooped in the butter and cracked the eggs into the skillet and laid the bacon into the other. Coraline yawned, but only because it seemed rude not to.

Honey, I'll finish that up, Batey said.

I'm up, she said. I'll just toss and turn wondering about what you boys are talking about. What are you talking about anyway?

Fielding almost got himself run over tonight, Batey said.

Don't joke, Coraline said.

Tell her, Batey said.

Fielding told her and by the end of it Coraline had forgotten about the eggs and they were burning in the skillet.

You tell the police yet? she asked.

Not yet, Fielding said.

Sounds like something they might want to know about.

We'll head over when they open up, Batey said.

You poor man, Coraline said. You don't look banged up.

Grass was soft, Fielding said.

Still, she said. She looked back at the burning eggs. Shoot, she said.

17

DRIVING TO THE STATION IN THE STILL-DARK MORNING, FIELDING flipped down the visor mirror and looked at himself.

Dang, he said.

I wasn't going to say anything, Batey said.

Well yeh should have. I look like a crazy man.

You might be.

Yeh got any eye drops?

Batey pointed to the glove box.

If I do, he said, they're in there.

Fielding opened the glove box and picked through the contents and found a small bottle at the bottom. He unscrewed the cap and squirted in a few drops and then did the other eye.

Looks like I'm cryin, he said.

That's not unreasonable, Batey said. Given all this.

I haven't been drunk in years, Fielding said. Maybe ten. Fifteen. Didn't even get drunk when Sara passed. Can't say I really care for it.

Well there's not any good in it, Batey said. I'll tell you that.

Yeh ain't a drinker are yeh? Unless yeh hide somethin in that ginger ale.

No I am not, Batey said. Not anymore.

It a problem for yeh? Alcohol?

Problem don't even scratch the enamel, partner.

Sorry that I showed up like this then, Fielding said. Probably stirs a few things up. For both you and Coraline.

Batey waved off the notion.

You got no problem with it, he said. I can tell. The ones who are invested are invested all the way. I can see it a mile off.

It's only a bunch of trouble ain't it?

Can be, Batey said. In the wrong hands.

How long yeh been?

Sober?

Yeah.

Well, Batey thought. Lola is twenty so that puts it at nine. Nine years.

That ain't easy. Quittin and all.

No it isn't.

Batey sipped some of his coffee.

Who was that fella, he continued, who had to push that boulder up the mountain for eternity?

Sisyphus.

Yeah, Batey said. Well, I believe old Sisyphus had the better deal.

Yeh both cheated death anyway.

I certainly cheated myself, Batey said. There're big blocks of time I don't even remember living through. That's what I missed out on. Lots of time. And that's a kind of death of its own. Years of my life. Years when the girls were just babies. Toddlers. Their first steps. First words. That's all a void to me. One big empty space. True darkness, partner. I might as well have been dead.

He sipped his coffee again. The road thrummed under the tires. The wind came at the Bronco sideways and tried to heel the truck like a boat.

I locked horns with the devil, Batey said. And the only thing the devil isn't ever going to do is lose. That's up to us. The thing about real good drinking is that when you're good at it, you're good at it. It's pedal to the metal. Time stops in your head and you start acting like you missed something and need to catch up for all that lost time.

Batey said, You know Cora loves to garden and when things got really bad, I used to watch her out there pulling up all them weeds around the carrots and the beans and lettuce and I remember thinking: if only she could pull out the weeds in me. And when I finally kicked it I told her that really dedicated drinking lets things get out of hand and when you ultimately want to kick it the addiction is like a weed that you've let go too long and when you finally do something about it and tear it up you can't tell which is which and you start pulling out all the good stuff too. That's what I was afraid of. By that point I didn't know what was good or bad in me. In a lot of ways it's like learning to walk again. But then one day a mountain of water rushes over you and you hear things more vividly and the sun feels good again and all that patience and all that perseverance—it pays you back. You tell the devil you've had enough. You tell him he won and then when his back is turned you run like hell.

Batey raised his mug of coffee.

And that's what I've been doing. Just trying to stay a few miles ahead of the devil.

Sounds exhausting, Fielding said.

You bet, Batey said. But Cora picks up on it. She can see it. Can see it when I'm worn out. Not a day she makes me go it alone.

You're a lucky man, Fielding said.

You bet, Batey said. Luckiest goddamn guy in the world. Back from the dead. Full-on Lazarus.

A stoplight turned red. He stopped the Bronco. Batey leaned

forward on the wheel with his wrist curled over the top and looked out the windshield. Said, I'm sorry I brought you into all this. I really am. We could've just been coffee and cigar buddies. Talking about the past and spitting in the dirt. But now. Well . . .

We still got time to smoke cigars, Fielding said.

Yeah, Batey said. But the devil's got his horns in this mess too. And this isn't something we can outrun.

No it ain't, Fielding said. Only way this ends is if the devil loses.

18

THE STATION WAS STILL CLOSED WHEN THEY GOT THERE.
Batey put the Bronco into park and sat there with the engine
idling. He leaned over the wheel and looked at the building.
There was a light on. Batey looked at his watch. He said, Marty's
usually early. Come on. He'll let us in.

They ran through the rain. At the door Batey started knock-
ing. Not long after, a head popped out of an office door. Rawlings squinted. You could tell he was having a hard time making
out the faces standing out in the rain. Rawlings came out from
the office and down the hall and through the double doors and
put his key in the lock.

What're you boys doing up so early? Rawlings asked as he
opened the door.

Need to make a report, Batey said.

Rawlings sniffed at the air around Fielding.

You been drinking, Amos?

Yes, Fielding said. Whole bottle.

Maybe you better get on home and sleep it off.

You'd a drank the same, Batey said, once you find out what
happened.

Okay, Rawlings said. His face now serious. Come on in.

They went up to the fourth floor and sat at the two chairs in front of Rawlings's desk. Rawlings brought a cup of coffee for each of them. Rawlings sat down and leaned onto his desk and laced his fingers together. He said, So? What happened?

Amos thinks he saw the guy who did it, Batey said.

Did what?

Lit that girl on fire.

Rawlings looked at Fielding.

You did? he asked.

I think so.

How do you know?

Sumbitch tried to run me over.

Where was this?

I went back down there.

Why?

Didn't feel right.

That's the understatement of the century, Rawlings said. He leaned back and opened a drawer near his feet and pulled out a form and took a pen from the cup on his desk. Rubbed some sleep from his eye then looked at Fielding and said, Okay, I tell you what. Chief isn't in yet, but I think he'd like to hear this. You mind hanging tight till he gets here?

You mind? Fielding asked Batey.

Nope.

It was 9:05 when Chief Price walked into his office. He took off his hat and his slicker and hung the slicker on the coat tree. Through the glass partitions Rawlings saw him and said to Batey and Fielding, Hold on a minute. He filled a mug with coffee and went into Price's office.

Thank you, Marty, Price said. Who's that with Dee in there?

Amos Fielding, sir.

He the one that bought the old Harris place? Fella from Iowa?

Yessir.

So what're they doing in your office so damn early? You boys starting a book club I should know about?

No sir, Rawlings said. Fielding there nearly got run down last night.

Run down?

Yessir.

By what?

A vehicle, sir.

Whereabouts?

On the spit. Where Summers was found.

Price was about to sip his coffee, but when he heard Rawlings say that he stopped and set the mug on his desk and furrowed his brow. His whole demeanor changed. He said, What was he doing out there?

Said something didn't feel right, Rawlings said. And when he was walking on the road a car came out of nowhere and tried to hit him. Thinks it's got some connection to the body.

That you talking or him?

Him, sir.

Why would he think that? Price asked.

I don't know, sir. Said he went down there again to have another look around.

Has anyone told him that's none of his business?

Want me to file the report and send them home?

No, Price said. He pinched the bridge of his nose and closed his eyes. Hell, isn't even nine thirty yet. Haven't even had my coffee. He exhaled. Alright, he said, send them in.

Chief Price's office was austere and seemed modeled after his personality. There was no clutter. There was a framed picture of the constitution on the wall. A framed National Rifle Association membership. An American flag hung in the corner. There was a crystal decanter and several tumblers on a silver tray next to his desk. Batey walked in behind Fielding, and Price extended his hand and Fielding shook it. Price was wearing a big gold ring with diamonds in it. When the chief stood Fielding noticed a .50 caliber nickel-plated Desert Eagle in his holster. Seemed an unusual choice for an elected official, Fielding thought. The chief noticed Fielding looking at it.

You a fan?

Fan?

My firearm.

He took it from its holster and popped out the clip and ejected the round from the chamber by pulling back on the action and spun it gracefully in his hand and held it by the barrel so that Fielding could take the grip.

Go on, Price said. Give her a feel.

I'm alright, Fielding said.

What you mean you're alright? Go on. Give her a taste. Ain't going to bite.

Fielding reluctantly took the pistol.

Heavy, Fielding said.

Hell yes, she's heavy, Price said. That's not some government-issued peashooter you're holding. He smiled. His teeth seemed too white. That'll rip a hole the size of a baseball in a shipping container. You ever fire one?

Fielding shook his head.

You were an old lawman, weren't you?

Yessir.

You telling me you've never taken something like that off a one of them gangbangers?

Can't say I have.

Well, you stick around long enough I'll find you one.

Mighty kind, Fielding said.

Going on ten years with this beauty, Price said. Got her off some wannabe hot-shit banger out of Vancouver running dope across the border. Took three shots at me. One nearly did the trick.

He unbuttoned his shirt to the sternum and pulled the fabric aside and tapped the scarred skin just above his heart.

Bastard aimed too high, Price said. Took the shot in fear. Adrenaline going a mile a fucking minute. Holding it all sideways like a real gangster.

Again, he tapped the skin above his heart.

Dumb son of a bitch, Price continued. Took off running when he was out. Trained him with my rifle. Deadnuts in the crosshair. One shot. Boom. Hit him right where I wanted. Dropped that fucker like a bag of gravel. I don't miss, Mr Fielding. You want to kill me, you better learn to fire your weapon first.

Fielding handed him the gun back and the chief popped back in the clip and pulled back on the action. He puffed some hot breath on the nickeled barrel and took a handkerchief from his pocket and buffed the silver metal. Then he put the gun back in its holster.

So, he said. He sat down on the corner of his desk. What is it you think you saw?

For a fourth time Fielding told the story. Just as he told it to Batey and just as he told it to Coraline and just as he told it to Rawlings. He didn't leave out a single detail so nothing could be inferred or speculated over and when he was done all the chief said was,

You been drinking, Mr Fielding?

Yes, Fielding said. I've also never seen a burned girl before. Wanted to try to forget that as quick as possible.

Thought you were a sheriff?

Different time, Fielding said. I don't know, maybe different place.

That some kind of commentary on the way I run things around here?

No sir.

Sure sounded like it, Price said. He looked at Rawlings. Sound like he was making some kind of commentary, Deputy Rawlings?

Rawlings did not answer and only looked down at his hands. He wanted no part of it.

Well, Price said, maybe I'm wrong. Maybe I'm jumping to conclusions.

He stood from the corner of the desk and walked behind it and placed his hands on the back of his chair and leaned against it and eyed Fielding for a long moment as if trying to parse out something within him. As if gauging his next move. As if deciding what kind of man Fielding really was.

People don't change, do they, Mr Fielding, Price said. Well, that's not really true. They evolve, I suppose. They mutate. I'd argue they've gotten better. Take criminals, for example. The bad guys. Empathy has seeped into the mind of the modern criminal. The heinous acts are not what they once were. Sure, there's some spooky shit happening with the cartels south of the border, but that's just a bunch of spick dope runners acting out of desperation. Notch above animals, if you ask me. But the truly great villains, there was no empathy in them. Genghis Khan used to fillet strips off his enemies and eat the meat in front of them while they were still alive. The Vikings did something called the blood eagle. Nasty stuff. They'd cut slits in the backs of their captured enemies and pull the lungs through the ribs and whenever the captive would breathe the bloody lung would flutter like a wing. Or the Judas Cradle. You ever heard of that? The guy or gal would be lowered onto this pyramid-shaped spear, with the point right up one of the holes and then weights were added to increase the effect. Can you imagine? Tore them apart. See, there's nothing like that now. Now they just shoot you. Hardly feel a thing. Pretty humane in the grand scheme of things.

That girl wasn't shot, Mr Price, Fielding said.

You can call me chief.

Okay. Chief Price. What happened to that girl is as bad as it gets. Make old Khan's stomach turn.

Well, Price said. He smiled at Fielding. He pulled out his own chair and sat and leaned back with his coffee resting on one of the arms of the chair. Listen, he said, I appreciate you coming to me with this. I really do. What happened was a tragedy. Not something we take kindly to around here. Despite what you've seen, Mr Fielding, Port Cook's a nice little town. Friendly. Nice place to raise your kids. And it's good to have another lawman of your stature kicking around, but we're all staffed up. If you catch my drift.

Price extended a hand and Fielding shook it.

Don't be a stranger, Price said. He stood and so did Fielding and Batey. And I'm serious about that Desert Eagle. Consider one yours.

Fielding and Batey left the office and nodded at Rawlings and walked out into the hall and as they did Price followed them with his eyes. Watched them until they disappeared and when they had Price rapped on the glass with his knuckle. When Rawlings came in Price said,

Keep an eye on him. I want to know exactly where Mr Fielding is and exactly what he's up to. You understand?

Back in the Bronco Fielding said, Charmin.

He's been like that as long as I've known him.

How long is that?

Nine years, Batey said. Which is nine years too long.

Thinks highly of himself.

Big dick swinging, Batey said. So what're your plans?

Plans?

For the day.

Sleep, Fielding said. I'm goin a feed the horses and then I'm goin a sleep for a few years.

19

IT HAD A BEEN A WEEK SINCE MOLLY SUMMERS'S BODY HAD been found. Dani was at the grocery store. Ruby was waiting in the car, complaining of a headache. I'll get you something for it, Dani had said before she left the car.

Dani was walking through the aisles when a tall man ran his cart into hers. Dani looked up.

I'm sorry, the man said. I need to pay more attention to where I'm going.

He had a ball cap pulled low. He had cold blue eyes like deep ice. He was bald, void of hair. Even his eyebrows were gone. Well over six feet. It was hard to look at him too long. And finally Dani looked back down into her cart and said,

That's fine.

She was pushing past him when he put out his hand and touched her arm. Said,

Don't you work at the shelter?

Yes, Dani said. Have you been? You don't look familiar.

No, he said. But I've seen you when I drive by from time to time. You're usually out helping those on the sidewalk. That's God's work there. It's very admirable.

Thank you, Dani said. It was nice talking.

She tried to push past on the other side but the man turned

his cart and blocked her. Dani glanced up with a harried sort of look. Closer to him now she could see his eyes from under his baseball hat. The blue had gone dark. Like burnt wood. Deep within smoldered something wicked that she couldn't explain. So wicked Dani had to look away and could not look in his eyes again.

How did you get into that kind of work? he asked.

I got to get going, she said. My shift starts soon.

The man looked down at his watch. It's 5:15, he said. Kind of late to start a shift.

I just got to get going.

Where are you going?

Work, Dani said. I said that already.

Yes, he said. I guess you did.

He did not move. Dani's eyelids fluttered like moths. He said, If I were to guess your name, would you tell me if I was correct?

Why do you want to know my name?

I'm not saying I do. I'm just asking if you would tell me if I was correct.

Listen I got to—

But he interrupted her and said, Stevie?

Stevie?

No, he said. That's not it.

She tried to force a smile. She said, I'm going to be late.

Tony, he said.

Then he said, No, that's not it either. Is it?

Is there something wrong? Dani asked.

Something wrong?

Yeah.

What would be wrong?

I don't know. Did I upset you somehow?

Do you think you did?

I'm not sure, she said.

Then why would you ask if you upset me?

Listen, she said, I don't know what you're onto but I'm—

Please, the man said, forgive me. He held his hands up as if in submission. I didn't mean to scare you. I just saw you and recognized you and wanted to say hello. I'm new in town and I don't know anyone. Gets lonely, I suppose. Just thought I'd say hi is all.

He moved his cart aside.

Maybe I'll come by the shelter sometime, he said.

Dani pushed past him. When she was a cart's length away he said,

We'll see you around, Dani.

She stopped her cart and turned back to him, though it pained her to do so. It was like holding one's hand over a fire.

How do you know my name? she asked.

I don't.

You just said it.

Lucky guess.

She turned away and pushed her cart on, one of the broken castors spinning in circles and rattling the cans and jars in the basket. The noise of it seemed to rise up into a roar as she pushed the cart faster. At the end of the aisle she turned back but all she saw were stocked shelves as though there had never been anyone there at all. As though the whole thing had been imagined. As though her mind had been playing tricks on her.

Ruby was sitting in the car and when Dani came back she sat there for a while watching the storefront, not saying anything. Ruby looked up and said,

Did you get some aspirin?

What? Dani said. She was looking in the side mirrors. The rearview. Back again at the storefront.

What are you looking for? Ruby asked.

Nothing, Dani said.

What is it?

Nothing.

Dani started the car.

Put your head in my lap, Dani said.

What?

Just put your head in my lap.

Dani put the car into gear and drove out of the parking lot. When they were out of sight of the supermarket Dani took her hand away from Ruby's head and Ruby sat up.

What was that for? Ruby asked.

I don't know, Dani said.

What do you mean you don't know?

Just a bad feeling is all.

Bad feeling about what?

Dani watched the rearview as they drove down the road. Ruby turned in her seat and looked out the back window.

What are you looking at? Ruby asked.

Nothing, Dani said.

When they got to Dani's apartment, Dani locked the door and went to the window and looked through the blinds. The glow of the town fighting against the fog. Lights of cars. Red taillights. Above that a sky black as soot holding nothing but countless drops of rain. Couldn't see a thing out there even if there was something to see.

What are you looking at? Ruby asked again. What's going on?

Nothing, Dani said.

I'm starting to not believe you.

Dani stayed at the window.

Is someone out there? Ruby's voice heightened. Talk to me, would you? You're making me nervous.

Just someone at the store, Dani said. Creeped me out.

Did you know them?

No. But he knew me. He knew my name.

How did he know your name?

I don't know. Said he recognized me from the shelter.

That seems normal.

No. He's never been to the shelter. I'd have remembered him. Looked different from anyone else I've ever seen.

And you never seen him before?

No.

Dani moved away from the window and sat down on the sofa and looked down at her tattooed hands.

He terrified me, Dani said. I felt like I was standing on the edge of something and looking into oblivion. His eyes were like pits and looking into them I felt like I'd never be happy again.

Ruby went to the window and was about to look for herself when Dani said, No! Don't!

You're scaring me, Ruby said.

I'm sorry, Dani said.

Should I be? Scared, that is?

Ruby stood in the middle of the room and watched Dani. Her hands were trembling.

I want to go talk to the police tomorrow, Dani said.

The police? Why?

We have to tell someone about you. About what has happened.

No, Ruby said. She started to pace. She started shaking her head. No, she said. We can't do that.

What if he's still out there and someone knows something? Or maybe he's not and someone caught him and then we don't have to worry?

He's not caught. If he were caught we'd hear about it.

So you're just going to give up?

You weren't there! Ruby screamed. Her voice sounded like sheet metal being shook.

Ruby collapsed onto the floor and Dani threw her arms around her. In her arms, Ruby felt to Dani as small as a child huddled against the sounds of thunder.

20

THE NEXT MORNING RUBY AND DANI DROVE TO THE POLICE
station and parked the car and sat there with the engine running.
Sat there looking at the austere building like it was a mirage.
Then Dani shut off the engine and they sat there some more.

There were only a few lights on in the station. From time to
time they'd see an officer walk past a window and then walk past
again like a tin character in a carnival shooting gallery.

It's not too late, Dani said.

We're here, Ruby said. We've made the trip.

Could just as easily turn around.

We've come this far.

All of this has an end, Dani said.

I know, the girl said.

And that can start right now.

Ruby was picking at her nail.

I'll be right beside you, Dani said. You're not alone. Those
days are gone.

Dani reached for her hand.

She said, It's you and me now, you understand? You and me.

She lifted Ruby's hand and kissed the back of it. Ruby nodded. They got out of the car and walked through the rain to the
station. They walked through the doors and took the elevator to

the fourth floor. Rawlings was sitting at his desk and he looked up when their figures daubed out the light through the glass. Dani opened the door. Rawlings knew Dani and said her name. Then he asked who the girl was.

There someone we can talk to? Dani said.

With me, I guess, Rawlings said. What's the problem? You looked spooked.

There somewhere we can talk in private?

In another room Ruby told Rawlings everything she could remember and when she was done Rawlings didn't know what to say. Finally, he said: When did all this happen?

About a month and a half ago, Ruby said. I think.

Then he said: He violate you?

No, Ruby said. I don't think so.

Were there any marks or anything of that nature?

Marks? Ruby asked.

Yes mam, Rawlings said. Abrasions or cuts. You know ... vaginally.

Dani shot Rawlings a look that could start a fire.

Just a question, Dani, Rawlings said.

She already told you no, Dani said.

Just a question I have to ask, Rawlings said. Don't know how else to ask it.

Differently, Dani said. You ask it differently.

Okay, Rawlings said. He held up his hands in surrender.

So is there anything you can do for us? Dani asked.

I can file all of this and put it out there. But if we don't have anything to go on, no description, no name, no forensics, then ...

He pursed his lips and hunched his shoulders.

He said, I just don't want to give you any false hope is all.

False or not, Dani said, we need something.

Rawlings looked hard at Ruby. Hard and long and he didn't

say anything for a while. He knew what she had told him was true. About the dopers in the house. About the looming figure and the horns. About being drugged up and so scared that she ran out of the house into the woods and tried to push it all from her memory. Didn't doubt her for a second. He knew hope was exactly what she needed. False or not. He took another deep breath. He said, I tell you what. I'll put it out there. Make it a priority. I'll ask around. Shake some trees. You never know.

Just then Price walked into his office. The light went on and they could see him through the glass two rooms down. He was about to take off his Stetson when he looked at them. He kept his hat on and walked out of his office and down the hall and stepped into the doorway of the room and looked at Ruby, said, Who we have here?

Rawlings told him. And he told him about the girl's situation. Told him his plans to put out a person of interest.

Sounds fine to me, Price said. Can't have monsters roaming free, can we?

Thank you, Dani said.

Price went and sat in a chair in the corner of the room. The chair was behind the women and Price was talking to their backs. He crossed his legs at the ankle and rubbed at a smudge on the toe of his boot and ceremoniously removed his hat and propped it on his bent knee and smoothed his hair with his hand.

Does seem a reach though, Price said. Hundreds of sickos out there. Hundreds of dopers. They come and go every day. Though I am curious. Why it take you so long to come to us? Someone might get the impression you're hiding something. That what you're doing? You hiding something?

She was scared, Dani said.

You let her tell it, Price said.

Ruby looked at Dani and Dani nodded to her.

I was scared, Ruby said.

Of course, Price said. Who wouldn't be?

We've established that, Dani said. How many times you need to hear it?

What'd I tell you about interrupting?

He uncrossed his legs. He stood from the chair and went to the corner of the desk and sat on it. He looked down at them. His eyes were shadowed under his hat. He looked at the tattoos on Dani's hands. The tattoo of the woman being carried by the raven on her chest. He looked at her cleavage. Dani sensed it and did her best to conceal herself.

That's kind of a spooky tattoo, Price said.

He pointed at Dani's breasts.

Have any meaning? Price asked.

It's a long story, she said.

I'm here to serve my community. My job is to listen, sweet-heart. I'm all ears.

He reached down and with a finger tried to move aside the fabric of the collar to see the full tattoo but she shied at his touch and cast her eyes into her lap.

Sir, Rawlings interrupted. I think we got everything we need. I'm sure these ladies are tired after such an ordeal.

Price laced his fingers together on his lap. He smiled his too-white smile. Yeah, he said. I'm sure they are.

He stood and squared his hat. He extended a hand. First to Dani, who shook it reluctantly. Then to Ruby.

Thank you girls for stopping in, he said. We'll let you know what we find out.

He walked out of the room and all three of them watched him walk to his office. When he sat down at his desk he took off his Stetson and smoothed his hair and turned and winked at them through the glass.

Yeah, Rawlings said to Dani and Ruby, Well, we'll let you know.

When they had gone Rawlings went out to get coffee. When he was passing Price's office Price said,

Deputy.

Rawlings stopped at the door.

Where're you headed?

Coffee, sir.

Get me one, would you?

Sure.

And Marty.

He stopped again.

Kill that person-of-interest case.

Sir?

You heard me. If there even was someone like that, they're long gone. Don't want to waste resources going on a ghost hunt.

Rawlings didn't speak for a while. Price just stared at him.

That all, sir? Rawlings finally said.

Price nodded. Rawlings put his hat on and was walking away from the door when Price stopped him a third time.

Sir?

Black, Price said. Little bit of sugar.

21

WILSON WAS ALREADY IN THE CAFÉ WHEN FIELDING AND BATEY arrived. He was sitting in a booth at the back of the place. He had papers laid out around him. He had his head in the palm of his hand like he was studying for an exam. There was a cup of coffee on a white saucer to his right. Across the table was a plate of eggs that had gone untouched.

Batey and Fielding stopped in the doorway and looked at Wilson and then looked at each other. Batey raised his eyebrows.

Suppose we shouldn't be rude, Fielding said.

Maybe he likes his breakfast alone?

Guess we'll find out.

The two men walked to the table and stood a moment before Wilson noticed them. It was Batey who cleared his throat. Wilson turned up his face and squinted at them as if he'd never seen them before. Then he sat back and put his palms on the table and smiled thinly.

A little homework? Batey asked.

To what do I owe the pleasure? Wilson asked.

Nothing, Batey said. Just come in for some breakfast and saw you sitting here. Amos thought you might want some company.

Wilson looked at him like he was speaking a different language.

Well, Batey said, want some company?

Wilson looked at the table. His eyes poring over all the papers and photographs spread out. He looked up at Fielding and Batey again. He took a deep breath. Then he reached over the table and began to stack the papers and photos in assorted piles. Fielding reached to help in the matter but Wilson put out his hand and Fielding got the point. When it was all tidied up Wilson motioned a paltry welcome to the seats across the booth. Fielding and Batey slid in. Fielding looked down at the plate of cold eggs in front of him.

Yeh didn't eat yer eggs, Fielding said.

Not a big fan of eggs, Wilson said.

Then why'd yeh order em?

The waitress said I must be hungry.

Which one said that? Batey asked.

Wilson pointed to a young woman behind the long counter. The counter was busy. Men shoulder to shoulder. Most of them were Hispanic farm workers. The young woman was walking up and back with a carafe of coffee. She smiled a lot. Had a booming laugh.

That's Cheryl, Batey said.

Okay, Wilson said.

That's something she would do. Bring you eggs even if you didn't ask for them. Won't charge you either.

Super, Wilson said.

He lifted his cup from its saucer and took a delicate sip and then set the cup back in the saucer and then laced his hands together before him on top of the table.

Well, Wilson said, what should we talk about?

Suppose you heard about the girl, Batey said.

Yes, Wilson said.

Molly Summers, Batey said. Confirmed it. Only eighteen years old.

Yes, Wilson said.

He looked over at the stack of photographs. The top one was of her blackened naked feet. Arranged perfectly together.

Yeh get the autopsy report? Fielding asked.

Wilson tapped one of the stacks with his middle finger.

Is it as bad as we thought? Batey asked.

That's a subjective idea, Mr Batey, Wilson said. The notion of *bad*.

Okay, Batey said. Well, would I think it's bad?

Yes, Wilson said. I think you would consider this bad. I think you might even consider this worse.

We saw an eighteen-year-old girl who had her throat cut and then was set on fire, Fielding said. How can yeh top that?

Not cut, Wilson said.

Excuse me?

Her throat. Not cut. She was garroted.

What the hell is *garroted*? Fielding asked.

Strangled, Wilson said. The skin of her throat was damaged but not cut. The report states that her larynx was collapsed. The weapon was probably some type of collar. About an inch and a half wide.

Like a dog collar? Batey asked.

Wilson shrugged.

Could be a thing of his, Wilson said. Or perhaps hers.

A thing? Fielding said.

Yes, Wilson said. A kink, if you like. An act of submission. But more than likely it was imposed.

What do we know about this girl? Batey asked.

Runaway, Wilson said. Picked up twice for prostitution down in Seattle.

Probably how he found her, Fielding said.

So what's the *worse* part? Batey asked. You said *worse*. What's worse?

There were several samples of semen found in the vagina staggered over a few days.

A few days? Batey asked. Two? Three?

Four, Wilson said. All postmortem. They also found ketamine and heroin in her system.

What is ketamine? Fielding asked. What does that do?

It is a dissociative drug, Wilson said. Typically used as an anesthetic. It acts on different chemicals in the brain to produce visual and auditory distortion.

A detachment from reality, Batey said.

Yes, Wilson said.

So the victim doesn't even know what's happenin, Fielding said.

Correct, Mr Fielding. Completely unaware.

A woman cleared her throat at the end of the booth. The men looked up at her.

Oh hi, Cheryl, Batey said.

Didn't want to interrupt, she said. Looked like you boys were onto something good.

There ain't any good in this, Batey said.

Cheryl was holding the carafe of coffee. She started to say *Can I top you off,* but she only got to *Can I top* before she saw the photograph of the burned foot at the opposite end of the table. And then she didn't say anything. She only stared. Didn't even attempt to pour the coffee.

Yes mam, Fielding finally said, I'll take a bit more. If yer pourin. Dee, yeh want some more?

Batey slid his mug across the table. But Cheryl didn't move. She was paralyzed. Then she said: That the girl from the beach?

Yes mam, Wilson said. Molly Summers.

She stood there with her hand covering her mouth. Finally Wilson reached for the photograph and turned it over. That shook Cheryl out of it. She smiled with her mouth closed and left without filling their cups.

When she was gone, Wilson said, Do you remember Amy Barnhardt?

The girl found up in the hills by that father and son? Batey said.

Yes, Wilson said. I pulled the report on her.

Let me guess, Fielding said. Detachment from reality?

Yes, Wilson said. The same mixture in fact.

So they aren't taking this on their own, Batey said.

No, Wilson said. I don't believe they are. I think the word is *administered*. And let's go back a bit further.

How far are we talking? Batey said.

Eight years.

Eight years? Batey frowned. I think I know where you're headed.

That girl you found all those years ago, Wilson said. Can you guess?

Same cocktail?

Wilson nodded.

We've got a pattern, Batey said. Don't we?

Yes, Mr Batey, we do.

22

THE SUN WAS SHINING THAT MORNING AND THE AIR WAS COLD
and the foothills were dusted with snow. The white mountains
to the east were stark against the blue sky like a diamond in a
dark ear. Dani suggested they go shopping. Get Ruby some new
clothes.

Shopping?

For clothes, Dani said. How's that sound to you?

They drove to the department store and they walked in together and started looking at the clothes on the metal circular
racks.

What do you think about this?

Ruby held up a dress.

Dani shrugged.

Okay, Ruby said. How about these?

It was a pair of Levi's.

Dani shrugged again. You like them? she asked.

Yes, Ruby said.

Then that's all that matters.

Maybe I'll try them on first.

They got the key from the attendant. A bored-looking teenager reading a gossip magazine. She said, while blowing a bubble: Only five items at a time.

I only got six, Ruby said.

Only five.

Dani grabbed the dress from the collection and set the rest on the counter.

Five, she told the attendant.

The girl went back to her magazine.

In the dressing room Ruby tried everything on like royalty. She turned at the mirror. Dani sat in a chair just outside the door and from time to time asked her how it was going in there. There was an old *Vogue* magazine in the rack beside her chair and Dani picked that up and flipped through the pages, and lost in all those glossy images she never even saw him come into the store.

23

NOON HAD FOLLOWED THEM THERE. WATCHED THEM LEAVE
Dani's apartment that morning. Followed them to the department store. Watched her pick out clothes. Watched her disappear into the dressing room.

He was loitering in the lingerie section. Waiting for the attendant to leave her desk.

Can I help you with something? a young lady said.

She appeared behind him. Noon looked at her. He had his ball cap pulled low. His eyes were cold and blue. She could look at them only for a short moment.

What was that you asked me? Noon said.

If you needed any help, she said. You need help with anything?

Why would I need help?

Sometimes men have questions.

Questions about what?

About what to pick out for their sweetheart.

Who said anything about a sweetheart?

I'm sorry, sir. She looked around. Is there something you had in mind?

In mind?

Yes, she said. There must've been something you were looking for?

Who said I was looking for anything?

I didn't mean anything by it. Just thought maybe you were looking for a gift of some kind?

You ask a lot of questions, Noon said.

Her eyes shot around. Hoping for something to bring a respite.

Sir, she said, if I upset you somehow, I apologize.

If you didn't know what you said then why would you feel the need to apologize? Do you apologize for things that you are not sorry for often? Is that a habit of yours?

The girl was silent. She bit her upper lip. She looked at the ground. She looked at the register. She looked for anyone else.

What is your name? he asked.

My name?

Yes.

Eunice, she said.

Eunice.

Yes.

That's an old-fashioned name.

It was my grandmother's.

Was she a nice lady?

Yes.

That's good. I have always wondered why a parent would give a newborn an old name.

I guess it's out of respect, Eunice said.

Respect.

Maybe.

Maybe?

Listen, sir, I need to see to the other customers.

Noon looked around. The store was empty. Only the attendant reading a magazine by the dressing room.

What customers? Noon said.

There are a few things I need to do in the back.

Do you need to see to customers, Noon said. Or do something in the back?

Sir, she said, I don't know what you're asking. But let me know if you need anything.

You already know the answer to that. That's why you came over here in the first place.

Okay, she said.

She started to walk away but he said her name.

Yes?

How old are you? he asked.

Nineteen.

Nineteen.

Yes.

It's the perfect age, Noon said. Isn't it.

I suppose.

Are you in school?

I go to the community college.

Uh-huh, Noon said. What is your focus?

My focus?

Of study. What are you studying?

Costume design.

Costume design. I see. You enjoy make-believe then?

I suppose, she said.

He lifted a black balconette bra from the rack and held it up.

Can I take this into the dressing room? he asked.

The balconette?

Yes.

I don't know why you'd want to.

To see what it would look like, he said.

That's for a girl, she said.

You're a girl, he said.

What I mean is, there wouldn't be anyone to try it on.

Who's to say I wouldn't try it on?

Would you?

No, he said. It's made for a woman after all. You said so your-self. Do I look like a woman?

No, she said.

But you are, Noon said.

Yes.

If I asked you to try this on for me, would you?

I could put it on a mannequin, she said, if you'd like.

I don't want to see it on a mannequin, he said. I want to see it on you.

She had been taking slow steps back, by the inch. Trying her best.

I'm afraid I can't, she said. It's against policy.

What policy is that?

Store, she said. Store's policy.

I would think the policy of the store is to sell. Wouldn't you? There was a noise by the attendant station and Noon and Eunice looked and Noon saw Dani and Ruby coming from the dressing room with the clothes piled in their arms. Dani gave the key back to the attendant and they walked to the register. Ruby spilled the clothes onto the counter and the attendant rang them up and folded them and slipped them into paper bags and then they left the store.

Suddenly Noon smiled. He took a deep breath. He made a sound like he'd just finished a good meal.

Of course, he said. You're right. I don't want to break policy. Nor get you in trouble.

He put the balconette back on the rack.

You have been very helpful, Eunice. I won't forget that.

He turned to leave. When he was at the door he turned back and waved delicately to Eunice and then walked out the door. The woman began to suck air like she hadn't taken a breath in a very long time.

24

ON THE WAY BACK TO DANI'S APARTMENT RUBY TALKED THE
whole time. She was pointing out stores she'd like to go into. She
was naming restaurants where she'd like to eat.

It's like this is all new for you, Dani said.

It is.

We'll go out to dinner tonight, Dani said. After I close up at
the shelter. Anywhere you want to go.

Ruby turned to look at her. Dani's silhouette was striking
against the glass.

I got you something, Ruby said.

When?

The other day.

What day?

The other day.

Yesterday?

No.

The day before?

Shut up and listen, Ruby said.

Dani smiled. Well, what is it?

Just something I bought you.

With what money?

Just some money I found.

You stealing my money again?

I've never stole your money.

My money's your money, is that it?

Would you just listen.

Are you going to make me guess or what?

Close your eyes, Ruby said.

I can't close my eyes, Dani said. I'm driving.

Okay, then open your eyes.

They are open.

Ruby took it from her purse.

It was a necklace. Silver and thin as a strand of hair.

You bought me jewelry, Dani said.

You don't like it.

It's not that at all, Dani said. You bought me something. You bought me a present.

So you like it?

Yes, Dani said. It's the most perfect necklace I've ever seen.

Later that night Dani moved about the quiet shelter cleaning up a mess here and there. A few plastic cups. A plate or two. Remnants of dinner. She walked among the rows of men and women sprawled on cots. Some asleep. Snores echoing back and forth like the calls of strange songbirds.

Pastor Lee walked about. He would talk to the ones still awake. Pray with them if asked to. Dani walked past him holding an extra blanket. Lee held out his hand to her.

Is our friend Ruby doing well? he asked.

Yes, Pastor Lee, Dani said. It's very nice to see.

I haven't seen her here lately.

Yes, Dani said. I found her an apartment in town. A small one-bedroom.

I see, Lee said, his eyes squinting with judgment. Are you helping with the rent? I assume so.

Yes, Dani said. Paying it forward, I guess. Following your lead.

Well, Lee said, not exactly my lead. It wasn't me who paid your rent. It was the church.

But you helped me and now I want to help her.

That's kind of you, Lee said. You are a kind woman. Here.

He took the blanket from her arms.

Why don't you leave early tonight, he said. I'll close up.

Are you sure? I'm happy to stay.

No, he said. Bring some of the leftovers from supper to Ruby. Tell her I'm thinking about her.

Thank you, pastor.

It was raining when Dani stepped outside. The lights of town ran in the wet streets. The colors looked like melting wax. It was a Tuesday night and the streets and the sidewalks were empty and the stores were all closed. The only things open were a bar down the street and a twenty-four-hour diner on the corner. She turned her collar up against the rain and tucked the plastic bag of leftovers under her arm and started for her car.

The little VW was parked three or four blocks away. She walked quickly. Her shoes were soon wet. There was a gap in the buildings where she could see the water of the bay. The water was dark and the only thing out there to see was the lighthouse with its beam revolving endlessly like a lost satellite.

The night was cold and it felt like it might snow. The kind of cold that left you damp even if you were dry. Kind of cold that made you tremble with weakness. She stopped and watched the lighthouse and for some reason the image frightened her. The isolation of it in such an inhospitable place. To be a beacon to all those unseen things prowling the darkness. Attracting both the good and the evil. She turned away and walked on with a great feeling of discomfort. For the three or four blocks she couldn't rid herself of it. Near her car was a pay phone. She was only a few minutes from her apartment but she opened the hinged door of the booth and set the leftovers on the floor and fished a quarter from her pocket and dialed the number to her apartment and leaned against the glass of the booth as the phone rang.

Hello?

Hi.

Where are you? Ruby asked.

Just left the shelter.

Are you coming home?

Yes, Dani said. I just wanted to check in.

What's wrong?

Nothing.

Are you okay?

I'm fine. I'll be home soon. Just wanted to hear your voice.

Dani said goodbye and hung up the phone. She picked up the bag of leftovers and opened the glass door. The rain had lightened. Only a drizzle now. She stepped out of the booth and closed the door behind her and walked around the front of the VW and set the bag on top of the car. She fumbled with her keys, tilting her face down and searching through the keys in the low light. She found the right one and put it in the lock and was about to turn it when she heard, Hello, Dani.

His dark silhouette was reflected in the glass. It seemed to rise up behind her, filling the window, consuming all of it. Before she could say anything the blade passed across her throat. A spray of blood like bird shot peppered the glass. She turned to him, trying to suck in air, but the blood was spilling into her windpipe. She was trying to speak but only the sound of her choking breath through the blood came through. She fell back against the door and he grabbed her by the arms and tenderly helped her to sit in the street. She was watching him all the while. Her eyes wide and unfathomable. He smoothed her hair. He tucked some of it behind her ear. Her blood was black as tar in the light and the last of it fell forth in a diminishing rill down the skin of her sternum to die out in the valley of her breasts, staining her tattoo of the woman being carried off by a raven.

Noon took a deep breath in and then he let it out. He lifted the necklace from her chest and popped it in one motion. He looked at it draped over his hand. He balled it up and put it in his pocket. Then he went around to the passenger side and opened the door and saw a few envelopes on the seat and found one with Dani's address on it and picked it up and folded it and put it in his pocket and then shut the door. Then he turned and walked to the alley across the street, to his camera on the tripod, and turned it off and put the camera back in the gladstone. Then he folded up the tripod and walked off down the sidewalk while the rain fell, washing Dani's blood into the gutter.

25

NOON STOOD NEAR THE BUILDING ENTRANCE WITH A BOOT jacked up against the wall and smoking a cigarette waiting for a tenant to come in or go out. He had smoked two before someone exited. He flicked the cigarette into the street and at the last moment deftly stuck the toe of his boot between the door and the jamb.

At the bottom of the stairwell he paused and looked up. It was only five stories. Dani's apartment was on the fourth. He put his hand on the banister and started up the stairs. The building was old and the smell reflected it. The stairs were some type of hardwood with green carpeting down the middle and the carpeting was wearing thin. The building was all but silent. Occasionally the muffled sound of a voice through one of the heavy wood doors. A baby crying. The yip of a small dog. But all these sounds were momentary and then the silence would return.

He stood in front of Dani's apartment. Number 404. Noon didn't move. Just stood there with his hands at his side. Looking intently at the door. It had been painted white at one time but the paint was chipping and the blond wood beneath was starting to show through. He stood there, savoring the moment. The missing starlet to his strange endeavors. He put his ear to the door. The wood was cold on his skin. He could hear the television going. He waited and listened for any sound of her but there was only the television. He took his ear away and tried the doorknob but it didn't turn. He took the knife and snapped it open and held it behind his back and was about to knock when the door two apartments down opened and a mother and her young son came out.

Noon snapped the knife shut and stowed it in his pocket. He made eye contact with the mother and the mother moved her son to the far side of the mezzanine, and they regarded one another intensely and she shooed her boy along saying, Come on, Joey.

When he heard the entrance doors open and close and when the building had gone silent again Noon snapped the knife open and knocked on the door. He waited. He knocked again. No one came. So he wedged the blade in the jamb and twisted it and the latch released and the door quietly inched inward. He stepped through and closed the door behind him and looked into the living room. Without taking his eyes away from the room he took off his boots by pulling the heel against the toe of the other. Stepped into the hall and in his socks he didn't make a sound. He went into the living room. All the cheap venetian blinds were closed. The television playing to an empty room. He went to the bedroom. The door was open. The bed was unmade. Some clothes on the floor. A lamp on the bedside table was on. Under the light was a photo booth strip of pictures. He picked it up and regarded their faces. The two of them smiling. The two of them making comical expressions. He folded it and put it in his shirt pocket. Then he went to the bathroom. He flicked on the light. It smelled like someone had recently taken a shower; the air was damp. Fog still in the corners of the mirror. There was underwear on the floor and he knelt and slipped the point of the knife through one of the holes and lifted the garment and pulled it off the blade like you might fruit from a skewer and he brought it to his nose and breathed in and then he balled it up and put it in his pocket.

He went back out to the living room and sat on the couch and watched the television for a moment. It was showing football highlights. Then he stood and went to the television and turned it off and the screen went a flat gray. He went back to the couch and sat in the silence and listened for anything to make a sound. He laid the knife across his lap. He tilted it back and forth and the blade caught the lamplight and he looked up at the dead television screen and the light from the blade was winking in the glass.

He waited like that for almost an hour but no one showed up. He looked at the time on the microwave over the stove. It read 9:10 in blue numbers.

He went back into the bedroom and lay down on the bed with the knife beside him. Then he turned off the lamp and lay there, waiting in the darkness.

26

RUBY HAD LEFT THE APARTMENT BUILDING A SHORT TIME AFTER talking with Dani on the phone. She had showered and dressed and gone out for some dessert to bring back for Dani. She was on her way to the twenty-four-hour diner when a police cruiser with its lights on went speeding in the opposite direction. Not long after an ambulance with its siren blaring came roaring up and turned where the police cruiser had. There was no reason for it other than premonition but she abandoned the idea for dessert and turned back and began walking to where the cruiser and ambulance had fled. She began to walk faster. Faster until she was running down the sidewalk, her shoes now wet and heavy with puddle water. And not far from where the vehicles had turned she saw the red and blue lights and a small crowd of people and the unmistakable shape of Dani's VW.

There were onlookers gazing down from the apartment windows and people loitering on the sidewalk and the police were holding them back with their arms held out like they were holding back livestock. One officer was beginning to string up the yellow tape. On the crowd's fringe Ruby lifted on her tiptoes to see anything. Some of the onlookers had umbrellas. Some did not. She could hardly see a thing.

Ruby pushed through. Some people jeered. Watch it, they said. They said: Hey!

But she didn't listen. She kept pushing and all of a sudden there was no more crowd, only the wet and gleaming pavement of the street between her and Dani's body. All the life drained out of Ruby as she stood there looking.

Pastor Lee had been called. He arrived at the scene and found her collapsed on the asphalt. He carried her to his car, got her in the front seat, and went around to the driver's side and started the motor. Ruby sat there slumped against the door. He didn't say anything. Just put the car into gear and drove away. They got to the shelter and he helped her to the room Dani had made up for her all those days before. Laid her down and pulled the blanket up to her chin. He was saying something but Ruby didn't hear it. It was like she was underwater and he was talking above it. He finally left, leaving the desk lamp on. Ruby just stared at the ceiling. There's a sadness that is incapable of feeling, and that was happening to Ruby: she didn't feel a thing.

She lay like that for hours. Not talking and not feeling. The only thing she knew was that her life had been altered and could only go one way. She could never go back.

She was suddenly roused from this state and pulled off the blanket and sat up and stood from the bed and walked barefoot through the big room and out the front doors. She walked down the sidewalk. The rain had stopped. Sometimes the moon showed behind the clouds. It was a crescent moon and the horn rode the clouds like a running sail. It was cold and she had on only a pair of sweatpants and a T-shirt but she didn't feel the cold and didn't feel the rocks under her feet.

She stopped once and glanced out at the lighthouse spinning

in the darkness. She might have stood watching it for a few seconds or a few hours. She didn't know. Didn't care. Time for her was no longer measured in minutes and hours. No longer in days. Just a single life, the only certainty of which was the commencement. All else was unknown. All else just debris in the tides.

She walked a mile. The road led away from town and bent lower toward the water. She walked over the beach and looked out at the lighthouse. The water over the bay was still as a millpond. The horned moon was mirrored upon it. Then from somewhere above a single flake of snow drifted down like a speck of ash. Then another. And another.

She stood on the shoreline with her toes just touching the water at that discernible place where one world ends and another begins. She undressed. She let her clothes fall where they did. Then she stepped into the water. It came to her ankles, then her knees. It rose to her hips and when she'd waded to her chest she began to gasp at the cold. She lurched forward in an awkward dive and began swimming toward the lighthouse. She kept her back to the fading shoreline so as to never see it again. The freezing water was lapping at her lower lip. The salt choked her. But she kept swimming with the ebbing tide, and she would keep swimming till it turned, and when the flooding water brought the flood of euphoria she wouldn't fight any of it anymore.

PART 3

I look back on all my years of sheriffin, all the maybes therein. I think about how lucky I was. When yer young the finality in everythin is vague. Like lookin out on the ocean and knowin there is land, another world entirely beyond the horizon, but truly believin yeh'll never see it. That's what old age is: comin, finally, upon that shore. Yeh can't cheat it anymore. Eventually the boat is goin a run aground.

When Sara was still alive I'd lament the fall. Autumn. The leaves would start to drop and the wind would carry them away. Because she knew this about me, Sara would say, Yes, but it's not like summer is gone forever. And that's what we had then. We had the future. Spring would always return and every year we'd cut down a Christmas tree and each summer we'd sit in the bleachers and watch baseball. That's what old age takes away from yeh. When yeh get to be my age there is no future and there's nothin to plan for. And I know that sounds morbid but I don't see it that way. I see a bit of solace in that. It's a burden I no longer have to carry.

27

NOON WATCHED THE ROOM PALE AS THE MORNING CAME ON
and the noise of the street grew louder. He swung his feet to
the floor and stood from the bed. He hadn't slept a moment the
night before. Hadn't even closed his eyes. Everything was just
as it was when he had entered the apartment. He looked at the
girl's clothes on the floor.

I guess you are not coming, he said.

He went to the kitchen and opened the refrigerator. He took
out a carton of orange juice and opened the spout and took a
drink. He looked around the apartment. He drank some more
of the juice and then put it back in the refrigerator and went to
the door and put on his boots and walked out.

Outside the sidewalks and streets were covered in a thin
layer of snow. The snow was wet and already melting from the
awnings and hoods of cars. The sky was a pale blue with a little
lavender to it and the sun had not yet crested the mountains to
the east. He walked across the street to a café and took a table
near the window and ordered a Coke and sat drinking it through
a straw and watching the building. The waitress had asked if
he'd like anything to eat but he said the Coke was enough. The
waitress was in her mid-thirties and sleepy eyed. She said she'd
be back to check on him.

An hour passed. People came out of the building and went in but none of them were her. The waitress came by again and refilled his Coke and asked, Would you like me to get some eggs going for you or something?

Noon watched her. She had nice hips. Then he looked up.

I already told you the Coke was enough, he said.

Figured you might be getting hungry by now.

What would bring you to that conclusion?

She waited for him to smile but he never did and she said, Okay.

Before she left Noon stopped her and said, Do you know this woman?

He took the photo strip from his shirt pocket and put it on the table. She bent over to look at it.

The one here, she said, that's a gal named Dani. Lives across the street. Did anyway. They found her last night.

Yes, Noon said. I heard. How about this one here?

She squinted. She furrowed her brow.

No, she said. I've seen her maybe a few times. But I don't know her name.

Her name is Ruby, Noon said.

Ruby.

Yes.

Sounds like you already know her.

Maybe I do and maybe I don't. I'm asking if *you* know her.

You some kind of private investigator or something?

Yes, Noon said. Something like that.

He took a pack of cigarettes from his shirt pocket and tapped the pack on the heel of his hand and shucked one from the pack and put it between his lips and flipped open the Zippo and was going to light it when she said, You can't smoke that here.

Why?

You're in the nonsmoking section.

I've never understood that, he said.

Understood what?

The sections. Do you have different air being pumped into this section?

No, she said. Same air.

Same air.

Yes.

Same air as the smoking section.

Yes.

I see.

He snapped closed the Zippo. He laid some money on the table.

How old are you? he asked.

Thirty-four.

You're quite beautiful.

She blushed but not from flattery.

What are you doing tonight? he asked.

Tonight?

I want to take you to dinner.

Dinner?

Yes, he said. I want to take you someplace where you can eat food and then I want to have sex with you. And I want to film us having sex. Would that be something you would enjoy?

Again she waited for him to smile but again he never did. She held up her left hand to show him the ring on her finger.

Lucky you, he said.

He stood and walked out of the café and she watched him go and he turned and looked at her through the window and there was not a single emotion on his face and then he walked on and disappeared.

28

RUBY'S BODY WASHED UP A DAY LATER A QUARTER MILE FROM
where she had swum out. It was reported on in the paper. The
body was still listed as unidentified but the moment Noon saw it
he knew it was her. He took the paper from the newsstand and
went to a café on the other side of town and took a table near
the window. A waitress came and asked if he would like to order
anything. No, he said.

He sat there for almost an hour just looking at the paper. At
the headline of the washed-up girl. No one had ever gotten away
from him and now someone had and he couldn't decide if what
he felt was anger or amusement. The waitress came back at some
point and asked if he had made any decisions. He looked at her
as if she were speaking a foreign language. Then he smiled. Yes,
he said, I believe I have.

He left the café with the paper folded in his hands and walked
back to his car. He started the engine and swung out of the parking lot onto the street and drove to the shopping mall. He parked
three or four rows back and at an angle so that the entrance to
the mall could never be obscured. He shut off the engine and sat
back and laid his arm across the seat and watched the entrance
with hardly a blink. For long periods he sat so still that one might
think a mannequin had been placed behind the wheel.

The hours passed. The sky grew darker. The rain had given way to a fine mist. There were sweet gums planted around the parking lot and tall fir trees out behind the mall and the clouds were low and the tops of the taller firs were hidden. In the cracks of the sidewalks weeds were pushing through.

Noon chain-smoked cigarettes, lighting a new one with the cherry of the old and dropping the butts out the window and listening to the hiss of each on the wet asphalt. The image of the mall was bespeckled through the windshield. Maybe a shopper would pass or a car would drive by but other than that it was quiet. For hours it was completely silent.

It was a little after five when he saw her. She was walking with a friend. It was dark and all the parking lot lights had come on. The two of them were walking quickly. Almost running. Under the cones of streetlights Noon could see they were smiling. Making a game of running through the rain. Noon watched them get to their car and open the doors. Then taillights flared. The wet pavement washed in red.

Noon watched the car pull out of the space and swing around and come toward him and as the car passed he could see the girls laughing together.

Hello, Eunice, he said.

Noon started the engine and followed them at a distance out of the parking lot and onto the road.

Their car pulled into a burger joint a ways down and Noon pulled to the shoulder and waited for them to get out of their car. Once they were in the restaurant Noon pulled in and backed into a space and left the engine running and turned off the headlights and watched them sit in a booth.

He must have sat for an hour or more. Never once did he take his eyes from her. Never once looking at the girl across the table. Only her he cared to look at. Only Eunice that mattered.

The parking lot was full of puddles and the restaurant's lights were mirrored on the surface. Sometimes the wind gusted and the puddles rippled and all those reflected lights went fuzzy.

He watched her eat. He watched her sip her milkshake through a straw. He watched her tuck her hair behind her ear. It was all perfect.

Almost two hours later they finished up and paid their bill and left the restaurant. The wind came at them and they shrieked as they ran toward their car. Noon cracked his window and listened to them scream. Their feet bursting puddles like children playing in the rain.

The girls drove off and Noon followed them for twenty minutes. It seemed aimless. They seemed to be wasting time. Avoiding going home. Doing all the things teenage girls like to do.

The rain abated and the wind swept the clouds away like dust and the sickle moon appeared. He followed them into a quiet neighborhood. The speed limit read fifteen miles per hour. One of those neighborhood watch signs. All the houses were modest but nice. Certain covenants with regard to decorum. Little lights for the landscaping. Newer cars in the driveways.

Noon pulled over and waited to see what house they were going to pull into. Their car pulled into a driveway and both girls got out and hugged behind the car and Eunice walked off alone down the street. Noon reached behind him and lifted a long piece of fabric. He wrapped it around his arm and shoulder several times and made a makeshift sling. Threw on a ball cap and pulled it low over his eyes. When the other girl had gone inside Noon shifted into drive and drove slowly past Eunice. The girl didn't look up. Noon drove on ahead a couple blocks and pulled to the side and shut off the motor and got out and went around to the trunk and got out the tire iron and jack. He placed the jack under the chassis and fitted the tire iron over a lug nut.

As the girl approached Noon began to struggle with the tire iron. The girl slowed as she came up on him.

Are you alright, sir? she asked.

Noon startled for effect.

Heavens, he said. Scared me.

I'm sorry, she said. Do you need any help?

She pointed at his bad arm.

Tire went flat, he said.

She looked down at the tire. Her eyes pinched.

It looks fine to me, she said.

Would you hold this a moment? Noon said. I need to get something from the glove box.

He handed her the tire iron and opened the passenger door and leaned in and opened the glove box and pulled something out. He turned to the girl and smiled. His face was shadowed under the cap.

I really appreciate you stopping and helping me like this, Noon said. You've made my night.

No problem, she said. What happened to your arm?

Nothing is wrong with my arm.

Why do you have it in a sling then?

I don't.

She frowned slightly. Noon's unslinged hand was behind his back.

Well, she said. Here's your tire iron back.

Thank you, he said.

She handed it to him and when she did he pulled his good hand around and stuck a needle into her shoulder and depressed the plunger. She looked down at it, uncomprehending. Then looked back at him and in the fleeting moments before she blacked out she recognized his face from that day in the store and he said: Hello, Eunice. He caught her as she went limp and he carried her like a sleeping child to the trunk and laid her gently in it and closed the lid and looked around. The street was empty. Nothing. Not even a dog.

29

DEPUTY RAWLINGS WAS OUT IN THE COUNTY THAT NIGHT
driving around on patrol. Wasn't much traffic and there wasn't
much to see. He could see the lights of town glowing against the
clouds. Gave himself twenty minutes before he'd throw in the
towel and call it a night.

On his way back he passed what looked like an abandoned
house except in the driveway was a burgundy Ford Fairlane that
looked anything but abandoned. He had no reason to stop but
he also had nothing else to do, so he pulled the cruiser off the
state route and parked behind the Ford. Rawlings took note of
the plates. Snapped on the dome light and wrote it down and
then snapped off the lights again and sat there for a moment
trying to talk himself out of getting out of the cruiser. He finally
took the flashlight from the glove box and put on his hat and
stepped out into the rain.

At first it seemed empty and nothing compelled him. Rawlings swung the beam about. First at the car then at the house.
For some reason the car looked familiar but he didn't think anything more of it. The house was boarded up with plywood covering the windows and graffiti all over the siding. The roof was
more moss than roof and one end of the gable was collapsing in.
It reminded Rawlings of a rotting pumpkin.

The ground was all wet mud. Rawlings walked to the trunk of the car and shined the light at it. Then he dropped it to the mud below and in the light were boot marks. Rawlings knelt and touched their outline. Rain could have softened up an old print, he supposed. But these looked new. Rawlings tilted his head forward and the rain ran off the brim of his hat. He stood and trained the light at the house. Then back down at the prints.

He walked to the house and stepped lightly up the rotting stairs. The wood was spongy. It was like walking on damp grass. He shined the light at the door but the door had a big hasp and a heavy-duty lock. A sign with a court-ordered condemnation bulletin on it. He went to one of the windows and pressed the flashlight to a crack in the plywood and peered in. Inside was completely vacant. More than vacant. As if no one had ever lived there. All manner of nature had taken over. Rawlings stepped back and turned the flashlight back at the Fairlane.

The boot prints led away from the car and around the side of the house. Rawlings was careful not to disturb them. Walked by keeping the prints between himself and the house as if herding them. From time to time he stopped and shined the light behind him to make sure he was still alone.

When he finally caught up to where the boot prints ended he was looking straight down at the doors of a storm cellar. The paint peeling. The wood covered in a black film. The boot prints just disappeared. No meandering. Just straight in. There was no lock on the doors and Rawlings shook his head at what he was going to do next.

The iron handle was rusty and cold against his skin. He hoped the door would not budge but it did. Even through the small opening and even over the strong odor of mud the smell of mildew was overwhelming. He heaved the door open and let it fall. Trained the light down the stairs, cutting the darkness.

He stood there a long moment. Not sure he wanted to go any further. Not sure he even wanted to have come this far.

Sheriff's department, Rawlings called out. Anyone down there?

He waited a moment longer. Waiting for someone or something to come into the yellow light of the beam.

Ain't in trouble, he said. Just asking is all. This house isn't safe to be in. Condemned.

Still there was no answer. Rawlings groaned. He unsnapped the leather band on his holster.

With his first step the wooden stair moaned. He tested it. Then took another. He took each step carefully, slowly. Never once did he let the light get out of sight of exactly where he was going. He half watched the step directly below him and half watched the stone floor.

When he got to the bottom he swung the flashlight. Trained it up overhead. Old pipes and black joists. There was a string for a single bulb hanging and he pulled it but nothing happened. He stood there listening for a sound. There was water dripping somewhere but that was it. Rain falling outside the cellar door.

As he was turning to leave the flashlight caught sight of a small wooden chair that stood in the corner. Rawlings studied it a moment. Seemed odd there being a chair in an otherwise empty cellar. Or maybe not odd. Maybe completely normal. Rawlings went to it and tilted it and turned it and stood it back where he had found it. He turned back toward the stairs and a pair of burning eyes were caught in the beam of the flashlight. Startled Rawlings so that he almost dropped the light. The rat went skittering.

Back in his cruiser he turned on the headlights and backed out of the drive and drove off down the road.

———

When he was certain the deputy was gone Noon came from the only corner of the cellar Rawlings had failed to search, the girl limp in his arms. He went to the breaker panel and switched on the light and the single bulb flared. Then he sat the girl in the chair. He carried her to the center of the cellar and tied her to the compression post. Then he pulled the string and the light snapped off.

30

NOON PULLED INTO THE STRIP CLUB A LITTLE AFTER NINE THAT
night. More like a roadhouse. A small neon sign out front: EX-
OTIC DANCERS. ALL NUDE. Noon parked the Fairlane and
sat watching the place with the engine running. It was a Friday
night and the parking lot was full. It was a concrete building that
was painted black. You could tell it had held some other kind of
reputable commerce in another life but now it was the French
Maid Gentleman's Club. All the windows had been bricked over.

When Noon finally went in, a bouncer nodded at him without asking for ID. The music was loud. Hair metal rock and roll.
There was a runway stage with a pole and two women were dancing topless with folded ones and fives stuffed in their G-strings.
The seats below the stage were full and the men were packed in
like tinned fish.

Noon went to the bar and ordered a Coke. He stood with his
back to the bar and watched the audience. The lights were flashing an array of colors. There was a mirror ball twirling. A DJ in
the corner would announce the next girl and she'd strut out and
turn and smile and the men would jeer and wave dollar bills like
ranchers at an auction house.

Two men caught Noon's eye. Sitting a few rows back from
the stage. They'd stand and cheer but the girls paid them no

attention. Noon sipped his Coke like it was wine. These two men seemed overly eager and by their gestures and expressions one could tell they felt they were being dealt a great injustice by being ignored. One had a perm-like haircut and the other wore his long and with a ball cap on the top of his head like a trucker. Both were a little overweight.

Noon watched them for the better part of half an hour. They were going to be perfect. Noon was turning to order another Coke when a hand touched his arm.

You looking for a date tonight, baby?

It was a dancer wearing a fishnet shirt that stopped just below her breasts. She was wearing a black G-string and had a huge head of blond hair.

A what? Noon asked.

You looking for a date? A little fun?

I'm having fun right now.

Want to have a little more fun?

What kind of fun would that be?

She leaned in and whispered into his ear.

I'm not sure you're my type, Noon said.

And how's that?

You're a little too . . . what's the word. Lively.

Lively.

Yes.

Want me to play dead? she said. Is that it? I'll play dead.

Noon sipped the Coke. He cocked his head oddly. He said: If I gave you five hundred dollars, would you go down to that table there and ask those two men a question for me?

What kind of question?

Just a question I've been wanting to ask them.

Let's see the money.

Don't you want to know the question first?

Sure, she said. What's the question?

The question is: Would they have sex with you and my girlfriend while I videotape it?

You want me to fuck them in front of you?

And my girlfriend.

Who's your girlfriend?

Why does that matter?

The woman leaned against the bar.

You some kind of sicko? she asked. She smiled at him.

No, Noon said. No more than anyone else in here.

Noon reached out and touched the bend at her shoulder.

You have very beautiful skin, he said. Has anyone ever told you that? It would look incredible on camera. My girlfriend would love it. She has a thing for older blonds.

I'm only twenty-five.

Yes, Noon said. How about this? Five hundred for the question. Another seven for the rest?

Twelve hundred?

If my math is right, yes. Twelve hundred just for being your charming self.

Noon reached into his pocket and showed her the money. She glanced down at it and then took the money and walked down to the men behind the stage and leaned and asked the question. Noon watched them balk in disbelief. The woman flashed her breasts as an incentive and then she turned and pointed up toward Noon. Both men squinted against the flashing lights at the dark silhouette at the bar.

A couple minutes later they were all seated at a table in the corner going over Noon's proposition.

What do you mean you want to film it? one said.

It's very simple, Noon said. I want to set up a camera and I want to film you having sex with this woman and my girlfriend.

Like a foursome?

There would be four of you. So yes. You are good at math.

What would you be doing? the other said.

I've told you that already.

So they ain't going to fuck you?

No, Noon said. I don't know how I can explain this any easier.

He turned to the stripper. He said: Do you find this woman attractive?

Well, hell yeah.

Have you ever had sex with someone as attractive as her?

They were both silent. Just staring at her.

That means no, Noon said. I'm offering you a very rare opportunity.

You some kind of pornographer?

Do you like pornography? Noon asked.

We have cocks, the other said. Don't we?

I don't know, Noon said. I have never seen you with your pants off.

The one looked at the other. Frowned a little.

And she's cool with it? he asked.

Cool with what?

Your girlfriend. She's okay with all this?

What kind of person do you think I am? Noon said. Everyone has a choice in this world.

Well, bud? The one looked at the other. What do you think? Could be fun.

How much you say again? he asked Noon.

A thousand.

A grand?

Yes.

Each?

How about this? Noon said.

He took the money clip from his pocket and pulled several hundred dollars from it and laid the money on the table.

That's half, Noon said. Earnest money.

What kind of money?

A good faith gesture, Noon said. Go on. Take it.

They hesitated. One scratched his chin. The other licked his lips. The stripper twirled a strand of hair around and around her finger.

We can have that now? the one said.

Of course, Noon said.

This don't seem real, the other said.

It's real, Noon said. It's very real. Nothing from here on out will ever be this real. Everything you do from this night on will all seem like a dream.

Well? the one said.

Giddy up, bud.

Noon smiled. He wrote down an address. He said: Meet me here in four hours. All three of you.

I can't go with you? the woman said.

No, Noon said. It has to be this way.

He stood from the table.

Four hours, he said.

31

NOON WAS LYING ON HIS BACK ON THE BED OF HIS MOTEL
room but he wasn't sleeping. Just staring at the crack in the plaster. Looking at it in what dim light was offered from out on the road. Outside he could hear a pack of coyotes yipping in the opaque night and a lone dog answering them. He heard snoring through the thin walls. Then he sat up and placed his feet on the floor. He turned on the lamp beside the bed. He put his hands on his knees and took a breath and closed his eyes. His back was straight. He looked like some kind of strange monk in meditation. Then he opened his eyes and lifted the phone from the receiver and dialed a number and listened to the tone and waited for an answer on the other end.

Hello? a voice finally said.

Noon sat with the receiver to his ear for a moment. Didn't speak, just listened.

Hello? the voice said again. This time with impatience.

Answering your own calls? Noon said.

There was a long pause on the other end. Then: How'd you get this number?

I have all of your numbers.

How do you have all of my numbers? Actually, I don't give a shit. Why you calling in the middle of the night?

Is it the middle of the night?

Cut the cute shit.

The girl is dead, Noon said.

Girl?

Yes, Noon said. You let her drown.

I didn't let her do shit. Why the hell am I talking to you right now?

Because I want to tell you something.

You have any idea of the scrutiny that little fire you started put me under?

Fire?

I suppose you're going to tell me someone else burned down that shack out in the woods? First the fire then that gal with her throat cut. Not to mention the Barnhardt and Summers ordeal. You know the kind of heat you're putting on me?

Is that some kind of pun?

Cut. The. Shit.

I think there would be a lot of people interested in hearing the kind of activities you're into.

There was silence on the other end.

Noon said: Are you still there?

That's called extortion, the voice said.

Okay, Noon said.

You know I got a call from the governor the other day? Asking if we need any assistance out here. The fucking governor!

People love to help people, Noon said.

You think this is a joke?

No.

You need to lie low.

Why are you upset?

Because you're being reckless. Because you're making your business my business.

My business is your business, Noon said.

He sat with the phone to his ear. He looked out the window.

It's raining outside, Noon said.

Why do I care if it's raining?

You'll want to wear a jacket.

Why would I want to wear a jacket?

Because you're going to meet me in about thirty minutes.

I'm not going anywhere.

There's someone I want you to meet.

Middle of the night, fucko. I don't want to meet anyone right now.

Yes you do, Chief, Noon said. Yes you do.

He said the place then he said the time. Then he hung up the phone without saying another word and laid back down and laced his fingers behind his head and listened to the rain falling on the asphalt.

32

THE TWO MEN AND THE STRIPPER PULLED UP TO THE HOUSE A
little before two in the morning. Everything was dark. The Fairlane was parked near the house and the headlights of the man's
car shined on it and they could see Noon sitting behind the wheel.

The one driving leaned over the wheel and said of the place:
Thought it'd be nicer.

The other said: How about you, sweetheart. Still want to
have a go?

It's two weeks' worth of dancing, she said.

Okay.

Noon stepped out of the Fairlane and walked toward their
car. His hat was pulled low and they couldn't see his face. He
walked to the door behind the driver and opened it and got inside and sat a moment. The girl and the guy in the passenger seat
were looking at him with suspicion. Finally the guy behind the
wheel turned in his seat.

Well? he said.

Well what?

Are we doing this?

Doing what?

Listen, the driver said, you—

I am only teasing, Noon said. You all need to lighten up.

He smiled strangely at them.

You all seem nervous, he said. Are you nervous?

No one spoke.

Here, Noon said.

He reached into his pocket. He pulled out a glass pipe. He handed it to the girl. Handed her a lighter.

What is this? she asked.

Something that will help you, Noon said.

She watched him. She looked down at the pipe. Then finally said: Fuck it.

She brought the pipe to her lips and lit the end. The glass flared. The flame scorched the crystal and the crystal pulsed a deep orange and when she dragged on it the flame bent and righted and then bent again as she pulled in the smoke. When the lighter clicked out and the pipe smoldered and the crystal went black, a ribbon of glaucous smoke spun into the air. Then she handed the pipe and lighter to the guy in the passenger seat and he did the same. The driver was the last to hit it and when the smoke left his lips Noon said, Another?

They all agreed and hit it again and when Noon was satisfied with the state they were in, he said: Shall we?

They walked to the house with Noon leading. Then he stopped and turned to the woman and said, I want you to wait in the house.

Aren't we all going into the house? one guy asked.

Stop asking questions, Noon said. Then to the woman: Wait in the house, please.

The woman climbed the steps. At the door she said, It's dark.

Yes, Noon said. Are you afraid of the dark?

She stared at him for a moment. Then she pushed through the door and stepped inside.

Follow me, Noon said to the two men.

He led them around the house. He slid an iron bar through the handles of the cellar and opened the doors. The smell of mildew and human waste tumbled out. The two men covered their noses. One used the collar of his nylon jacket. The other a bandanna. The one with the bandanna said, Jesus Christ. He said, What the fuck am I walking into?

Noon led them down the steps and pulled the string. The girl flinched lazily at the sudden light. She was seated on the chair and her arms were tied to the post. Her pants were soiled and there was vomit on the cellar floor beside her. Noon turned to the men.

You can get undressed now, he said to the men.

There was a camera mounted on a tripod in the corner of the room.

What the fuck is all this? one said.

This is where you are going to have sex with my girlfriend.

The fuck is that over there? the other said.

That's a mask, Noon said.

Just then there was a knock on the cellar door.

Your girlfriend? one of them asked.

You have a bad habit of asking questions, Noon said.

A man stepped in and came down the stairs. He was wearing expensive boots. A Stetson hat. When he reached the floor he nodded at Noon.

Is this what got me out of bed?

The two men looked at him. Then they looked at one another. Then back at the man again.

Are you Conrad Price? one said.

Let's get one thing straight, Price said to him, I'm Chief Price to you.

Yes sir.

Price looked at the girl and then back at the two men. Price said, Tweedle Dee and Tweedle Dumb. Though for the life of me I can't tell which one is dumber.

Noon was standing in the shadows. Price turned to him.

Come on out of the shadows there, Price said. You're being too dramatic.

Noon came into the mephitic light. He removed his ball cap. The bones of his cheeks under the tight skin were like palette knives. Noon didn't take his eyes from the men.

What are we all doing in this basement together? Price said.

He said we were going to . . . , the one said.

Going to what? Price said.

Said he wanted to make a movie.

A movie? A movie about what? Two dipshit speed freaks looking to get their dicks sucked?

The two men were silent.

Price walked over to the girl. He knelt and balanced on the toes of his Lucchese boots. He took off his Stetson and held it in one hand and with the other he lifted the girl's chin. Her head was heavy. Her eyes could not focus.

You don't have to worry, sweetheart, Price said. These two here, they aren't going to hurt you. I'm going to take you out of here, okay. Getting you out of here tonight. Get you cleaned up, get you something nice to eat. Get you some good clothes. How does that sound?

He pointed back over his shoulder.

Those two over there, he said. Those two are bad people. Degenerates. Junkies. They didn't touch you at all, did they?

He looked back at Noon. They touch her yet?

Noon shook his head.

That's good, Price said, looking back at the girl. I'd hate to have that happen. Those two are like stains you can't remove on a nice piece of fabric.

He patted the girl's knee.

This will all be over soon, he said. I promise.

What the fuck is going on here? one of them said, interrupting.

Price winced. He closed his eyes and pinched the bridge of his nose. He stood up and turned toward him.

What's wrong with your voice? Price asked.

Nothing, he said.

That's the worst sounding voice I've ever heard, Price said. Your voice makes me want to cut off my ears. What was it you so rudely asked me?

What the fuck is going on? he said.

I suspect you're going to have sex with this girl and my friend over there is going to film it. And then he'll probably kill you.

Both men were beginning to shake. The crystal had hit them hard. Even their teeth were chattering.

Price looked at them and cocked his head.

You two get high before I showed up? he asked.

He gave it to us, one said. Just to take off the edge.

What edge?

I don't know, he said.

Price took a step closer.

You seem nervous, Price said. Do I make you nervous? Do they seem nervous, Mr Noon?

Yes, Noon said.

Seem nervous to me too, Price said. It's insulting.

Insulting? the other said. We ain't trying to be.

Oh, but you are, Price said. Because you're not taking this seriously. You're not taking this seriously just like you don't take me seriously. Do I seem serious to you?

Yes sir, one said.

That's good, Price said. Because I'm a serious man and this is a very serious thing. You kidnapped a girl and locked her up like a dog and let her shit herself and then you were going to rape her. Does that sound serious to you?

Whoa, one said, holding up his hands. We didn't kidnap her.

We didn't tie her up. She was here when we got here. This is how we found her.

Is that true? Price asked Noon.

Noon shook his head

My friend says you're lying, Price said.

There was silence for a moment. It was broken by a loud thud overhead. All the men looked up into the joists.

You got a friend up there? Price asked.

He looked at Noon. Noon nodded.

Ah, Price said. That must be the stripper they killed.

Killed? one said. His eyes widened. Look, just let us get out of here.

Get out of here? Price said. I don't think that's a very good idea. That'll screw up the plan.

Plan? the other said. What plan?

Were you not listening to my soliloquy about stains, Price said.

Your what?

Soliloquy, Price said. Speaking one's thoughts aloud. Stains on a piece of nice fabric. Sometimes to get rid of them you just have to cut them out.

He turned to Noon and said nothing, only nodded, and Noon took out a pistol with a silencer sweated onto the barrel and pulled the trigger and opened a hole between the guy's eyes. The guy dropped to the floor. The other one stood there uncomprehending. Noon stepped toward him and the guy looked up just in time to see Noon drop a noose over his head. Price threw the other end over the joist and Noon hauled against it. The joist moaned under the weight. The guy kicked and flailed like he was riding some ridiculous bicycle. He was twisting in and out of the shadows. His fingers were working in vain against the rope. Finally he quit moving and hung there with eyes aghast. The blood from the other one ran over the uneven cellar floor.

Price stood over the girl a moment. Then he looked back at Noon and said, She'll do.

Price walked up the steps and left Noon with the girl. Noon walked over to her and pulled a syringe from his pocket and uncapped it and stuck it in the girl's arm. Her head fell forward. He pocketed the syringe and stuffed the pistol in the waistband at the small of his back and unchained the girl and lifted her from the chair and carried her up the steps, over the gravel drive. He opened the back door of the men's car and laid her inside. He straightened up and looked off down the road. He could see the taillights of Price's truck receding in the darkness. Then Noon walked to the house. Up the rotting steps and into the house. The woman said something then the quick flash of a single shot lit up the open doorway and then it was dark again.

Noon carried the dead woman into the cellar. He sat her in the chair and tied her to the compression post. Her head bowed forward. He crossed the cellar to the mask then returned to the hanged man and put the mask on him and gave him a push and he swung, a slow pendulum, like the weights of a morbid clock. He went to the camera and pressed record and for a long time he taped the man just swinging.

When he left the cellar he went to the Fairlane and opened the passenger door and went into the glove box and took a videotape from it and set it on the dashboard. Took a screwdriver and went around to the plates and removed them. He went to the dead men's car and removed their plates. Went back to the Fairlane, swapped the plates, and wiped the car clean of his fingerprints. Then he went to the dead men's car and got in and started the engine and drove off with the girl in the back seat.

33

NEWS OF ANOTHER GIRL GONE MISSING SPREAD THROUGH town like a barn fire. Two days later half the state of Washington was out there with the state patrol and the FBI asking questions to anyone they could. The murder of Dani was also in question. The newspaper had a front-page shot of both Dani and Eunice with a predictable headline. Missing posters brandishing Eunice's young face were everywhere.

Fielding had to stop watching the news. Instead, he busied himself with the animals. Taking Snake for walks both morning and night. He'd brush Buckshot like he was a dog shedding its winter coat. He put a little radio in the barn and he'd play them Vivaldi and Chopin and a lot of the time he'd bring a metal folding chair in and just sit with them, drinking some whiskey or coffee or both and listening to the music.

A week went by and one afternoon the phone started ringing. Fielding let it go. Then it started up again. Finally he picked it up.

Yes?

Thought you'd hit the road, Batey said.

No sir.

What are you doing?

Mucking stalls.

You going to be there in ten minutes?

I'm goin a be here all day. And all day tomorrow. And probably the day after that.

On my way.

A little before three in the afternoon Batey's Bronco pulled into the drive and seeing the bay doors of the barn open and the lights on Batey parked it there. Fielding was pitching forkfuls of hay into the stalls. He turned and saw Batey get out and then he saw Rawlings get out of the passenger side. Fielding stood the pitchfork on its tines and gripped the handle and rested his chin on his hands.

Fielding said their names and Batey and Rawlings nodded and both took off their hats and slung the rainwater into the dirt before entering the barn.

To what do I owe this visit? Fielding said.

Need to talk, Batey said.

You and everyone else, Fielding said.

He went back to his pitching and Batey said, You might want to hear this.

I don't want to hear anything, Fielding said. In fact, that's why I moved so far from everythin. It's because I want to be left alone and left out of anything anyone might find interestin.

You got any coffee on, Batey said.

Up in the house.

Want to talk up there?

No, Fielding said. No I do not.

I think you might find what Marty has to say very interesting.

What did I just get done sayin about being left out of anything interestin?

Neither Batey nor Rawlings spoke. It forced Fielding to stop and exhale. He put the fork aside.

Okay, Fielding said. What will I find so interestin?

Rawlings started talking about the girl gone missing. He said the night she was reported gone she had stopped with a friend to get some milkshakes at a diner.

Okay, Fielding said.

I went out there and asked around, Rawlings said. I checked in with the waitress who was on shift. I checked with the manager. They all said they saw her. Said she came in and ate and left.

Seems like somethin yeh'd do at a diner.

So I go around to all the businesses in the strip mall. Asking if they'd seen anything odd. Last place I go to someone says they seem to remember a car parked in the lot with its engine running. Said no one got out. No one got in. Just parked there. I asked them what kind of car. They said something older. I said, how old? They said maybe ten, fifteen years old. Big, they said.

So what? Fielding said.

Well, I saw a big old car like that recently. Parked out in the middle of nowhere. Out at some abandoned house. A Fairlane. For whatever reason that car stuck in my mind.

A Ford?

Ford Fairlane.

Okay.

I'm racking my brain as to why I got that car in particular stuck in my head.

And what did yeh shake loose?

It hit me that I saw a Fairlane the night Dani died. That girl from the shelter. The one with her throat cut.

Lots of Fairlanes in the world, Fielding said.

Not this kind. Both were burgundy in color. Same year. I looked it up. A '78. When was the last time you came across a car like that?

Hmm, Fielding said. Yeh tell the chief about all this? Seems like somethin he'd like to know.

Rawlings looked at Batey.

What? Fielding said.

So that's another thing.

Rawlings told Fielding how Dani and this younger woman had come in telling him and Price about someone trying to track her down. How she was on the run from this guy. How when the women left the station Price had told him to sweep all of it under the rug. How he didn't want to waste resources and whatnot.

So the girl with Dani was Eunice? Fielding asked.

No, Rawlings said. The girl with Dani was a runaway. No one has seen her since Dani was killed.

Yeh think the runaway's a suspect?

No.

Fielding nodded.

We also got a call that a dancer over at the French Maid hasn't showed up to work in a week, Rawlings said.

Maybe she skipped town? Fielding said.

Maybe.

So yeh think Price knows somethin he's not tellin?

I don't know, Rawlings said.

Yeh think this Fairlane guy might know where Eunice is?

Don't know yet.

Fielding shook his head.

And what's Wilson said? Seems like somethin he'd have fun with.

Thought we'd start with you, Batey said.

Fielding nodded again.

Well, good luck, he said. He went back to pitching hay.

We got an address, Batey said. This old abandoned house the Fairlane was parked at. Thought we might go have a look-see.

Good for you, Fielding said.

Come out there with us, Batey said.

Pass.

You don't want to know? Batey asked. Aren't you curious?

No, Fielding said. Matter of fact, I'm less and less curious the more I know.

What if it were one of your daughters, Batey said.

I don't have daughters, Fielding said. I don't even have a wife.

Okay, Batey said. Well, what if it were one of my daughters? One of Cora's daughters? What if it was Lola or Emmy Lou out there missing? Then what? Would you keep pitching that hay if you knew it was one of them?

Fielding stopped and turned back to look at Batey.

You're already up to your knees, Batey said.

And I can still turn around, Fielding said.

Or you can dive in and start swimming.

Fielding looked at the two men. They were earnest and eager and Fielding knew they hated what was happening in their town. Anyone could see that. Fielding put the pitchfork aside again. He wiped his hands on his jeans.

I see how yeh got such a beautiful woman like Coraline to marry you, Fielding said.

How's that? Batey asked.

Relentless goddamn perseverance.

34

THEY PULLED OFF THE STATE ROUTE INTO THE DRIVE OF THE
abandoned house at twilight. A fog had come in from the sea.
The gate to the cyclone fence was left open. The grass was long.
Hidden in the tall grass were husks of trash metal sinking into
the ground like the rusting bones of a dismal feast. A cast-iron
bathtub turned on its side. A dented water heater. Snares of
blackberry seemed to be using the house as a ladder. The Fairlane was parked in front of the garage. Batey left the Bronco running and leaned over the wheel.

Well, Batey said. There's our Fairlane.

Well, Fielding said.

Yep.

They got out of the Bronco and stood in the drive a moment. The high-voltage lines were thrumming overhead, lost in
the fog. They sounded like they were trying to burn their way
through. The three of them hooked their thumbs in their jeans.
No one wanted to make the first move because to make the first
meant there was no turning back.

A good plan violently executed right now, Fielding said, is far
better than a perfect plan executed next week.

What? Batey said.

General Patton, Fielding said.

What's Patton got to do with this?

Means let's get this show on the road.

Rawlings led them toward the house. They stopped at the Fairlane and peered into it. All but empty save the videotape on the dash. They went on. They were stepping though all manner of trash. Near the open garage they saw a rat skitter. They had to push through the tall grass and weeds like they were on a safari. At the wooden steps of the porch Rawlings toed a rotten board to see if it would bust through. The door had been pushed aside and the condemned sign was askew. The three of them stood on the porch a moment as if not sure what to do next.

Well, Fielding said to Rawlings, go on. Yer the law around here.

Rawlings knocked then he tried the door. It fell inward. A foul smell billowed out. Like cat urine and vinegar and mildew. The floorboards were curling or punched through. Blackberry vines grew up the walls and piles of garbage were scattered everywhere.

I think Mr Fairlane has skedaddled, Fielding said.

Think you're right, Batey said.

They exited the porch and started off toward the Bronco.

Feel like I need to take a shower just standing there, Batey said.

That ain't the last time yeh'll be standin in that spot, Fielding said. Yeh just opened a whole drum of somethin. Better start buyin yer soap in bulk.

Walking back Fielding saw something in the grass. Something foreign, like a gem lying in a bucket of tar. He toed it. It was a shoe. He said Batey's name. Batey came over and looked down at it.

What's that look like? Fielding said.

That's a shoe.

Yeh have daughters. What kind of shoe is that?

That's a girl's shoe, Batey said.

What kind of girl?

The kind that might have gone missing.

That'd be my guess too.

Fielding knelt and picked it up. It was new. There was very little scuffing on it. He turned it in his hand. Then he looked back at the house in the forlorn light.

They got in the Bronco and Fielding handed the shoe to Rawlings.

Yeh go ask Eunice's folks and see if this shoe is hers, Fielding said. I'd be willin to stake everythin I own that it is.

Rawlings looked at the shoe.

Raise your right hand, Rawlings said.

Why? Fielding asked.

I'm deputizing you.

I don't think yeh can do that.

Maybe not, Rawlings said. But I'm doing it anyway. Right hand.

Fielding raised it.

Rawlings said what he had to say and then said, Okay?

Alright, Fielding said. And then he said, And don't tell Price about the shoe. We won't let the wolf in the henhouse quite yet.

35

THE GIRL'S SHOE NAGGED AT FIELDING. HE DIDN'T KNOW WHY but he was getting pulled back into it. Not getting pulled—he was already in. Not his business he kept telling himself. Leave it alone, he said. Said, Yeh don't need to be the hero here. He was lying on the couch telling himself this when the phone started up.

He stood and went into the kitchen and took the phone off the wall.

You a gambling man? Batey asked.

No.

Let's say you are.

Okay, Fielding said.

Would you still stake everything you own on that shoe being Eunice's?

I think I would.

Congratulations. You haven't lost a thing.

What'd I win?

Not sure there's a winner in any of this.

Not sure that's a fair bet.

Want me to come get you?

Why would yeh come get me? We goin somewhere?

We're going to go talk to this creep.

Which creep is that? Lot a creeps out there.

Mr Ford Fairlane.

Not me, Fielding said. I've taken this ride as far as it goes. About time we handed it over to Wilson. I think yeh should get off as well.

Can't do that, partner.

Why not?

Cause I have girls of my own. Plain and simple. And that missing girl could easily be one of mine. Can't go backward now.

But she ain't yers, Fielding said. She ain't Lola and she ain't Emmy Lou. And havin yeh dead over all this ain't goin a help anyone. Especially yer girls.

You going to tell that to her folks? You going to look her father in the eye and tell him she isn't yours to find? Nope, Batey said. Can't do it. I can't anyway. And I don't think you can either.

Fielding knew he was right. If this had been anyone coming to him for help in Oscar, Iowa, he would do the same thing. And he knew a hundred others who would have helped right alongside him and he knew they wouldn't stop helping until she was found. He said that to Batey and then he said, Alright. All in.

An hour later they were driving in Batey's Bronco. Turned onto the state route and went south. The macadam was wet but it wasn't raining.

I feel suspended out here, Fielding said.

He'd just been sitting there in silence when he said it. Just sitting there looking out the window.

Suspended? Batey asked.

Like a piece of Styrofoam on the water.

How do you mean?

In Iowa it would get cold in the winter and hot in the summer. In the summer it would rain and in the winter it would snow. Some days it was sunny and somedays it was cloudy.

You know you're describing weather, partner. That's what weather is.

Not out here, Fielding said. Out here it never stops rainin. Out here it's not too hot and it's not too cold. Out here the sun never comes out and the sky is always gray.

I get the feeling you're wanting to tell me something.

No, Fielding said. Just that I'm livin a life in suspension.

Nothing suspends forever.

No. I suppose it don't.

Goes up and it goes down.

Sounds about right.

Well that's good, Batey said.

What's good?

Get all the crazy stuff out before we talk to the real crazy.

At the abandoned house Batey slowed the Bronco and pulled off the blacktop and onto the gravel apron.

Batey parked behind the Fairlane. He put the transmission into park and they sat there looking at the house for a moment through the windshield. They noticed that the dome light was glowing faintly.

You remember that light on yesterday? Batey asked.

No I do not.

Batey said, I think the water under that Styrofoam is about to get bumpy.

Outside the air was thick. Overhead the high-voltage lines droned on like broken cicadas. Batey followed Fielding up to the house and when they passed the empty Fairlane Fielding stopped and peered in. He couldn't see much. But it was all but empty. On the dashboard was a videotape.

What's yer opinion on that? Fielding said.

Batey looked in.

Oscar winner, if you ask me.

They looked up at the house.

We go burstin through that door, Fielding said, there might be somethin waitin to burst back.

Batey expected Fielding to say something more but he didn't. He just tapped his lower lip with his forefinger.

What do you suppose is on that tape? Batey asked.

I don't think I care to know.

Without a word Batey turned back to the Bronco and opened the driver's side door and leaned in for something and then shut the door behind him. He came out with his gun belt and his 9mm Beretta in its holster. He put that on so that the gun was on his right side. Fielding looked down at it and raised his eyebrows.

Never know, Batey said.

They made their way up to the house. The grass was tall and wetted their legs as they walked through it. Near the house a rat shot from the brush and gave Fielding a start and he tried to kick at it but it disappeared under the rotten porch.

At the foot of the steps Fielding said, How yeh want to do this?

I guess we just knock.

At the slumped door Fielding knocked on the jamb with the heel of his hand.

Sheriff's office, he said.

Batey gave him a look. Fielding shrugged and knocked again. Then he stepped over the door.

What are you doing? Batey said. He was almost whispering.

I'm goin in.

That's trespassing.

Our little secret.

The necrotic light from the headlights was lapping against the moldy walls like scum on the shoreline of a dead pond. In the middle of the floor was a wide black oval. Fielding crossed the room. The wood floor was sticky and his boots made sounds like they were fighting glue. He stepped in something like tar. Or asphalt sealant. He looked down at it. It was the same color as tar. He said, Dee, pitch me that flashlight. When he clicked it on and trained it at the floor he found the color was not black but very dark red. He swung the light around but the room was empty.

Yeh seein this? Fielding said.

Batey came into the house and crossed the room and toed at the blood on the floor.

Ain't dry, he said. But it ain't fresh neither.

He clicked the safety off on the gun. He said, You think anyone is in here?

No I do not, Fielding said.

Batey took stock of the room. He looked off down the hallway. Then he took stock of the room again.

Where you think that hall leads?

Rooms, I suppose, Fielding said. Keep that pistol ready.

They went down the hall. The floor was sagging in places. There was nothing on the walls. The first room they came to had no door and no trim and the Sheetrock was exposed and crumbling. Inside the room was nothing but stacked boxes. Some of the stacks were piled to the ceiling. The room smelled like moldy oranges.

The next room had a door but it was closed. Fielding nodded at it. Batey stepped forward and was ready with the Beretta. Batey nodded and Fielding opened the door. The room was empty and dark and musty. There was a mattress on the floor. A greasy sleeping bag laid out. Fielding swung the flashlight around and lit up some graffiti. There were dirty clothes spread over the floor and cigarette burns in the carpet.

There's got to be something waiting for us, Batey said.

That's what I'm afraid of, Fielding said.

Back in the living room they stood looking at the stain of blood. Batey said, You think we're onto something here?

Yes I do.

Fielding looked around the room. He said, This place have a pump house or a cellar of some kind?

Your guess is as good as mine.

Outside they followed a well-trodden path that looked like a game trail from the porch steps to the side of the house and then around to the back. Fielding watched for any light or movement in the windows but there was no light and nothing moved. Batey kept turning around like something was following them.

The backyard was full of junk and brier and old wooden crates and pallets and leaning columns of bee boxes and rusted engine parts and bald tires and it was all half-hidden or half-sunk. All was perfectly still and nothing but the power lines made a sound. Absolutely dead quiet.

Could be anything hiding out there, Batey said.

There ain't nothin out there but ghosts, Fielding said.

They kept on and came to the far side of the house and their eyes fell to the cellar door at the same moment and neither of them wanted to say what they were both thinking.

There was an iron bar slid through the handles.

Found the cellar, Batey said.

What spooks me is what we're goin a find inside it.

Inside it?

Come this far, haven't we?

You get the bar and I'll get the door.

Deal.

The bar weighed more than it looked. It was rusted and bent and did not slide well. It jammed once or twice and Fielding cursed it under his breath and when it finally slid free he pitched it into the grass and spat into the dirt. The door was heavy and awkward and the handle was wet and Batey's hand slipped and the heavy door slammed down. The thick air muffled the noise and they expected an echo or a dog to bark in return but there was no echo and no dog. Just the cellar to be opened. Just the silence.

The smell that escaped was like poking a bloated dead animal. The odor got the best of Batey and he spun around and threw up into the grass. Fielding took a bandanna from his back pocket and held it to his nose. The wood of the stairs leading down looked punky and Fielding wondered which one would break on him. The night air was cold but a strange warmth spilled out from within. Fielding looked down the stairs. They disappeared into a darkness absolute. Into the throat of some beast without a name. Into the dark heart of the unthinkable.

Batey came up behind Fielding. He was wiping his mouth with the back of his hand. Fielding looked at him but didn't say anything. He only nodded.

We go down there, Fielding said, we might not come back out.

You wanting to call it in? Batey asked. Get Marty out here? I'd be fine ending this nightmare.

Somethin tells me we call it in that chief of police might throw the book at me. Might throw the whole damn shelf.

I don't think you're wrong on that.

So we're goin down?

Lead the way.

Fielding clicked on the flashlight and pointed it down the stairs. It made a white circle on the concrete floor.

Okay then, Fielding said.

Batey raised the gun and they started down the stairs. Each step creaked. The wood sounded like the moaning of a ship's planks. At the bottom of the stairs and straight ahead the flashlight caught the image of a chair and a dead woman tied to the compression post. Her top had been removed. Her skirt hiked up and torn. Fielding seemed transfixed on her. Batey tapped Fielding on the arm. He said: Partner. Then he pointed.

Fielding swung the light around and caught a hanged man lifeless at the end of a rope. His face was blue and swollen. His eyes were glassed over and bulging in the skull. A shot man was collapsed on the floor. Fielding shined the light on the wall. It was covered in blood and gore and small fragments of bone. Shined it back on the dead man on the floor.

Mr Fairlane? Fielding said.

Your guess is as good as mine, Batey said.

Fielding shined the light back at the chair.

What do yeh think happened here? Fielding asked.

Haven't a clue.

Looks like they did somethin to the girl.

You think that one shot the other then hanged himself?

Yeh better call this in, Fielding said.

Yep. And you better make yourself scarce.

What're yeh goin a tell them?

Going to tell them I came out here alone on some anonymous tip about some poaching activity and that I found the cellar door open. I'll call Marty and tell him. I'll come back out here with him and let him find these three himself.

Seems thin.

Like new ice, Batey said, but I don't think we got another way.

Batey went to the hanged man. Found his wallet in his back pocket. Opened it and saw all the money. Looked at his driver's license.

Lot of money, Fielding said.

Too much.

Batey put it all back in the wallet and put the wallet back in the guy's pocket.

Back outside they stood under the low clouds and the humming power lines and Fielding put his hands on his hips and looked out at the junk in the field and then down the cellar stairs and then at Batey and shook his head. He said,

None of this is right.

No it ain't.

I mean it ain't right. The three of them down there. One hanged, the other two shot. But here's my question.

What question is that?

How are three people goin a slide that iron bar through the handles from the inside?

Hmm.

Yeah, Fielding said. Hmm.

A long moment passed and then Fielding said: They were put down there, weren't they?

I'm starting to wonder.

That shoe we found. That was Eunice's shoe. Eunice was in that basement at some point, wasn't she?

Batey nodded. We got to find that girl.

Yes we do.

Fielding slid the iron bar back through the handles. He said: We'll let Marty find it the way we found it.

Going back to the Bronco Fielding stopped at the Fairlane and opened the door.

What are you doing? Batey asked.

Nothin, Fielding said.

He reached in and grabbed the videotape.

I wouldn't, Batey said.

I won't.

But he knew he would. Fielding set the tape on the dash of the Bronco. Then they drove away.

36

THAT NIGHT A TERRIBLE DREAM. ONE IN WHICH THE LIGHTS OF the world were melting down upon him. The sun was a black dot and gave off a heat so intense that the very air felt a repudiation to breathing. He was cast about over the wet sand of low tide and the tidelands were infinite. It was snowing lightly despite the awful heat and the flakes were drifting down to the sand as if gravity did not hinder them. On closer examination, it was not snow but ash and he held out his hand to catch one and the falling ash appeared like sheds of dead skin. And within this the demented warble of a nameless songbird kept ratcheting out. It seemed to be heralding dawn but dawn could not happen here. Out in front of him there were figures lying in repose and spaced evenly at ten feet or so in a perfectly straight line. He walked away from the shoreline. In the tide pools there were neon crabs and balls of eels thin as pencils and barnacled flounders all huddled at the pool's drying edges with mouths agape and sucking air on the surface. He walked on. Closer he came he saw the burned body of Molly Summers. Beyond her was the hanged man and further on he saw the bodies of the dead woman in the chair and the man who'd been shot and all of these bodies were lying naked over the sand.

The air was still and the only sound was of the bird somewhere in the distance. He knelt beside the body of Molly Summers. Her skin was no longer burned; she looked almost peaceful, like she was sleeping. The warble of the bird grew louder and with it the dull roar of water. He stood and looked toward the black sea. A gnashing line of white spilled toward him. He took a step toward it in disbelief. It seemed miles away and then all at once it was upon him. He turned to run. The water rose up. His feet pounded over the wet sand. He turned once and saw the wave lift up the body of the girl. The bodies of the two men and the woman. The dead limbs flailing like kelp. The birdsong was gone. There was only the water. The black sun's heat raging in his lungs. Then like a giant hand it scooped him up and he rolled in the water. His eyes were closed and it boomed all around him. Then it all went silent and he opened his eyes and looked down at his feet to a deep ocean where no light could reach. He saw the corpses suspended in the water, their limbs and hair lifting and falling in slow undulation. And then as if on a timer their eyes snapped opened and they started swimming toward him and the fright made him take in a bellyful of water. And then he woke up.

37

HE AWOKE WITH A START. HE WAS SWEATING. THE SHEETS
were damp and his hands were trembling. Sara, he said. Sara.
But when he looked at the bed next to him she was not there and
he remembered she never would be again.

He swung his feet out of bed and put them on the floor.
The heeler was asleep at the foot of the bed and did not move.
Fielding went to the bathroom for a drink of water. He drank a
glass and then another. He looked at his reflection in the mirror.
There was a little rain tapping on the glass. He knew he should
go back to bed but the haunted world of that dream had left him
wary. So he put on his robe and went downstairs and made some
coffee.

The clock on the wall read 3:49. The coffee maker was starting to bubble. He stood looking through the big windows out
at the darkness. Nothing to see there but looked anyway. Kept
looking until the coffee was done. He went to the cupboard and
took down a mug. That's when he remembered the videotape
he'd taken from the Fairlane. A sinking feeling came over him.
Its very existence frightened him. He put down the mug and
went to the front door and pulled on his boots and dressed in his
slicker and put on his hat and went out into the rain. He crossed
the drive toward the truck. The dirt of the drive had turned to

mud. His boots made sucking sounds as they pulled free. He opened the door of the truck. Right where he had left it after Batey dropped him off. The danger it seemed to possess. Like coming across a sleeping pit viper.

Back in the house he stood looking at it while his coffee steamed in the air. Going this far, he knew, had already started it. It was like nudging a boulder from a mountain. It would only stop when it reached the very bottom.

He took the tape into the living room and slid it into the VCR and turned on the television. An awful unsettled feeling washed over him. He hit the play button. A static line fell down the screen like a theater curtain. There was no sound to it. At first Fielding didn't know what he was looking at. His heart was pounding against his ribs. It was like it wanted to flee his body. To have no part in this.

The video opened on a dark room. Nothing but darkness. So black anyone watching might make the mistake of checking the VCR to confirm the video was even playing. Then came the switch of a breaker and there she was. The pale subject. Drugged looking and naked, but somehow alert. Her head turned about like it was chasing a hummingbird. She'd been decorated with feathers and what looked like twigs of sagebrush done up in her hair. A halo on her head. The same kind he had seen on Summers. Her eyes were painted black. Like a kind of mask. She appeared to be alone in the room. There was a long close-up of her breasts, like some obscene art house film. The same kind of shot between her legs, the skin smooth and hairless. The last close-up was of her face. She was crying and the tears streamed through the black paint and the tears mixed with the paint and ran in black rivulets down her face.

There was a smash cut to an abandoned factory. All the large boilers and bent and twisting pipes looked to have been out of use for years. In the middle of the wide concrete floor was a wooden table and on the table was the same naked girl. Fielding felt his palms go slick with sweat. His stomach balled up. Everything was humming. The camera closed in on her. She was tied to the table and she had a piece of black cloth tied around her eyes. The camera backed up and from the dark voids of the factory a parade of six figures emerged. They were holding candles and the votive flames seemed suspended of their own volition. The men too were also naked but their faces were hidden in grotesque carnival masks painted wildly like something out of Dante. They came and surrounded the table like acolytes. They stood motionless. Some fat, some skinny. The girl on the table writhed sluggishly. The flames of the candles leapt about like moths.

Another smash cut to the girl's tortured face. All the sound had been removed and she was crying out in silence. Then one by one each of the men moved toward her. They tilted their candles to spill the hot wax over her isabelline skin and then one by one they took their turns.

When the last of them had stepped away a towering figure came forward. The mask he wore was made out of some kind of animal skin. Some stiff mangy hair coming off the chin like a billy goat. A broad set of antlers with feathers and sage dangling like distorted ornaments. Holes cut for eyes, but no mouth. Just the mindless facade of a nightmare that plagues a soul's empty corners from the moment a soul is.

The antlered one approached her. He stood behind her. Her supine head level with his waist. He removed the blindfold. In a distinct moment of awe the girl looked up and did not cry. She did not scream. Only for a moment she went totally still. Completely calm. As if in recognition. As if in awakening. Her eyes gleamed with a crazed light as though the flames of every votive candle in that room were captured within her black pupils. And for a moment it was not fear in her eyes but salvation.

But there was no salvation and this was no awakening. This was the first dimming of the eyelids' closing that shuts out all light to come. A darkness that would be forever. Infinite. And with one hand the man held the girl's chin. Then Fielding cried out as the blade winked in the candlelight and erupted a thin crescent across her throat and the black blood pumped onto the table, to wash over the wood like wine and spill finally to the cold floor. Her eyes glazed over and eventually went flat. And one by one each man came to the table and buried his face into her throat.

38

HE DID NOT SLEEP. NOT A SECOND. NEVER EVEN CLOSED HIS
eyes. The light was grainy with the coming dawn. The doves in
the maple trees were waking and beginning to call. Buckshot
was standing in the pasture with his head turned eastward to
watch the morning come up. Fielding was sitting in a chair looking west over the flat green country. He glanced at the television
screen. It was gray and lifeless. The videotape sat on top of it. He
checked the wall clock. Seemed late enough to call Batey.

Later that morning Fielding stood at the window of Wilson's
hotel room with his arms crossed chewing on his thumb while
Batey and Wilson watched the video. Fielding looked down at
the traffic. Down at the people walking back and forth on the
sidewalk. Mothers with small children. Men taking their coffee
at the café. All of them ignorant to what was happening on the
screen.

Neither Batey nor Wilson uttered a word. Wilson sat there
jotting notes. He was watching it like some instructional work-
place video. When the screen went black Wilson hit pause and
turned back to Fielding at the window.

How many times have you watched this? Wilson asked.

Just the once.

And how did you happen to come across it?

Bad luck.

I am going to need you to be very specific on this, Wilson said.

I told yeh that already. Side of the road.

That sounds awfully suspicious.

I know how it sounds.

Wilson stood and went to the bureau. He straightened his tie. He brushed his hair over with his fingers. He poured a little bourbon into a crystal tumbler and brought it to Fielding.

It ain't even noon yet, Fielding said.

It is somewhere, Wilson said. Somewhere it is.

Fielding took the glass but he did not drink it. Wilson went back to the television. He pressed rewind on the VCR.

He backed up to the point when the men started drinking the woman's blood. Then he hit play. Each man would remove his mask momentarily before lowering his head. The image was a little fuzzy. It was hard to make out any discerning qualities.

Do any of these men look familiar? Wilson asked.

Most of them have their backs turned, Batey said.

Wilson said, Say you saw Mr Fielding walking down the street. You were behind him. Would you know it's him?

Sure, Batey said. But that's because I know him. I don't know any of these men.

But maybe you do, Wilson said. And you just don't know it.

What are yeh gettin at, Wilson? Fielding said.

Same thing you are.

And what's that? Fielding asked.

Truth, Wilson said. These men on the tape, they're not make-believe. Neither was that girl. And what they did to her really happened. All of this is real. That's what I'm getting at.

Alright, Batey said.

Alright what? Wilson asked.

Roll it again.

Wilson nodded and rewound the tape. Then he pressed play.

Fielding and Batey were seated at a bar with a neon Rainier sign glowing above them. Leaning on their elbows. Not talking. The barman came and took their empties and brought fresh ones in their place and then he went away without saying a word. Better part of an hour must have gone by before Fielding said,

How's yer club soda?

Sucks, Batey said. How's the Rainier?

Sucks.

You know what I've been thinking about this whole time?

What have yeh been thinking about?

You think those guys we found in the cellar had anything to do with that tape?

I don't know, Fielding said.

I had Marty run their names.

What did yeh tell Marty?

Told him I went out there on a poaching claim. Told him what I found.

Well, Fielding said.

Does it make sense to you that two guys with no criminal record would find themselves shot and hanged with a dead stripper?

No, Fielding said. No it does not.

I don't think so either, Batey said. You know what else makes me think these guys were in the wrong place at the wrong time?

What's that?

I think I know where that video was taped. And anyone without a criminal record would have no business being there.

What do yeh mean?

I think I know where that factory is. Where that video was made. I think I've seen it. Hell, I think I've been there.

Yeh gettin spooky on me? Fielding asked.

Might be spooking myself.

How do yeh know it?

Past life, Batey said. My DEA days. That factory shut down in 1956 and has been empty since. Old paper mill. Fifteen years ago we had some entry-level dope runners setting up in there. Some kind of hideout or something. Stashing the stuff coming in from Canada.

It's by the water? Fielding asked.

Everything is by the water around here.

Why didn't yeh mention this to Wilson?

Same reason you told him you found the tape on the side of the road.

Fielding nodded at the back mirror. Not at anyone in it. Just at it.

Okay, Fielding said. Well.

Well what?

This factory have a location or do yeh want me to guess?

Down in Tacoma, Batey said.

Are yeh proposin somethin here?

I don't know what I'm proposing.

I think they'd call this an obstruction of justice.

I'd say that'd get us five to ten.

We're building up quite a rap sheet between us, Fielding said. Aren't we?

39

WILSON CALLED RAWLINGS'S OFFICE AND EVELYN SAID THEY were out.

They? he asked.

Yes, Evelyn said. Deputy Rawlings and Chief Price.

He asked where and she told them, and when he arrived their cruisers were already parked in front of the abandoned house. Wilson pulled in and cut the engine. His clipboard was in the seat beside him. The sun was out and the light was flashing off the polished metal of the coroner's truck. A few officers were standing around near the porch steps. An officer was coming out of the house holding a camera. Wilson got out of his car with his clipboard. The first officer he saw he asked: Where might I find Chief Price and Deputy Rawlings?

The officer pointed around to the side of the house.

At the open cellar door Wilson found two officers talking with their arms crossed. Wilson flashed them his badge and they nodded at him and he stepped into the cellar and walked down the stairs.

The room was lit with floodlights and little numbered markers around each body. The coroner was standing over the shot man on the floor. The flash on the camera going off constantly.

Price was standing near the woman in the chair. When he saw Wilson come down the stairs he sucked his teeth and said: Decide to sleep in, Agent Wilson?

I got a call that Miss Roma here failed to show up for work this week? Wilson said.

You got a call? Price said. Who from?

Whom, Wilson said. From whom. And I believe it was the proprietor of the French Maid Gentleman's Club.

Do you pride yourself on being insufferable? Price said. And what's with, *you believe?* I would think a detective of your clout would know without equivocation who—*whom*—he was speaking to.

You're using that word incorrectly.

What word?

Clout.

What?

Never mind, Wilson said. I just came from there. Had a nice little chat.

Is that a fact?

Seemed to have as many questions as I did.

And what kind of questions did Mr French Maid have for the detective?

Mostly if I knew anything about the tall man who seemed so intrigued with one of his best dancers.

Tall man? Price said. Lots of tall men. Hell, I'm tall. Maybe it was me.

Yes, Wilson said. I said the same thing. This one, he said, was very tall. Showed me the surveillance video and everything.

Surveillance video?

Yes sir.

And?

Certainly very tall, Chief Price.

Price turned to Rawlings.

Deputy, he said. Put out an APB for a very tall man. Mr French Maid give you anything else, Agent Wilson?

Wilson knelt to the woman. He took a pencil and with the eraser end he lifted the hem of her skirt.

You got a thing for cold ones, Price said.

She appears intact, Wilson said. Has the coroner found anything?

I hate to argue with you, Agent Wilson, Price said, but she's got a big hole between her eyes. Hardly call that intact.

Wilson smiled thinly. He looked at Rawlings.

I assume the three of them weren't here the first time you checked on the place?

First time? Rawlings said.

Yes, deputy. The first time you searched this cellar.

How did you know I searched this cellar?

I know a lot of things, Deputy Rawlings.

How about the reason these three are down here, Agent Wilson? Price said. Do you have an answer for that?

Wilson stood. He said: When you found these bodies, deputy, was the cellar door closed?

Yessir.

How about that iron bar lying in the grass up there?

What about it?

Was it lying in the grass?

No sir, it was through the handles.

Isn't that interesting.

Sir?

Hard to slide an iron bar like that from the inside. Don't you think?

I'd say so, Rawlings said.

So would I, deputy. I might even say impossible.

Perhaps someone came by and slid it back into place, Agent Wilson, Price said.

Perhaps, Wilson said. He tapped his chin. So here's my next question: Why?

Why what? Price said.

Why are there three dead people in here with no motive as to why? They didn't know each other. She wasn't raped. One man is shot through the head, the other hanged. And they're all down here together. Left for us to find. Why? It's almost like someone's trying to cover something up.

You saying this is some kind of red herring, Agent Wilson?

Wilson looked at Price.

Yes, Chief Price. I think it might be.

Wilson took some photographs. He jotted some notes. Went to the man hanging from the joist and examined him closely. On the collar of the man's shirt was an odd stray hair. It was short but coarse. Wilson plucked it off. He put it in a little plastic bag.

What are you doing over there, Agent Wilson? Price asked.

Wilson turned and smiled.

Just looking, Chief Price.

He walked to the foot of the stairs.

I'll be in touch about the autopsy report, he said. Enjoy the day, gentlemen.

Back in his car Wilson held the plastic evidence bag up to the light.

Where have I seen you before, Wilson said. He stared at the package.

Then he put it in his jacket pocket and started the car and backed out and drove back to his hotel.

40

WILSON WATCHED THE VIDEO ON REPEAT. WATCHED IT SO much he was afraid he was going to ruin the tape. In his hotel room he had erected a corkboard and brought up all the photographs and information he kept tacked to the wall in his apartment and reassembled it all and drew new lines to new suspects. Some with names. Some just a question mark. The three found dead in the basement were a concern but he hadn't been sent here to solve that. The mask, the ritual, that was his purpose.

His first move was to find out who the girl in the video was. The missing persons list at that point in the state of Washington was very long and she could have been anyone. If she was even missing. Or worse, if she was even missed. He had only the color of her skin and a rough sense of her age. Her face was shown but the black paint hid a lot and comparing her likeness with the photos on file helped very little.

The sun swung in a perfect arc from one horizon to another. A rare brilliant winter day. No rain and no snow and no wind. Perfectly calm and perfectly at ease. But Wilson didn't notice the nice weather. He didn't notice that it was daytime, and he didn't notice when it became night.

He had the curtains drawn and had moved the cheap hotel chair close to the television so he could more easily start and stop and rewind the video. The only inconvenience was that the cork-board was across the room so he moved the dresser over to the corkboard and set up the television and VCR atop the dresser. Satisfied, he pressed play again.

It was a bit of an exercise in insanity. He watched the same scenes over and over with the expectation of seeing something new. He was missing something. He knew it. But every time it was the same. Always the same ending. Same tortured expressions. Same muted pleas. But there had to be something more. Some mistake. Some slipup. Something. What he was watching was crude and made by crude people and the thing that Wilson could always count on was that crude people always, at some point, made mistakes. There had to be a mistake in there somewhere.

Later he stood from his chair and went to the window and drew back the curtain and saw that the sun had fallen some hours ago and that night was well advanced and that the weather had changed and now snow was falling.

He stood at the window looking down at the street. The snow was falling through the cones of light from the streetlamps. There was a restaurant across from his hotel. The name BAY-SIDE GRILL was glowing red. The neon name coruscated on the wet pavement. It burned there like an image in a warped mirror until a car passed through it and the name washed out.

There was a fair number of people on the sidewalk. Going into the cafés, the restaurants. Coming out. In and out of the corner bars. Men and women coming home from work. Dour faces and tired faces and faces filled with worry or exaltation. Some of the men still wore the hats and long coats of an older era. Half of the women he noticed wore heels. Since it was a port town some of them wore coveralls, condemning them to the cold storage of the fisheries or canning lines.

He leaned closer. Pressed a single palm against the glass. His nose nearly touching the glass. He could feel the cold passing through the pane. A cold that went through him, that chilled him in a way that made him feel like a child with a fever.

Among the crowd his eyes were attracted to a lone figure standing at the mouth of an alley. The figure was leaning against the brick wall and smoking a cigarette. The burning tip raised and lowered mechanically. When the cigarette was done, the figure in the alley lit another. Wilson saw the flare of the lighter and the hot glow of the cherry as his lungs inhaled. Wilson watched as the man held the cigarette to his mouth and dragged on it again.

A sound came out of the television that took his attention away from the window. The video had almost run out. The screen had been blank for a while. Then there was a man's voice. Almost unintelligible. Wilson went to the television and watched it. What he saw was an old factory framed in the shot. He knew it. The old paper mill in Tacoma. As recognizable as Smith Tower. Then the mill vanished and the screen went full of static.

41

AT SOME BLEAK DARK HOUR WILSON AWOKE. HE TURNED ONTO
his back and blinked at the ceiling. The light was dim. Only the
streetlights. The stoplights going red to yellow to green. He had
to pee. Pulled the covers off and crossed the room.

Halfway to the bathroom something stopped him. Call it a
feeling. Call it a premonition. But it stopped him. And instead of
the bathroom he went to the window. He pulled aside the curtain and let his eyes adjust. Through the warped glass and wet
snow, Wilson saw the same figure standing in the alley just as
before. Same stance. Cigarette in hand. It was like he had never
moved. Wilson cupped a hand to the glass. He blinked to make
sure what he was seeing was real. Nights that have been lost in
dreams can often stay that way. So he blinked again. The burning end of the cigarette lifted from the man's side and when he
pulled on the cigarette the cherry flared and the glow illuminated his face and then that face was bedimmed by a cloud of
smoke.

Wilson stepped back from the window. He left a thin sliver
of glass showing and through that sliver watched the man as
he pulled on his clothes. He went to the bureau and picked up
the Galco holster and slid each arm through and then put on a

jacket. He went to the window one last time. The man hadn't moved.

The elevator dinged as it opened onto the lobby. The tired night clerk looked up from a magazine. He said Wilson's name but Wilson ignored him. At the front door he stopped and turned back to the clerk.

Anyone come in here asking about me? he asked.

No sir.

No one?

No sir. Just me tonight.

Wilson nodded and walked out of the hotel. He stood under the hotel's awning for a moment. Eyeing the street and the alleys and what they might be hiding. When he was confident he stepped out into the snow and crossed the street. The man standing in the alleyway flicked the cigarette in a long arc then turned away from the street and walked into the alley.

Hold it, Wilson called.

The man didn't listen. Wilson set off into a jog. The wet street was crashing under his feet. He stopped just before the sidewalk, his shoes damming the gutter. He took a quick study of the alley. He had to squint his eyes. He could see trash cans and dumpsters. A pile or two of garbage in plastic bags. There were fire escapes with stairs and landings Z-ing up the buildings. Wilson stepped onto the sidewalk. He put his hand inside his jacket. His hand closed around the grip of the pistol.

My name is Agent Wilson, he said. I have my firearm drawn. If there is anyone in here you had better make yourself known right now.

He waited a belabored second. He listened for a clumsy footstep. The crashing of a trash can. Nothing. He stepped forward and pulled his gun from the holster. He trained the pistol up and as he walked, he took note of everything around him. The alley was deep and seemed like it had no end.

At a dumpster he stopped and rested his back against it and waited. Both hands were on his gun. He looked up at the buildings. The fire escapes were empty and all the lights in the windows were out. The alley was like a cave and the farther he got from the street the darker it became.

He slid along the dumpster till he hit its corner and there he paused and breathed in and spun around the edge with the gun pointed. A feral cat leapt and Wilson could feel his finger almost flex on the trigger.

He went a little farther. Peering around dumpsters and piles of trash bags. The alley seemed all but empty. The tenants of the buildings were asleep and only the cats seemed to be prowling. Wilson knew the alley had an exit and for all he knew the alley was empty. He stepped out into the middle and let his gun fall to his side and for a moment let his guard down. He said,

Anybody back here?

He felt the first shot before he had even heard it. Didn't even really hear it. More like a lump of bread dough hitting the floor. The stinging pain came second. What he felt first was the sticky wet of the blood running down his left arm into his fingers. Each fingertip dripping like rainwater from a leaf. He had time enough to see the flash of the second just as he was diving behind a stand of trash cans. The bullet clipped him in the side. Wilson bunched himself up behind the cans and pressed his good hand to his side. When he took it back it came away warm and all slick with blood. His back was against the brick of the building. He was suddenly exhausted. He tried to quiet his breathing. He listened for the shooter to make his next move. He expected lights to go on all up and down the alley but only two shots had been fired and both had come from a silenced gun.

Wilson sat there holding himself. He listened for footsteps. He cocked back the hammer of his gun. The definitive click was immediately followed by the starting of a big-block engine and Wilson saw the length of the alley come to light. He heard the transmission dropping into place and the tires snapping over the wet pavement and he knew what was about to happen so he lifted himself as best he could and started running toward the street. Wilson turned once and fired three shots at the approaching car. One hit the headlight and the alley went a little dimmer. Wilson heard the engine growl behind him. Heard the car smashing through everything in its path.

He was loping along as fast as he could. It seemed futile. When he had just about given up the alleyway ended and Wilson leapt to the side and the car came bellowing out onto the street. Fishtailing over the wet road. Its tires spinning wildly. Wilson lay there with his face on the sidewalk. And with the last of his strength propped himself up and fired twice more but missed his mark and watched the car vanish down the street.

Gasping, Wilson reached for his side and winced at the pain. He felt thirsty. Most of the lights in the buildings had come on and he heard people leaning out of their windows wondering what the hell was going on. There were dogs barking. In the distance Wilson heard the unmistakable sound of a siren. He scooted himself up against the stone wall of a building, the warm blood pooling in his crotch.

42

BATEY AND FIELDING DROVE SOUTH IN THE MORNING WITH THE first paling light. There was snow in the foothills. The clouds were low and the color of sheet metal. Their bottoms were panned out like they were laid on a vast plate of glass.

They had driven almost an hour before either of them really said anything. Maybe because it was early or because neither of them knew exactly what they were doing. But for almost an hour they listened to a country-western station, the interstate under the tires. It was Batey who finally spoke up.

Cora made a thermos of coffee, he said, if you want some more. She also packed us a lunch in the cooler back there.

Nice of her.

Nice has got nothing to do with it. It's out of preservation. She knows I'll stop by a McDonald's or something. Eat three or four cheeseburgers. Try to blow up my heart.

Ain't a bad problem to have.

No it's not.

Coffee yeh say?

Help yourself.

Fielding twisted open the lid and poured the coffee into his mug. He poured some for Batey too. He screwed the lid back on and set the thermos on the floor behind him and blew the steam from the coffee.

The country was lower and flatter the farther south they got. The valleys were wide and the fields were furrowed with old crops gone brown. A lot of it was flooded. There were large banks of trumpeter swans picking at the leftovers. Fielding watched a wedge of them come gliding in. Not one of them moved their wings till the very last moment.

Yeh miss it? Fielding asked.

Miss what?

The agency.

DEA?

DEA. The way of life. Gettin the bad guys.

No, Batey said. People are cruel to one another when there's money involved. And that's all I saw. Money and cruelty.

Now look at yeh. Drivin south with some retired hick sheriff. Two-steppin with the occult.

How about that.

They were quiet a moment. A semi passed them on the left. It sent up a cloud of dirty water and Batey had to turn up the wipers.

Fielding finally said, So that's why yeh quit?

I suppose, Batey said. Same reason as you.

The cruelty of mankind?

What I started seeing went beyond cruelty. Things were starting to get pretty creative there at the end.

Like what?

Creative, Batey said.

They didn't talk again for a few minutes. Fielding looked at Batey and Batey had the look like he'd rather not talk about it. So Fielding looked out the window and drank his coffee. Then Batey said,

It was me and two other guys. We were working this bust going on a year. Maybe more. Long time anyway. This was down in Arizona, right on the border of Mexico. All you had to do was mention the first syllable of this cartel to anyone in that town and they'd clamp up quicker than a nun's legs. Real strange. I mean you'd be having a nice conversation with some dude at the café, just drinking coffee and chewing the fat, and the first whisper of that cartel and you'd think you just insulted the guy's dead mother. No one said shit. Even the police department wouldn't give you anything. Can't blame them. They had three officers killed in one week. Shot dead. One of them just because he was in uniform. The other two stopped a jacked-up truck for speeding and when the two officers went up to the windows they opened fire on them with little machine guns. Little MAC-11s and Škorpions. Opened them up. Once they were dead they roped them to the truck by their feet and paraded them through town. Right down Main Street. Broad daylight. Then they noosed them up in a big tree next to a playground.

I can see why no one talked, Fielding said.

Me too, Batey said. There was a lot of that. Random shit. All of it more violent than the last.

Sounds bad.

Hell, that's not even the worst of it. The day I quit we got a call from border patrol saying they stopped a bus of Mexicans at one of the crossings. I asked if they were illegals. Guy on the other end tells me they all have visas or the correct paperwork and that some of them are even U.S. citizens. So I ask why he stopped them. Routine, he told me. So we drive over there and I see this big bus pulled over at the station. A couple patrolmen have their rifles out. Almost looked like a standoff. I got out of the car and asked one guy why he had his rifle drawn. Routine, he tells me. Odd to me but what do I know. So I'm just standing there in that awful sun looking at this bus. I can see all these faces turned toward me. All these eyes and every one of them looks terrified. I walked to the bus and got on. Smelled awful in there. Smelled like an outhouse. And all those eyes watching me. That's a feeling that never leaves you. All those people trapped in there and you're the one trapping them. I don't speak Spanish so I have a guy translating. Where are you coming from? Nogales, they said. Where are you going? Tucson, they said. Every one of them had that answer. Not out of the ordinary, it's a bus. People in a bus are often going to the same place. As I'm walking up and down the aisle I'm keeping my eyes open. They all look innocent. Like they've never done so much as steal a candy bar. There's old men and old women and younger women holding babies. Some children sitting next to each other. Just sitting there. We were there for maybe half an hour and then for some reason it dawned on me how quiet it was in the bus. There were probably a dozen babies, all of them infants. Not one of them making a peep. I walked down the aisle with my translator and asked one woman what her baby's name was. She stammered a bit. Like she wasn't entirely sure. Like no one had ever asked her that before. It looked like a little boy. I said, *Dormido? Si*, she said. I reached down to touch his head and the woman pulled the baby away. Really aggressive like. To the point that the baby should have startled but it didn't. It just lay there. I looked at the woman and I looked at the baby and then back at her and she was starting to shake like a rattle. *Esta bien*, I said. I reached for the baby again and the woman let out this awful scream and lunged up and threw the baby at me and tried to run out the back of the bus. One of the guys grabbed her before she got out and I'm left holding this baby. I look down and see it isn't alive. I'm holding this dead baby in my arms, all swaddled up. I pulled back the fabric of the swaddle and there's this big line up the belly where the skin has been sewn together. Didn't look real. Its little lips and its little eyes, the skin on its cheeks gone cold. Awful. I handed the baby to the patrolman behind me and he had to go vomit out the door. I walked through the bus and told each woman to show me their baby. They all acted the same except no one ran this time. Every baby was dead. And stashed away in each was a brick of uncut heroin. This cartel, these monsters, had killed these infants and opened them up and put drugs in them and forced these poor women to carry them across the border. It turned out to be a huge bust. Millions of dollars' worth. But that was it for me. I left that very day. Turned in my badge. Told Cora what was up. Got the hell out of there.

Both men were quiet. The interstate was hissing like a frying egg. Fielding took a sip of his coffee.

And now yer here, Fielding said.

Here I am, Batey said. But that was the cartel and the cartel wants power and money, but this . . . This is something new.

To film it all, Fielding said. To put it into a movie. That takes someone special.

Yeah, Batey said. Special.

What gets me, Fielding said, is where Mr Fairlane even got it. The tape that is. Assuming he didn't film it himself. He raised his eyebrows.

Can't just go into the local Blockbuster and ask.

They were quiet again. Only the country music. The interstate beneath them. Then Fielding said, Maybe we can.

Can what?

Ask.

Batey gave him a look.

Maybe we make a pit stop in Seattle, Fielding said. I got a idea.

Uh-oh, Batey said.

Fielding raised his eyebrows again and poured some more coffee.

43

WILSON AWOKE IN A ROOM PAINTED EASTER YELLOW WITH A window that overlooked a small patch of grass. There was an IV in his arm and a nurse looking over something on a clipboard. The blinds were open and Wilson blinked at the fog and then he heard a foghorn somewhere within it.

The nurse said, Okay, I'll let you two be.

Huh? Wilson said. But when he turned his head he saw who the nurse was referring to.

How are you feeling? Price said.

He was sitting in a chair next to the bed and there was a plate of cookies on his lap.

I've been better, Wilson said.

I brought you cookies, Price said. Would you like a cookie?

No, thank you.

I was going to bring flowers, Price said, but I was unsure of how you would feel about being given flowers by another man. Might give the wrong impression.

Price shrugged.

He asked, May I have one? One of your cookies?

Wilson turned his head on the pillow and looked at the ceiling and made an ambivalent gesture.

Price took a cookie from the paper plate and ate it in two bites. He brushed his hands together to get rid of the crumbs.

Made it out of there okay, Price said. Didn't you?

I wouldn't say it like that.

How would you say it then?

I would say I just barely made it out of there.

It could have gone much worse.

I consider this much worse, Wilson said.

How old are you, Agent Wilson?

Thirty.

Thirty, Price said. I would have guessed thirty-five or so. But thirty makes sense.

Why does that make sense?

That answer you gave. Your reasoning. That's the kind of answer a young man would give. Immortality is something all young men believe in. Feel like it's been bestowed upon them solely. Like death isn't real and you'll live forever.

Is this some kind of philosophical lecture? Wilson asked.

No.

Then what's your point?

My point is that it can always be worse. And at its worst, it's you six feet in the ground.

Wilson looked out the window. Price put the plate of cookies on the counter behind him and then took off his Stetson and propped it on his knee.

How is it that you found yourself in that alley, Agent Wilson? Price asked.

I walked there.

Randomly? Just by coincidence?

I was looking out of my window and I saw someone that piqued my suspicion.

Piqued your suspicion, Price said. So you just decided to go take a look?

Yes.

Alone?

Just me, yes.

Did you think it was him? The Port Cook Killer?

Is that what you're calling him?

Price shrugged.

You're dealing with a pretty serious man, Agent Wilson, Price said.

I know exactly what I'm dealing with.

Do you? Price said. Because if you did, you'd run. You'd get the hell away from here and quick. And you certainly wouldn't be tracking him down dark alleys in the middle of the night all by your lonesome. Shooting at the car like you did. Trying to bust it up.

Price snapped his tongue. Shook his head.

This is a dangerous game you're playing, Agent Wilson, Price said. Thirty is awfully young to die.

Price's tone instantly darkened.

You might want to let the grown-ups take over from here, he said.

A game? Wilson said. He let his tone match Price's. Again with the games. Games are big with you, aren't they? For playing the role of such a serious guy, you sure like to keep things light.

Price smiled with his lips together. His eyes went flat. He stood from his chair and squared his Stetson. He pulled up on his belt. When he did Wilson caught the glint of the nickel-plated Desert Eagle .50 holstered at Price's hip. Wilson's eyes snapped quickly at it and then snapped away. Price noted the exchange and levered his eyes to admire the gun.

Desert Eagle, Price said. You like it?

No, Wilson said. Not really.

Pity, Price said. Hope you feel better.

He touched the brim of his hat like a cowboy. At the hospital-room door he stopped and turned back to Wilson. Said, You try to stay out of trouble. Then he left.

It was a strange conversation, and it was strange for many reasons but the strangest part, and by far the most interesting to Wilson, was that he hadn't told anyone about shooting at the car or even about the car itself.

44

THE CITY OF SEATTLE SPRAWLED LIKE A RIPPLE IN A POND.
The outer limits were almost unnoticeable. Then farmland was
replaced with strip malls. The buildings got bigger. Like the
far-flung remnants of a great disaster, with trash and shards of
blown-out tires beginning to blanket the ditches. There were
more cars and trucks and soon the roadways were all clogged
and there was nothing but brake lights.

I hate this town, Batey said.

Car horns were blaring. There were angry faces behind the
windows. Batey stayed in the far-right lane and now and then
someone flipped him off for going too slow. At some downtown
exit Batey pulled off the interstate and Fielding pointed at a
7-Eleven and said, Pull in there.

Fielding got out and went to the phone booth and started
scrolling through the phone book. When he found what he was
looking for he tore the page from the book and folded it four
ways and put it in his pocket. Back in the Bronco, he said, First
Avenue.

First Avenue and what?

Just First. Rick's Fantasy Land.

Rick's?

First Avenue.

———

Coursing through downtown they saw the legions of street people huddled in their cardboard squalor. Their shopping carts of garbage and aluminum cans. Their prizes covered with tattered tarps. Some of them smoking the abandoned butts of cigarettes. Torn nylon jackets, wet from rain, draped across their shoulders and hanging like shredded Mylar balloons.

On First Avenue the words RICK'S FANTASY LAND burned in a small red neon sign behind the barred window. The front door looked like a sheet of metal. It was in a brick building. All the other windows were boxed out with newspaper and cardboard from within. It was a discreet place. If you weren't looking for it you wouldn't see it.

Batey parked the Bronco across the street. The rain fell and the wipers went back and forth, back and forth. Batey turned off the radio. Only the sound of the engine running and the rain on the hood and the wipers on the windshield.

So what are we doing here? Batey asked.

I'm goin a go ask if they have videos like the one we saw.

Why you going to go do that?

If they have some, Fielding said, they got to get them from somewhere. Someone's got to be bringin them in.

Okay, Batey said. You know how you're going to ask that tricky question?

No I do not, Fielding said.

The wet sidewalks were full of people. Only a few umbrellas. Men in suits and trench coats held newspapers over their heads as they raced in and out of buildings. Women ran in high heels. Taxicabs parked along the street, their doors opening and their doors slamming shut. There was a hooded sweatshirt in the back seat of the Bronco. Fielding said, Mind if I borrow that?

Be my guest, Batey said.

Fielding reached back and put on the sweatshirt and pulled the hood over his head. How do I look?

Like someone who doesn't want to be seen going into Rick's Fantasy Land.

Keep the truck runnin, Fielding said. I'll be right back.

Fielding jogged across the busy street and pushed through the crowded sidewalk to the front door. Inside, the mat at his feet was wet and said WELCUM. CUM INSIDE. The place was lit in sallow fluorescent lighting that droned on like crazed insects. There were rows of videos and the walls were full of sex toys and novelty lingerie. A man in his early thirties was working the register. Behind him a television was playing an X-rated video with the sound just audible.

Fielding went to the counter and the attendant looked up from a gun magazine.

Yeah? he said.

He had a wispy mustache and bad teeth and his cheeks were full of acne scars.

I'm wonderin if yeh got somethin I'm lookin for, Fielding said.

The attendant was already annoyed and said, You got to tell me what it is, old man. I'm not a fucking mind reader.

What I'm lookin for is pretty extreme.

S & M or something?

Go further, Fielding said.

You got to tell me what you're into, the man said. Got to give me a little direction here.

Let me ask yeh this, Fielding said. How far is too far?

The man had an odd look in his eye. He put aside the magazine.

You talking something like . . . he swiped his hand across his throat.

I might be, Fielding said. Yeh got anythin like that?

What you're talking about sounds pretty illegal.

Talkin about it ain't.

The man looked Fielding square in the eye.

You a cop or something? Cause you got to tell me if you are.

Ain't a cop, Fielding said.

After a long second Fielding said, So? Can yeh help me or not?

Not in the store I don't, the man said. But I can get one.

When?

Day or two. Isn't cheap either.

How much?

The man said the amount. The amount sickened Fielding. His heart pounded in his chest. His jaw muscles clenched.

You okay, the man said.

I'm fine, Fielding said.

The man wrote down an address on a scrap of paper.

Meet me here. Thursday night.

Where is this?

A parking lot.

Can't I come here?

What you're asking for isn't exactly legal, man.

Okay. Thursday night.

Back in the Bronco Fielding felt like taking a long hot shower. Batey sniffed at him.

You even smell funny, he said.

Think I need to burn my clothes, Fielding said.

Get what you need?

Thursday night, Fielding said. Little creep is goin a meet me here.

He showed Batey the scrap of paper.

Where is that?

A parking lot.

A parking lot.

Thursday night.

Better clear my schedule, Batey said.

45

THEY ARRIVED IN TACOMA JUST AFTER FIVE. THE TRAFFIC
was slow. It moved like floating trash in a slow deep river. The
rain hadn't let up and the hillside of the city was masked in fog.
All the freighters moored in the port were beaming into the
clouds. The port was so bright that Fielding and Batey almost
had to squint at it. Past the chain-link fences they saw men in
coveralls and hard hats going about their work. Forklifts and
cranes. Teamsters and their semis lined up like dominoes. They
drove on and the light faded and that light receding seemed an
omen of what was to come. The darkness that lay ahead. Pulling
them deeper whether they liked it or not.

The road split from the water and soon they were on an
abandoned road that ran straight as a plumb line.

Batey followed it till he was forced to stop. The headlights
caught the tall fence ahead. An old iron sign half hanging on
the fence and covered in lichen and rust. NO TRESPASSING.
There was thick chain coiled around the gate and an old ABUS
padlock keeping it all closed.

End of the road, Fielding said.

Just the beginning, Batey said.

Batey got out with the engine still running and went to the
back of the Bronco and opened the door and pulled out a set of

heavy-gauge bolt cutters and went around toward the gate and laid the chain in the jaws and popped the chain like he was cutting paper with a pair of scissors. Batey pulled on one end. The severed chain slipped through the fence like a snake with its head cut off. He pitched the length into the grass. Then he opened the gate on its rusty hinges and it made a sorrowful sound.

Back in the Bronco Batey turned off the headlights and looked back at Fielding without saying a word.

They drove through the gate in the new darkness. Batey stopped the Bronco again and got out and closed the gate behind them. Then they drove on.

Their eyes started to adjust to the dark. Things became recognizable. To either side of the Bronco were acres of flat concrete, deserted parking lots with old streetlights with the glass busted out. The paper mill in front of them looked like something out of a gothic fairy tale. The kind of place that haunts children's dreams.

Fielding leaned forward and looked through the window. The factory seemed to rise up like a giant wave.

What'd they make here? Fielding asked.

The stuff sweethearts wrote their sweet little nothings on, Batey said.

All that, Fielding said, pointing, for a little paper?

A mechanical nightmare, Batey said.

The front entrance was boarded up and the boards were all covered in graffiti. Over the entrance was a sign covered in moss and the O of whatever name used to be there was all that was left. Batey swung the Bronco around toward the mill. There were clusters of thick tubes. Stacks where the burn-off had once escaped. Now all was still. Valves seized. Thousands of tons of steel arrested in time. Batey pulled up to a side entrance. A small metal door with no windows.

They sat in the Bronco watching the door as if waiting for someone to come out. Finally Batey turned off the engine.

Okay, he said.

The dome light shined for a moment as both doors opened and for a moment Fielding watched his shadow over the concrete and it seemed to be moving of its own volition and he had the urge to warn it to go no further. To shout out the mistake it was making. But then he closed the door behind him and the shadow disappeared. Batey came around the truck and the two stood side by side looking at the door leading in.

You know that feeling you get watching a scary movie, Batey said, when the character is about to do something dumb and you're sitting there yelling at the screen telling him not to go through that spooky door of an old, abandoned paper mill?

Sure do, Fielding said.

Me too.

Well.

Yep.

The handle of the door was cold against Fielding's hand as he touched it. The metal was rusted and the rust was boiling up and was so thin in spots you could put your finger through it. Fielding tried the handle. He thought it would be locked but the handle swung down and the door opened.

Convenient, Fielding said. He pulled the door.

The smell that came from inside was like a cave. Within was a blackness absolute. A void without end. The rain had started up again. Batey snapped on his flashlight and the bigger drops fell through the beam with a kind of impatient determination. They stepped through the door. There was water at their feet.

Don't let that shut behind yeh, Fielding said.

Batey wedged a rock in the jamb and then lifted his flashlight to the room. There were miles of overhead tubing. Bent pipes.

Tanks and valve wheels. Dials with shattered glass faces and the indicator pins frozen in place. There were prison-like elevated walkways. It looked at once orderly and chaotic. The flashlight caught only glimpses of it in its narrow spectrum as Batey swung it around. Fielding was squinting as if it were blinding. The roof was leaking and there were pools of stagnant water all over the floor. They stood and listened. They didn't know what for but still they listened. There was only the sound of the rain on the roof. The water dripping through.

Yeh want to lead the way? Fielding asked. I'm already lost.

Batey led them down the only way they could go. At the end of the corridor was an airtight door like in a ship. It had been left open. They stepped through one at a time. The air seemed to be getting worse. Sulfuric. A faint smell of sweet rot. And heavy. Like they could drape it over their shoulders. Like it could smother out their lungs.

This lookin familiar? Fielding asked.

He pointed his light across the room.

Through that door, Batey said.

Stinks in here.

I'm hoping that bad smell isn't what I think it is. Here.

He handed Fielding his gun.

What am I goin a do with this?

Shoot it, Batey said. If it comes to that.

They walked to the door on the far side of the room. Batey put his hand on the handle.

Ready?

Fielding nodded. He raised the gun. Batey opened the door slowly. The hinges didn't make a sound. The door eased in. It was like it was being inhaled. Neither man moved. The flashlight cut a stark line over the floor where the door had stopped.

They waited as if something was going to cross the path of light but nothing did. Not even a single speck of dust.

Yeh keep that trained upward, Fielding said. Don't let it go dark in here.

He walked through the door with the gun raised. Neither of them knew what they were expecting but what they saw was not it. The room was large with high ceilings and was completely empty. Every bit of machinery had been removed. The tanks, the boilers. Not even a forgotten bolt. As if the place had been scrubbed clean. All the glass was gone from the windows near the ceiling and the rain was coming in.

Where'd everythin go? Fielding asked.

I don't know.

This is the room, Fielding said. I recognize it.

Yep.

They walked out to the middle of the room and stood in the very spot where the girl on the video had been tied to the table and murdered. Batey looked down at the cement floor where a stain should have been. But there was no stain. Only the anemic gray of the concrete. Batey walked around with the flashlight trained on the ground in an attempt to find a bloodstain but he couldn't find anything. Fielding was looking up at the punched-out windows where a lighter shade of black was printed in the open frames.

Maybe we got it wrong? Fielding said.

No, Batey said. This is the place.

Blood don't come out of concrete easily.

A sound came careening from the far side of the room and Batey wheeled around with the flashlight and stunned there in the yellow light was a wharf rat the size of a house cat. Its tail more than a foot long. The oily hair on its back was clumped with wet. It hunched there blinking at them. Fielding raised the gun and aimed it at the animal and said, Git. Then the rat ran off and again they were left with an empty room.

Well? Batey said.

Yeah.

They retraced their steps back to the Bronco. Outside the rain was coming harder. Inside the Bronco the rain was loud as it crashed against the roof. They sat there silent. Fielding handed Batey back the gun. Then he faced the window looking out at the mill.

Bit of a wasted trip, Batey said. Not even sure what we were looking for.

Wasn't a waste, Fielding said. Got Thursday night after all. Might tell us somethin.

Yeah, Batey said. How you going to navigate that, by the way?

I do not know, Fielding said. Suppose I'll have to beat it out of him.

Batey grinned but when he turned to look at Fielding he saw Fielding was not grinning and judging by the look on his face they were thinking the same thing. That by the end of this someone was going to die. Batey did not know who was going to die, if it was going to be one of them or someone else, but someone was going to die. That he knew.

46

THE GUN PRICE CARRIED HAUNTED WILSON IN THE FOLLOWING
days of his recovery. It was an odd gun. It was more like an em-
blem, a stance. There was some kind of pride in it that a typical
lawman would not foster. It nagged at Wilson. It was the kind
of symbol that demands attention. One that forces you to take
notice and never forget.

For three days and nights he lay in that hospital bed. A cycle
of nurses. A doctor or two. A gale on the second night throwing
water at the stalwart institution like a child with a garden hose.
The morphine drip tilted the weather to something out of *The
Odyssey*. Being there in bed with no company and no one to hold
him accountable to separate fiction from reality, Wilson turned
the image of Price's gun over and over in his head. Had no idea
why he was fixated on it. But it became an obsession. Every time
he closed his eyes he saw it. Behind the black curtain of his eyelids the polished metal winked. It was on display. It taunted him.
Cried out to be touched.

Then on the third night Wilson came reeling awake. Sweat
coursing past his temples, the hospital gown wet against his skin.
He sat up and pulled the IV from his arm. He rubbed his face.
He kicked his feet to the floor. Went to the window and looked
down the corridor toward the nurses' station. At that late of

an hour the post was held by three sleepy-eyed women. They were talking and drinking coffee. Wilson found his clothes in a drawer. He dressed in the dark room then went to the window again. He waited there ten minutes. Fifteen. Two of the nurses had left the station to do rounds. One still sat there looking at a magazine. He waited until he was sure she wouldn't look up. Then he opened the door and walked down the corridor away from the nurses' station, turning once to check that no one was following him. Slipped under a sign marked EXIT and then loped-ran down the stairs and out of the hospital.

At his hotel the night clerk nodded at him.

They let you out? he asked.

Something like that, Wilson said. He was holding his side. The clerk looked where Wilson's hand was pressed. Wilson didn't dare move his hand. He was afraid that if he did it would come away all full of blood.

Anyone to see me? Wilson said.

No one.

Don't let anyone know I'm here quite yet. Can you do that?

Of course.

He went up to his room and sat down on the bed. Took his hand away from his side. He went to the bathroom and took a hand towel from the rack and pressed it into the blood. Then he went back to the bed and looked at the corkboard.

Doesn't make sense, he said. Two guys with no record just happen to be found dead? Chief of police just standing around? Doesn't make sense.

Then he picked up the phone and dialed a number.

Hello?

Deputy, Wilson said. Did I wake you?

Agent Wilson?

I wake you?

No sir. What can I do you for?

You hear anything back from the coroner on those two men, Evan Nesbit and Conor Hogan.

Yessir.

What'd you hear?

One asphyxiated. One from a gunshot.

How about the woman? Kimberly Roma.

Gunshot.

Yes, Wilson said. Anything in that report regarding their blood? Anything in their system?

No sir.

Nothing?

No sir.

Thank you, deputy, Wilson said. He hung up the phone without saying goodbye.

He went to the television and turned on the VCR and pressed rewind till he saw it. For three days and nights it had eluded him. He pressed pause. He stood there shaking his head. He was almost embarrassed. But there it was. Very discreet, seemingly out of the shot. Hanging from the wall. Slung in its holster. Desert Eagle .50.

47

WEDNESDAY DAWNED COLD AND BRITTLE. THE RAIN HAD
turned to snow sometime in the night. It was a wet snow and all
the branches of the cedars were heavy and they frowned toward
the white ground like they bore the weight of not only the snow
but also something else. It was just after eight when Fielding
awoke. The yard was white, the pasture. Reefs of purple clouds
stacked toward the paling eastern sky.

Fielding put the coffee on. He made a morning fire in the
stove. When the coffee was done he took it in bed with the down
comforter pulled to his chest. The room felt cold. The heeler lay
asleep at the foot of the bed. Sometimes he would yip at the
deer or grouse he was chasing in his dreams. Fielding listened
to the cedarwood popping in the stove. Listened for anything
else but there was nothing else to hear. Totally quiet. Like every
morning.

Late in the morning he went to see the horses. When he
opened the door of the barn their heads swung up from the stall-
boards. Their eyes were big and wet. Snake was looking through
the hair of his mane. Fielding walked toward Snake and Snake
tossed his head. He pressed his long face into Fielding's hand.

Yeh boys warm enough? Fielding asked. Got cold last night.

He rubbed Snake between the eyes. Rubbed down the long

bridge of his nose. Snake's nostrils were working the air. The bone beneath the skin was like rock. Fielding let his hand rest where it was. Through the caged mane Snake's dark eyes looked back at him and dished within that dark world Fielding saw himself and the somber expression on his face. And looking into them he knew there were things in this world he would never know or even care to. And he said to the horse, Yeh got no idea what's goin on out there, do yeh? The Appaloosa blinked at him. Fielding said, I envy that.

He opened the stall door and walked in and closed the door behind him. Snake turned his head and watched him. Fielding took down the hackamore from the nail in the wall. The bosal was a pale color and made of rawhide and the rope cinched to the bosal was made of horsehair. Fielding liked the way it felt in his hands. There was a certain amount of weight to it, like it would never wear out. Like it would outlive the horse it was used on. Outlive the rider. He slipped the bosal over Snake's nose and laced the thin leather strap behind his ears and buckled it just below his eyes. Snake tossed his head once.

I know, Fielding said. But we'll get it.

He led the horse from the stall and dallied the rope and went to get the saddle. The tack room was at the far end of the barn and Snake watched him as he walked the length. Inside the room was nice and dry. Fielding snapped on the light. The old Rowell saddle hung on a thick wooden post. He lifted the saddle and the Navajo blanket and carried them out and snapped off the light and shut the door and walked them back down the barn where Snake stood watching him. He draped the blanket over Snake's back. Then he lifted the saddle and buckled the girth strap. He undallied the rope and led Snake through the barn and into the falling snow.

The wind was perfectly still. The snow fell in silence. The

snow was wet on the ground and wherever the pair stepped their prints turned dark in the mud. Snake's breath smoked in the waxen light.

He stopped Snake and told him what he was about to do. Said, Just let me get my boot in here.

He stuck a boot in the stirrup and then said, Just goin a swing my leg up.

He sat the horse for a moment and together they watched the falling snow. He snapped his tongue and tapped his boot-heels into Snake.

Uh-oh, he said.

And once again the horse took off in a pounding gallop. More than once he attempted to stop him by reining back but it was like trying to pull a log from water. With the bosal taut against his nose Snake ran with his neck erect and his face turned down in a calamitous fashion. Again Fielding lost his hat. With his head jostling and hands and reins aloft, he looked the part of an ill-fated buckaroo. And not sure what to do with the fence line approaching, he kicked his right foot out of the stirrup and leapt from the saddle.

He hit the ground with his back against the earth. His face staring up at the sky. He lay unmoving for fear something was broken. But he felt around and everything felt as it should. Nothing busted, only his ego.

Snake returned and stood above him, blinking his large eyes like he'd never seen a man lying on the ground before.

If yeh kill me, Fielding said, who's goin a feed yeh?

A little breath of wind kicked up and Snake's long mane lifted with it.

I'd yell at yeh if yeh weren't so pretty, he said.

Out over the snow he heard the hooves of another horse. He thought at first it might be Buckshot escaped from his stall but the gait was not the gait of a mule. He lifted himself up to sit with his elbows propping him and he saw a rider approaching over the white pasture. The horse was a dun-colored Morgan with a dark mane. The woman riding it had a long black braid over her shoulder and a broad flat-brimmed hat the color of flour and she had set the Morgan into a trot and she moved with the horse in a way Fielding had never seen before. Closer she came he could tell she was smiling. She slowed the horse and then sat it with her hands laid one atop the other on the saddle horn.

So this is what happens when yeh die? he said.

Excuse me, she said.

Some pretty lady on a horse comes to take yeh away.

You aren't dead, Mr Fielding.

Mrs Batey, Fielding said. To what do I owe the pleasure?

Figured it might be a good morning for a ride.

Yer too late, he said. Already rode him.

She was wearing a worn Carhartt jacket and a pair of Wranglers that came up high on her waist and they made her legs look longer than they already were.

Can't help but wonder, Coraline said.

What's that?

Why a grown man is lying in all this wet snow when there's a perfectly good horse standing over him.

Thought I'd give him a break, Fielding said.

She leaned in her saddle and offered him a hand.

My knight in shining Wranglers, he said.

He took her hand and made a painful kind of sound and stood and tried to clean his hands on the thighs of his jeans. Coraline swung out of her saddle. She draped the reins over the Morgan's neck and the Morgan stood there without moving. She went over to Snake and leaned into him and spoke Spanish in a soft voice Fielding couldn't understand. She closed her eyes as she spoke and she rubbed Snake's neck and spoke to him some more. She slipped her fingers under the girth strap to check it. Oh, she said. *Pobrecito.* She unbuckled it and loosened it by a notch. Then she went around him and looked at every part of him. Snake tossed his tail like it was chasing flies. She came around again and held Snake's face in her hands and looked into his eyes.

What made you choose him? she asked.

Yeh mean Snake?

I mean an Appaloosa.

What's wrong with an Appaloosa?

Absolutely nothing.

Then why yeh askin me?

They're a bit spirited is all.

Spirited is good.

Sure, Coraline said.

What's that look for?

Nothing.

That look yer givin me, Fielding said. That ain't nothin.

You want my unsolicited opinion?

I got a choice?

I'd have you set up with a quarter horse. Around nine years old. Broke and trained so even a toddler could ride him. And you're riding a hackamore?

Yes mam.

Ran through your hands, didn't he?

Yeh saw that, did yeh?

Caught a glimpse.

She rubbed Snake between the eyes. She rubbed her hand down his nose.

Why are you riding a hackamore, Coraline asked, and not a snaffle?

I don't know, Fielding said. I don't know what a snaffle is.

It's a bit, she said.

She put her finger between her teeth and bit down.

A bit?

A bit.

So a hackamore ain't a bit?

No, she said. A hackamore's a hackamore.

What's the difference?

It'd be like driving a race car in roller skates.

Yeh mean it'd be tricky?

Means you better be a good driver.

I haven't worn roller skates in years.

Then I wouldn't recommend taking them to Daytona.

Come to think of it, Fielding said, I ain't ever driven a race car either.

Coraline smiled at him. She smiled with her eyes and it was those eyes that made him believe that things could turn out all right if one really worked at it.

You mind? she asked.

Mind what?

If I take this Appaloosa for a spin?

If yeh feel like gettin bucked.

She smiled again but this time for a different reason.

She spoke to the horse in Spanish again. Whispering something. Then she put her foot into the stirrup and swung into the saddle. Snake stepped uneasily at first. His eyes wild looking and unblinking. He jostled a bit and he stepped quickly in circles. Her hands popped the reins, correcting the horse. All the while Coraline's braid did not move from its place on her shoulder. Then all at once Snake stopped. His breathing seemed easier. He tossed his head a time or two then stood like the statue of a horse.

Ahí está, she said. Take him for a little walk now.

She set the horse forward. She circled Fielding standing there in the snow. As she circled she called out the horse's steps.

Right hind, right front, she said. Left hind, left front.

She repeated it like litany.

What's that yer sayin?

You got to become acquainted with a horse's cadence. Right hind, right front. Left hind, left front. To get him to do what you want you got to know what hoof is leaving the ground.

She rode in circles. The snow grew dark with the wet mud.

Right hind, right front, she said. Left hind, left front. Now I'm going to get him going a little.

On the right hind step she set the horse into a lope. Loping in circles in the wet snow. Fielding was turning with them like a ribbon on a maypole. Like he had never seen a horse lope before.

See how he's just going now? she said. I've got the reins loosened up. If you can control the hind quarters you got the whole horse. He's just doing his thing now. Like I'm supposed to be up here. Then she said, Now I'm going to pick up some softness here.

Coraline tightened the reins a little and the horse slowed and she set him into a walk again and then abruptly she stopped him. She patted Snake's neck. She said, I'm going to try something.

She turned the horse and trotted off. At a good distance she turned back to Fielding, who was just standing there like a scarecrow. She clucked her tongue and Snake pounded off. She was high in the saddle. Snake's mane and Coraline's braid were straight out and sawing like fire. Ten feet from Fielding she said something and the horse drove its hind hooves into the ground and squatted its quarters like it was trying to sit and they slid to a stop.

Huh, Fielding said.

Coraline walked him over and patted Snake's neck again.

You got a good horse here, she said.

She lay the reins over the saddle horn and put her hands up as if in surrender and with just the pressure from her legs Snake started backing up. Then she set him forward. Then she turned him in circles.

Now yer just showin off, Fielding said.

She took up the reins and swung out of the saddle.

Yeh ain't afraid of anything, Fielding said. Are yeh?

Everything frightens me, Coraline said. I'm a mother. The whole damn world frightens me.

But not horses.

No, she said. Not horses. There isn't a single horse alive that I'm afraid of. That horse doesn't exist.

She handed Fielding the reins.

Swing on up, she said.

I told yeh I've already ridden him today.

Swing up.

He put a foot into the stirrup and swung his leg over and stood up into the saddle and sat down and looked at Coraline.

Don't look at me, she said. I can't tell you where to go.

He tried to nudge the horse on but Snake did not move.

He tried again but it did no good.

He ain't goin, he said.

You haven't told him anything yet.

What should I tell him?

You tell him whatever you want, she said. It's your horse.

Right hind, right front, Fielding said. Left hind, left front.

He didn't know if it was those words or something in his body or something deep within the union of horse and man but Snake started walking. He did not take off. Just walked and Fielding rode him as if he was meant to be there.

Coraline went to her own horse and passed the reins over its neck and stood into the saddle and turned the horse and rode up alongside Fielding and looked at him once but did not say a word and they rode side by side into the pasture over the snow in the ash-colored light till the fence line stopped them and then they rode back again. They rode for nearly an hour with the only sounds coming from the horses' breathing and the leather of the saddles creaking in the cold morning air.

At some point they rode back to the barn and Fielding dismounted and dallied the reins on the post and walked Coraline to her truck. It was a big 350 diesel and it seemed overkill for a single horse trailer. Coraline stepped down from the horse.

How about that, she said. She looked at him. A cowboy.

Yeh mean me?

I mean you.

Coraline leaned and undid the girth strap and lifted the saddle from the Morgan's back and walked it to the truck and swung it into the bed as if it weighed nothing at all. She folded up the blanket and put that inside the truck and came back with a brush and started rubbing that over the Morgan's coat. And as she did she started talking and it was as if she were talking to the horse but what she spoke of had no concern to the horse. She ran the brush down the horse's neck to the withers. Still Coraline was talking and not letting Fielding rebut any of it. He stood there and listened and when she finally said all she had to say she turned around to Fielding and spit into the snow.

So that's why yer here, Fielding said.

Yes.

He told yeh all that? Fielding asked.

Yes sir.

I wish yeh wouldn't call me that.

Yes, Amos, she said. He told me all of that.

Tell yeh about tomorrow night then? Tell yeh what we're aimin to do?

He told me everything.

Huh.

Huh what?

Don't seem right, Fielding said. I don't know.

What doesn't seem right?

Yeh knowin. Or maybe yeh havin to know.

Cause I'm just a purty little woman? Is that it?

No.

Let me ask you something.

Ask it.

You tell Sara all this?

All this what?

What you do, what you did? You tell her all about what you had seen? About what you had to go and do?

Sure, he said. Some of it.

Some of it?

Okay, Fielding said. I told her.

Then how is this different? How is me knowing any different?

I guess it ain't.

You guess?

Sara and I were like the same person. Even if I didn't tell her, she knew. She knew the whole story before I even said a word.

What makes you think Dee and I aren't like that?

Ain't my place to say one way or another. Guess what I'm tryin to say is that it's different bein on the outside. To see what yeh expose people to. People yeh love. Thinkin about it now, I wish Sara didn't know what she did. I wish I came home and she saw the man she married. The man full of hope. That's what yeh lose in all this. Yer sense of hope. I just hope yeh can still see the good in it.

The good in what? she asked.

Life, I guess. Livin. I hope yeh still see Dee just as yeh did the day yeh married him.

I do.

That's good.

You boys can stop you know, Coraline said. You can stop.

Yeh ever been on an escalator? Fielding asked. Sometimes yeh can't get off. Sometimes yeh have to ride it till it's done.

This isn't that.

Maybe, Fielding said. But I'm movin somewhere.

This isn't a department store, Amos.

No, Fielding said. And I'm bad at metaphors. Don't matter neither. Someone killed those girls. Someone shot those two guys. Someone took that Eunice girl. And that girl might still be out there. That's why I ain't gettin off this ride till it's done.

And when's that going to be?

I don't know. Ain't got there yet.

You know how this could end. Don't you?

Could end several ways.

You know what I'm talking about.

Yes mam.

Don't make it end that way.

I don't plan to.

Promise me.

Dee ain't a Boy Scout out there, Fielding said. He can handle himself.

Promise me.

Okay.

Say it, Coraline said.

Her eyes were becoming wet.

She said, Say the words.

I promise.

You promise to what?

I promise I won't let it end that way.

A teardrop fell from her eye and it streamed in a thin rivulet down her cheek. She did not attempt to wipe it away and it fell to her jaw and with nowhere else to go the weight of everything pulled on the drop and it fell to the ground, where it vanished in the snow.

Coraline led the horse back to the trailer and inside and closed the door and dropped in the lever and then chained it. She came back around and said, You better not be lying to me.

I don't tell lies, he said.

Good, she said. Cause if you are and the worst thing happens I'll kill you both myself just for putting me through it.

48

BY THE NEXT MORNING ALL THE SNOW HAD MELTED AND THE falling snow had turned to rain and all the beauty the snow carried with it was gone. The trees were bare and gray. The leaves on the ground in the woods were rotting. The air smelled heavy. The stench of winter was so thick you could almost chew it.

They were driving south on the interstate and not saying a word because to say anything might talk them out of it. So they went on like that, not talking and only thinking.

The interstate was dark and ribboned on before them. It was all different shades of black. The sky was low. The tall firs set back from the interstate were of the darkest shade and so close together they looked like a black wall to some storybook fortress. Fielding was looking out the window. The wipers smeared across the glass.

No Bronco tonight, Fielding finally said.

No, Batey said. Thought the optics of a government vehicle participating in what we're about to might look suspicious.

That's puttin it mildly.

What time are you meeting this guy? Batey asked.

Eleven.

Cora said you two had a nice chat yesterday.

I listened, Fielding said. That's what I did.

She can talk alright.

She can ride too. She tell yeh about that?

She told me she watched an old man nearly break his neck.

She's got a way with horses, Fielding said.

Did she lean in and talk Spanish to it?

Yep.

In the light from the dash Fielding could see that Batey was smiling.

Yeah, he said. She's got a way with horses.

Fielding had a hard leather case and an envelope stuffed with strips of paper sitting in his lap. Batey eyed it. First the envelope. Then the case.

That what I think it is? Batey asked. He nodded at the case.

That depends on what yeh think it is, Fielding said.

Your old peacemaker on its comeback tour?

Yeh know I've only fired it a couple times? And only then at a target. Never even pointed it at another human.

Fielding unlatched the case and opened the lid and the dark metal glinted in the light. There was a space beside the gun carved out for a box of bullets. Fielding sat looking at the gun.

Yeh want some truth? he said.

Okay.

I don't even like lookin at it, Fielding said. No good can come out of it. No good at all.

He shut the lid and put the case on the floor between his feet.

Think the guy will buy that ringer? Batey asked, nodding at the envelope.

I'm hopin he won't get the chance.

They didn't speak again till they reached the outskirts of Seattle. Batey asked about the address. Fielding turned on the dome light and took the slip of paper from his chest pocket and read off the address. Batey told him there was a map in the glove box. With the map spread out on his lap Fielding traced a finger to the location. Where the tip of his finger finally landed was the warehouse district south of the city. Fielding checked his watch.

We going to make it? Batey asked.

How fast can this truck go?

North of the city they crossed an enormous bridge where far below the water was the color of oil. The skyscrapers rose into the night with their squares of yellow light awash in the Ford's glass. The interstate took them through the guts of the city, the buildings towering in the clouds. Lost up there, the shapes of bullets stood on end. They went under overpasses. Drab figures moving around barrel fires, their shadows pitched upward on the concrete like crude carnival spectacles.

South of the city the long tracts of industry took over. As they got closer, Fielding called out the road and Batey exited.

The lights of the warehouses grew dimmer the farther they went until soon there were no lights and the buildings themselves looked to have not been lit in quite some time. Most of them had temporary chain-link fencing around the perimeters and the warehouse walls were covered in graffiti. What little dirt there was in this abandoned place was consumed with tangles of blackberry vines and within those tangles were pieces of trash smeared like wasted bugs on the grill of a truck. Skinny cats prowled for a meal, their white eyes flashing for an instant in the headlights and then vanishing altogether.

Seeing the faded and moss-coated numbers, Fielding said, That's the place.

There was no fence and there was no gate. Batey stopped the Ford.

I don't see anyone, Batey said. Do you?

No I do not.

The Ford's headlights shined across the parking lot where a

large oval of water lay collected. It was big as a pond. Went from building to fence. No way around it. They sat there for a moment in the warm cab with the engine idling. Plotting their next move.

You sure this is the place? Batey said.

And then as if on cue a set of headlights flashed at the far end of the lot. Then everything was dark again. Even the shape of the car that had flashed them.

Okay, Fielding said.

Batey put the Ford into drive and set the truck ahead. At the edge of the pond he stopped.

How deep you think this is? Batey said.

One way to find out.

Batey let off the brake again and the water rose on the tires. It rose to the axle and then to the top of the fender.

I hope this asshole didn't put something in the water, Batey said.

The water on the undercarriage sounded like crashing surf. Batey was looking out the window, judging the depth. But Fielding looked straight ahead. Didn't take his eyes away.

The water fell away from the undercarriage and on the other side they could see the car now. Came closer and they could see it was a little rusted-out Civic. The driver was the same guy Fielding had talked to at the porn store. He was sitting behind the wheel. The truck's headlights lit up the car's cab. He was smoking a cigarette and the cherry flared from time to time. Twenty feet away Batey stopped the truck and put it into park and let the engine idle. The guy in the car held up his hand like a visor and then he opened the door and stood there smoking.

The rain had quit. It was cold and the exhaust from the truck and the breath from the guy lingered in the air. He held the tape in his right hand. It was wrapped in a plastic bag. Fielding reached down and picked up the leather case and laid it on his lap and popped each latch and opened the lid and lifted the gun from its felt bedding. Batey just looked on without a word. Fielding opened the cylinder and took the box of bullets from its cutout and with his thumb and forefinger slid a round into each chamber. Then he closed the cylinder and he closed the case and set it on the floor again. He leaned forward and jammed the gun into the small of his back. He stuffed the envelope of paper into his jacket pocket.

Alright, he said.

He took a deep breath. He looked at Batey.

Keep the engine goin.

Fielding opened the door and stepped out.

You're late, the guy said.

Got held up.

Who's that in the truck?

Friend.

Tell him to cut the fucking lights. Can't see a fucking thing.

Fielding turned back to the truck and made a motion and the headlights went out. Only the orange of the parking lights reflecting on the wet ground.

Nice truck, the guy said. It's always the guy who's into freaky shit that drives a nice truck.

That it, Fielding said. He pointed at the tape.

Yep.

Where'd yeh get it?

That's not part of the deal.

Yeh seen it?

I took a look-see. Didn't finish it. The ending isn't my cup of tea.

Am I goin a like it?

How the fuck should I know. I don't know anything about you.

I'm into knives. Fancy kinds. Masks and antlers. Any of them in there?

There might be.

How old's the girl in it?

How old do you want her to be?

How old are you?

You want the fucking video or not? It's freezing out here.

Just makin conversation.

The guy took a long pull of his cigarette.

Those will kill yeh, Fielding said. Yeh know that?

Listen, old man, he said, you got ten seconds to show me some dough or you'll have to jerk off to something else.

How much I owe yeh?

This is a rush order.

Like it was newly made?

How the fuck should I know when it was made.

Just askin a question.

Ten, the guy said.

Ten what?

Nine, eight, seven . . .

How much?

The guy said the number.

That's quite a lot, Fielding said. That's more than we agreed on.

Things changed.

Maybe my friend comes out here to help yeh change yer mind.

Maybe I got someone here too. Maybe that someone has got a gun pointed right at your fucking temple.

No yeh don't, Fielding said. There ain't no one. Just you.

Fielding saw a flicker of unease in him. Something fluttered in his eyes.

The amount we agreed on, Fielding said.

Let me see the money.

Give me the tape.

Fielding reached into his pocket and pulled out the envelope and handed it to the guy. The guy put the cigarette in the corner of his mouth and weighed the envelope in his hand as if he knew what he was doing.

Feels about right, he said.

He went to open the envelope and when his eyes fell upon all that shredded paper Fielding had already pulled the gun from his belt and before the guy could say a word Fielding pistol-whipped him on the side of the head. The spray of blood in the orange light hung for a moment like mist. He dropped the tape. Fielding hit him again. The guy fell to the pavement and Fielding began to kick him. He kicked him once, twice in the stomach. He kicked him in the chest. The guy gasped and moaned. Fielding didn't stop kicking him till Batey ran around and pulled him off. Fielding wavered on his feet like he might faint. He walked off a little ways and put his hands on his knees and vomited. He wiped his mouth with the back of his hand and then came back and stood over the guy, trying to catch his breath.

He dead? Fielding asked.

No, Batey said.

Yeh got cuffs in that truck?

You want to bring him in?

Yeah.

Where to?

I don't know. Figure that out later.

They carried him to the bed of the truck and lifted him in. More than once the guy tried to plead but Batey slapped him across the mouth. Fielding climbed up and manacled one hand and then slid the other cuff through a D ring and then cuffed the other hand. Then he jumped out and closed up the back.

Batey handed him a handkerchief. He had the guy's blood stippled across his face. Batey went around and picked up the video wrapped in plastic. Went to the guy's Civic and opened the door and leaned in and began rummaging through its contents. The upholstery was torn. The ashtray was overflowing with butts. He found the guy's wallet and opened it up and removed the license. He shut the door and looked at the license and read out the name. Then he put it in his pocket and walked back to the truck.

Fielding was already sitting inside. When Batey got in and sat down and looked over at Fielding he could see his hands were badly shaking.

We'll bring him in, Batey said. If he knows anything they'll get it out of him.

Fielding didn't say a word. He stared straight ahead. A vacant look on his face. Thinking about the guy in the back. Thinking about the horrors held within that video. Maybe daydreaming about what his life used to be. Wherever he was it was not in the truck. As far as far can go. Long gone, and never coming back.

Batey put the truck into drive and turned it around and drove out the same way they had come in. Batey kept checking the guy in the rearview but he was exactly where they had put him.

Batey said something that men like him do in an attempt to comfort someone but Fielding did not hear it. Finally he was roused as Batey repeated his name.

This was a good move, Batey said. We'll turn them over to Wilson. The guy and the video. Wipe our hands if we want. Call it quits. Over and done.

Yeh believe that?

I think I could.

Where's that leave the girl then?

Batey kept driving. Fielding said,

What about yer girls? Yeh remember what yeh told me?

I remember, Batey said. You remember what you told Cora? What you promised her?

Yeh ain't killed yet.

Not yet.

Yeh tellin me yer quittin?

No, Batey said. I'm saying what if there isn't an answer in this.

Maybe not.

You want to spend the rest of your lucid life searching for a ghost?

Fielding thought about that. Thought about what lurked in the future and what lay buried in the past. He looked out the window at the darkness, at the dark warehouses. The dark railcars motionless in the dark rail yards. Out beyond all of it to where the lights of the city spread out in a metastatic glow turning the low clouds pink. He said,

All I got are ghosts. That's the only thing I got left. Sara and that girl and that—

He was interrupted by glass shattering and his world going sideways as if jerked on a cable as a semi slammed into the side of the truck like some ribald meteorite crashing into the earth. The semi kept pushing until the tires of Batey's truck caught and flipped the truck and the semi pushing, rolling the truck like it was a bale of hay. And when the semi finally stopped the truck came to rest on its busted-out wheels. All the glass was smashed out and Fielding and Batey were still alive but unconscious. Their heads hanging forward as if asleep.

But this was no sleep. Their faces were battered. The canopy of the truck had been ripped off and the guy in the bed was dead with one arm severed at the wrist where the cuff had cut through. His bottom half gone and lying somewhere back in the road. The organs and viscera in his torso hanging out like a rag-ged piñata.

The semi idled where it was. The radiator was smoking. The headlights were all smashed out. The door opened up and a man stepped down. The clearance lights burned on over the cab and in their wash of amber light the totaled truck sat in full view. The man had a gun in his hand and he held it alongside his leg. He watched for a long time before stepping any closer. Watch-ing for any movement. And then he started toward the truck and Noon's shadow stretched out under the amber light as he reached in and took hold of Fielding's collar.

49

WILSON TRIED CALLING BATEY AND TRIED CALLING FIELDING
but neither of them answered. He had made a call to the captain
down in Seattle telling him about the deranged video and the
Desert Eagle and the corrupt chief of police. Captain thought
it sounded thin but Wilson told him about the missing persons
and the three found dead in the cellar. Told him about nearly
being run down. Told him about his strange conversation with
Price. Captain said, You telling me you think the chief of police
is trafficking young women?

Yes sir, Wilson said. And not just trafficking, but participating.

You got any evidence to back this up?

No sir, Wilson said. But my gut is telling me I'm right.

Your gut? the captain said.

I know how it sounds, Wilson said. But—

You're asking me to slander an elected official's name.

I know what I'm asking and I wouldn't do it if I weren't completely sure.

And that's what you are? Completely sure?

You got to trust me on this. Get me that warrant and I'll get
you a mountain of evidence.

Don't make me regret this, the captain said.

Wilson drove to Batey's house. He found Coraline with the

horses. She was leading a gelding into the barn when she saw him coming up the drive. Faster than one would consider reasonable. He parked the car and got out and called over to Coraline. Said, Is Dee here, mam?

No, she said.

She watched Wilson jog toward her with a limp. She said, What's going on? You hurt?

Where's Dee? Wilson asked.

With Amos.

And where's Amos?

The two of them went south.

Why'd they go south? What are they up to?

Coraline frowned. Wilson's voice seemed rushed. She knew little about him but what she did know was of a man not prone to panic.

You got me a little worried, Coraline said.

Where'd they go? Wilson asked.

Seattle.

Where in Seattle?

I don't know, Coraline said. Find the maker of some movie.

Movie? What kind of movie?

A bad one.

Have anything to do with a girl being murdered in it.

Yes.

Did he mention anything about an old paper mill?

Maybe, she said. I don't remember that.

They say anything about Tacoma?

No, Coraline said. Just Seattle.

They're not in Seattle, Wilson said.

He turned and loped back to his car. Coraline called after him. Where are you going?

But Wilson had already gotten in his car and peeled off down the drive.

50

THE WAILING IN HIS EARS WHEN HE CAME AWAKE WAS LIKE A forest of cicadas. The grass in the field he was lying in was tall and brown and wet. Fielding opened his eyes. The sky was gray. Night had turned to day. Fog had settled to the ground as if rooted there and it was thick and cold. Fielding tried to sit up but he couldn't. It took him several attempts. His blood was a brilliant red against the grass. He touched his face and winced at the pain. His ribs felt broken. He could hardly lift an arm. When he finally stood up and looked around he didn't recognize anything. Nothing but tall grass and fog. Not a tree, not a single distinguishing trait with which to get his bearings.

A small wind was blowing and the grass bent softly and the fog tumbled in the wind over the grass. He staggered forward as if drunk. And as if drunk held out a hand to brace himself but finding nothing he fell to the ground. The wailing in his ears did not relent. He blinked against the grass. His breath rolled over the ground like steam from a train. And when he could no longer keep them open he closed his eyes and the world closed out.

He began to dream and in this dream:

He was holding Sara's hand and they were walking on a path near the river back in Iowa. It was early summer and the flowers were out and the birds were calling in the trees and it was warm and the air was redolent. He looked down at their hands laced together and they weren't the hands of the old but the young. Her face too was young and her dark hair was piled atop her head and her neck was long and bare and the little hairs at the nape curled in ringlets from the humidity. He turned her hand up to better see it and looking at the wedding band, he said,

How long we been married now?

Forever, she said.

Yes, but when? When did we actually get married?

I don't know, she said. We've always been this way.

But there must've been a date? A day the weddin took place?

If there was I don't remember it. I think we were just born this way.

Yeh afraid of anythin?

No.

Nothin?

Nothing.

Are yeh afraid of dyin?

Are you asking if when I died I was afraid?

Yes. I guess that's what I'm askin.

No, she said. But that hasn't even happened.

What hasn't happened?

Me dying.

Yes it has. I was there. I was there with yeh.

I know you were.

So if yeh knew I was there and yeh didn't die and yeh aren't dead, where have yeh been? Why have yeh left me alone for so long?

Here, she said. I've been here. Waiting for you.

Why ain't yeh come to see me?

I see you all the time.

I wish yeh'd let me see yeh.

That's not up to me.

Who's it up to then?

She shrugged her shoulders. She kicked a pebble down the path.

I miss yeh, he said. I don't think I can do it anymore.

Then don't, she said.

Is it that easy?

Yes, she said. It's that easy.

What do I do?

You just stop.

Stop?

You just cease everything. You stop moving. Stop thinking. You just stop.

That seems easy enough.

It is.

I don't know if I could stop thinkin. Maybe not yet.

I know.

So why yeh tellin me this?

Because it seemed like something you needed an answer to.

That doesn't answer anythin though.

It will.

When?

In time it will, she said. You just have to be patient.

51

THEN FROM DARK TO DARK HE AWOKE. ALL THE LIGHT WAS
gone from the sky. The ground was wet as if it had rained but it
had not.

He rose up and stood in the grass. It came to his waist. There
wasn't a light to be seen. He could only make out a dark wall of
cedars at the edge of the field. And even that was diminished
in the fog. He turned in a circle. Any way, he figured, was better than just standing still. It was then that the first pistol shot
came. The sound was flat and soft in all that quiet and fog. It was
also unmistakable. He heard the whine of the bullet as it nearly
hit him. He turned to where the first came from and saw the
pop of the second flash in the dark. This one tore through the
grass to his right and he began to run. The grass was thick and
the running was difficult. All he could hear was his own breath
and the grass swishing against his legs. He felt his arm tug and
then a stinging pain. The bullet hit him just below the shoulder
and threw him to the ground. He labored up and clutched his
arm with his good hand and was running again. The warm blood
was running from the hole and down over his fingers. He looked
at it once. His arm and hand were black and it didn't look like
blood at all.

The next bullet spun him around and he fell backward into

the grass. Didn't even hear the shot. Just below his ribs his shirt was warm and wet. Fielding lay there holding himself. He was looking up at the sky. An odd sensation overcame him and he wished he was able to see the stars. To see them up there burning like they always did. He took them for granted, he realized. He regretted not looking at them every second they had been out.

Then he heard the footsteps of his shooter. He approached without hurry. Fielding heard him whistling like he was walking down a country road. Fielding lay there holding himself as Noon stepped up. He stood at Fielding's feet. Fielding couldn't make out any details. Just a black silhouette. Then a low, measured voice:

Hello, Mr Fielding.

And then the butt of the pistol came down and everything went dark.

52

A GLARING LIGHT LIKE THE SECOND COMING JOLTED FIELDING awake. His first instinct was to run or move and he tried both but both were impossible. His ankles were bound, his wrists cuffed to something cold. He was seated in a metal folding chair and the cold something his wrists were cuffed to was the piping of an oil boiler. Everything was out of focus until it wasn't and when it all came into view he realized he was back in that big empty room of the paper mill. There were studio lights on tall stands and the light was blinding. They were directed to a very specific focal point and beyond that ring of light the darkness could only be described as solid. The lights made a faint buzzing sound. And over the buzzing came the drugged sounds of Eunice Thompson tied to a table.

Fielding blinked heavily. He did it again. He didn't believe what he was looking at. She was laid out on her back. Her clothes had been removed. Her long hair hung from the edge of the table like a thick vine. It had been braided and within the braid there were feathers and twigs of sage. Fielding could see parts of her body had been painted. The paint almost looked like blood and the designs it left looked to be made by a sloppy hand, with the palm and all five fingers bold and distinct before fading out as the hand smeared across the skin. A black oval was painted over her eyes. Just like the others. The table she lay upon was the same table he'd seen in the video. Cut in a V and her legs tied to that shape.

Fielding tried to say the girl's name but only a mumble exited. A hot drip fell down his chin. In his lap there was a wide stain that glistened like spilled red molasses. He tried calling her name again but a voice not his own interrupted with,

Ah ah ah. I would not strain yourself, Mr Fielding. You have already lost a good amount of blood.

Fielding squinted into the darkness. The voice seemed to have no origin. It felt as if it were all around him. Fielding stayed quiet. Out of the gloom came a towering figure. Made taller by the gruesome mask he wore. The wild fringe of animal hair. The antlers wired in place. He came into view and stood just within the light.

Who the hell are yeh? Fielding said.

Through the mask Fielding heard the man laugh.

Who the hell are yeh! Fielding shouted.

Would that matter, Mr Fielding? Noon said.

What?

I asked whether or not that would matter.

Yeh get that girl off that table right now.

Why are you so angry, Mr Fielding?

Fielding spit a gout of blood onto the cement floor. A smell like iron and mold rose back up at him. Then the smell of urine. He wondered how long he'd been chained there.

Mr Fielding?

Stop sayin my name.

How shall I address you then?

Yeh don't.

But I am here. You are there. We are looking at one another. We have to make an attempt.

All I can see is some chickenshit pervert hidin behind some stupid goddamn mask.

Would you prefer if I removed it?

I don't care what yeh do so long as yeh untie the girl and then put a gun to yer head and pull the trigger.

Pull the trigger? That's awfully violent.

Yeh've already done it once tonight.

Yes, Noon said, but you were running. Running looks bad. Running is panic.

If yeh don't want panic then quit fuckin shootin at people.

Isn't this funny?

No.

Yes it is.

Why is this funny?

Choices, he said. How we have arrived here simultaneously. The minor decisions, the insignificant details that led you here. To this place. To this moment. It's remarkable, isn't it? How so many events had to align just so to bring you here tonight. And now here you are. Seated in that chair. Looking at me. Me looking at you. Remarkable.

Choices, Fielding said. Had nothin to do with choices.

He spit.

Please stop spitting on the floor, Noon said. I can get you a towel or a jar if you like.

Fielding spit again. The man took off the mask. He removed it slowly as if afraid to damage it. Even in the shadows of the studio lights his blue eyes were luminous.

So that's what a crazy person looks like, Fielding said.

I'm not crazy, Mr Fielding.

Yes yeh are, Fielding said. Batshit.

To be crazy is to not be in control. Do I look out of control, Mr Fielding?

Yes. Whatever the opposite of control is. That's what yeh are.

Chaos.

What?

Chaos. Chaos is the opposite of control.

Sure, Fielding said. Let's call it that.

Do you believe in movies, Mr Fielding?

Movies?

Film. Cinema.

I don't know what that means.

It is a very simple question.

It's a stupid question and I'm not goin a answer it.

I do, Mr Fielding.

Good for you.

Do you know why I do?

I could care less.

I believe in it because it's a way to see ourselves in our most extreme form. To see ourselves in a way we could never imagine in reality. On film anything is possible.

That's why yeh make that bullshit smut?

Again, Mr Fielding, choices. It's all about choices. I value honesty. Vulnerability. Intercourse, sex, the physical act of it all doesn't mean anything. Not really. Merely an amusing by-product. What I am searching for is that brief moment of vulnerability. That moment immediately preceding death. The exact instant one realizes and admits to the final outcome. That it is unescapable. A person will do anything in that moment.

Why are yeh tellin me this?

Because I want you to know. Because I want you to hear me say it. Because I don't want you to think badly of me.

I do think badly of yeh, Fielding said. In fact, I haven't thought worse of anyone before.

Noon frowned.

I'm going to let you ask me one question, he said.

I don't want to ask yeh any questions.

That's not true, he said. All you have are questions.

Okay, Fielding said. He spit. Yeh always been this sick?

That's not a question.

I don't care.

Would you like to know my name?

No.

It's Michael. Michael Noon.

That's a borin name for someone as fucked-up as yeh are.

I was named after the archangel Michael. It was my mother's idea to name me that. She believed I would trample the devil. Just like the archangel.

Yeh must've been a big disappointment.

Noon smiled with his eyes.

My mother was a good mother until she wasn't. It broke my heart to do it. She was a good woman for the most part.

Stop talkin, Fielding said.

She would take me to the beach and bake me cookies, Noon said. She would read to me at night. On Christmas Eve she would brine a big turkey. We had a Christmas tree with twinkling lights. A very good mother. And then one day she was different. She never smiled anymore. She began talking to herself. I now know she'd had a psychotic break. One day when I was eleven I knocked over a glass of milk and to punish me she held my hand atop the stove-top burner. Another time after returning home late from school she held me down and poured motor oil into my mouth. Not exactly loving behavior. It only worsened, of course. She chided me every chance she got. Belittling me in public. Laughing at my follies. Naturally I began to hate her. On my sixteenth birthday she made me brush my teeth with a wire brush. Happy sweet sixteen. My mouth filled with blood.

I told her I would kill her that night, after she fell asleep. Can you guess what happened?

She fell asleep? Fielding said.

Noon laughed.

I kept her head in an old trunk that she loved. I had to get rid of it after a while because of the odor. That really broke my heart. Anyway, that was my first experience with vulnerability. Do you want to know how I killed her?

No.

I strangled her, Noon said. Watching the life drift out of her eyes, I felt this supreme sensation of connection. A moment I cherished. I have been searching for that sensation ever since.

If yer goin a shoot me just do it and get it over with. Yer voice is annoyin me.

I'm not going to shoot you, Mr Fielding. I'm going to give you a choice.

I've already made my choice.

Your choice is this: your friend can watch it all happen or I can shoot him first so he doesn't have to. Two choices. Quite fair.

My friend?

Fielding suddenly looked up. The blood spilled off his chin.

Oh, Noon said. Yes. I forgot to mention that. My apologies. Mr Batey decided to join us as well. Let me get him.

Noon stepped again into the darkness. Then the whine of caster wheels over cement. What appeared in the light seemed a crude imitation of Batey. Drugged and naked and his body painted. He was vigorously duct taped to the chair, his head secured so it could not fall forward. Wrapped within that tape was a set of antlers. Five points a side. The sight overwhelmed Fielding and he cried out and lunged forward. The handcuffs cut into the skin of his wrists.

Yeh sumbitch, Fielding said. He said, Yeh ain't walkin out of here alive.

Is that my choice, Mr Fielding? Is that the choice you are imposing? Stay or go?

Yeh don't get any choices anymore, Fielding said. The last choice yeh made was a long time ago.

Is that the truth?

That's the truth.

If so then I have chosen wisely. He outflung his arms like a faith healer. He said, If what you say is true and I am not leaving here alive then what a beautiful culmination. I suppose I ought to thank you.

Thank me?

Yes. You have made all of this possible. You and Mr Batey. Miss Eunice Thompson. We have all made our decisions and now we are all here together.

Let me ask yeh a question, Fielding said.

Of course.

Why those girls? Why them specifically?

Noon cocked his head.

That is your question? Of all the questions one can ask in their final moments, that is what you want an answer to?

Yes.

If you were standing before God in your hour of judgment, Noon said, this would be the question weighing most heavily?

Yeh sayin you're God?

No, Mr Fielding. Because God does not exist. But I do.

Yes, Fielding said. That's my question.

Okay, Noon said. He pulled a metal folding chair across the floor and stood it before Fielding. Then Noon sat down in it and placed his palms on his knees and inhaled deeply through his nose like he was about to give a monologue onstage.

Vulnerability, I suppose, Noon said. Their lives could fall no further it seemed. To fall any further would be death. Their entire existence was balanced on that fulcrum.

Not Eunice, Fielding said. She wasn't fallin at all.

Let's say she made a few bad decisions. Then what?

But she didn't, Fielding said. She was perfectly innocent.

Innocent. Please, Mr Fielding. You can't possibly be that naive.

What about the woman who worked at the shelter. Yeh kill her?

Yes.

How about those three people down in the cellar?

Yes.

What about the girl found on the beach? The ones found in the hills?

Noon raised his hands in a gesture of guilt.

Were there others?

Yes, there were others.

Why did yeh do what yeh did to them after they were dead?

You mean have sex with them? Noon said.

Yes.

Noon shrugged.

Nothing ever really dies, Mr Fielding. Just another state we enter. We become connected. They have a piece of me and I have a piece of them, to wit, an eternal connection, Mr Fielding.

Yeh know how fuckin nuts yeh sound?

Do you really want your last conversation to be this way? We have a chance to be civil here.

So yer goin a kill me too.

I'm sorry.

Go on then, Fielding said. Who is it goin a be first? Me or Dee over there?

Again, Noon said. That is your choice.

I guess the coward's way would be to go first. Not have to see it all.

You do not strike me as a coward, Mr Fielding.

No, Fielding said.

Is that your decision then? Think carefully.

That's my decision.

Noble, Noon said.

Noon stood. He raised the gun from his side. The barrel winked under the studio lights. He stepped toward Batey. He laid the cold barrel against Batey's temple. Levered back the hammer. Batey in his horrifying articles looked up at Noon and blinked a slow drugged blink. A seemingly final regard of the world. Of everything he had known and lived through and loved. It could all be pinched out like flipping a wall switch. Life's terminus in this dismal place. Then the shot popped and echoed off the bare concrete walls and rang through the expired pipes and fled finally down the hard corridors and then it was silent, and all the memories and malice and evil escaped from Noon along with fragments of bone and brain matter through a star-shaped hole just above his left eye as his legs gave out and he fell to the floor.

The pistol shot had frightened Fielding and when he opened his eyes again he saw Wilson standing there under the lights. Then Fielding saw an officer. Then another. Wilson said, Get some attention going on that girl. Then he went to Batey and said, And get some help going on him too.

Finally he came toward Fielding with a look on his face Fielding had never seen before. It was relief and it was horror and it was empathy and it was the most honest anyone had ever looked.

Wilson moved behind him and removed the handcuffs and then handed Fielding a handkerchief for his bloody wrists.

Fielding took the handkerchief and dabbed at the lacerations. Then he went to stand but he fell forward onto his hands and knees. Wilson went to him but Fielding waved him away.

You don't have to get up, Wilson said.

Yes I do, Fielding said.

He labored to his feet with Wilson holding out his hands like one would to a convalescent. He walked to where Noon lay dead. Simply looked down at him without saying a word. He looked at the girl who now had a blanket to salvage some dignity. She moaned oddly. Then he looked at Batey taped to the chair. Fielding limped to him and pulled the garish horns from the tape and lobbed them into the darkness. He kneeled before him. Batey's eyes rolled. Clouded. Glassed as marbles. Fielding said,

Can yeh hear me?

Batey blinked.

Fielding said: It's all over, partner.

Wilson said, The good news, if there can be any in any of this, is that he won't remember it.

Fielding stood. Turned to Wilson.

I will, he said. All of this. No matter how hard I try. This is forever.

Exhaustion and pain and the weight of it all caught up to him and Fielding collapsed and again it all went dark.

53

CHIEF PRICE WALKED INTO HIS NICE HOUSE HIGH ON THE BLUFF
that overlooked the water. Too nice a place for a lawman in a
town like Port Cook to be called honest. Granite countertops
and vaulted ceilings and an enormous hearth with a big fire
going. The house was well lit as if expecting guests. He had a
woman who cleaned and cooked for him. She lived in a small
cottage at the far end of the property. Surrounded by tall cedars
and out of sight.

He came in and hung his Stetson by the door. He unbuckled
the holster and hung the Desert Eagle near the hat. He came
into the large kitchen and called the woman's name. There was
no answer. He crossed the kitchen to the bar. Adjacent the bar
was a tall picture window and because all the light was gone
from the sky the window was a mirror. He regarded the image
therein for a moment. Then he made himself a drink.

The house was silent. He took his drink to the living room
and turned on the television and then sat down on the sofa. The
nightly news was on and what he saw he couldn't quite believe.
A shot of himself and the words SCANDAL and DISGRACED
written below. Heard the name Eunice Thompson and the
words *human trafficking* and he sat up and even though he knew
it was true he couldn't believe it. The anchor said a warrant had

been issued for his arrest. That Price was suspected in the disappearances of several young women. His ultimate involvement, the anchor said, was still unknown.

And just then Price heard through all the gilded silence the clear and undeniable wail of sirens. From where he sat he could see where the road cut the forest along the shoreline and wending up was a glittering parade of police cruisers. The mirrored image of himself was frozen in the glass. He knew how this would end. There could be only one way.

Price stood calmly from the sofa. He went to the bar where he finished his drink and then took down a rare favorite bottle and poured a tall one. He drank half of it and then looked at the amber liquid through the crystal. Then he drank the rest. He crossed the house toward the door and took down his Stetson and his holster and went back out into the living room and stood before the tall windows contemplating the man he saw standing there. The evils committed. The breath that had been squandered. He squared the hat on his head then he pulled the Desert Eagle from its holster and bit the barrel. Then he pulled the trigger.

54

WHEN FIELDING OPENED HIS EYES IT WAS TO A PRETTY NURSE
with dark brown hair and eyes the color of almonds.

Good morning, she said. Nice to see those eyes open for a
change.

Fielding's voice croaked. He cleared his throat. He tried
again.

Where am I?

St Peter's.

Did I die?

The nurse smiled.

You tried to, she said.

But yeh wouldn't let me.

A few of us wouldn't let you.

He looked out the hospital window. It was sunny and the sky
was blue. Seagulls wheeling about in all that blue like scraps of
bleached paper. There was water in the distance and beyond that
mountains the color of coal.

So where is St Peter's?

Seattle, the nurse said.

How'd I get to Seattle?

An ambulance.

She was going about her tasks. Talking as she worked. She changed a bag of clear liquid in his IV drip.

What's that yer givin me?

Morphine.

It's doin the trick.

No pain?

Fielding shook his head.

Floatin on air, sweetheart.

Good.

What's yer name?

Maddie.

That's a nice name.

My parents think so too.

How old are yeh?

Twenty-four.

Twenty-four.

Yes sir.

That's young.

She gave him a look.

I didn't mean *too* young, he said. I didn't mean to imply yeh don't know what yer doin.

She smiled. Her smile was warm. When she looked at him the whites of her eyes reminded him of the moon and how bright the moon looks when it comes out from behind a cloud.

So you're the one to thank, she said.

Thank? Thank for what?

You put an end to it all? That's what they're saying anyway.

Not me.

But you had a part in it.

I wouldn't say that either.

What would you say then?

I would say I was in the wrong place at the wrong time.

If that's true then he'd still be out there. Thank you, she said. I guess that's what I'm trying to say.

Can I tell yeh somethin?

Sure.

My wife and I were married for forty-nine years.

That's a long time.

Yes it is, Fielding said. Not long enough though.

That's sweet.

Yeh married?

No.

Got a sweetheart?

Yeah.

What's he do?

He wants to be a writer.

A writer?

Uh-huh.

He any good?

Yeah.

Not much money in that.

That doesn't matter.

Yes it does.

No it doesn't.

Why not?

Because he loves me.

That makes sense. Yeh say that yet? The words.

The *I love you* words?

All three of em.

Yeah.

Yeh mean it?

Yeah. We mean it.

That's nice. It's the only thing that's really worth a damn.

What was your wife's name?

Sara.

I like that name.

So do I.

They heard a knock at the door. A soft tapping. They turned to look. It was Wilson. Wilson smiled as though he was unsure if he should even be smiling. He entered the room. The nurse said, I'll be right outside if you need me.

Wilson nodded at her as she passed him. He stepped toward the bed.

How you doing?

I don't know yet, Fielding said.

I spoke with the doctor.

What'd the doc have to say?

Says you're recovering well.

What does that mean?

Means you're recovering well.

How about Thompson? Dee? How they doin?

Fine, Wilson said. Both are fine. The girl's going to have a long road, but at least she's safe.

Doesn't seem real, does it.

No, Wilson said. Rarely does.

Thanks for comin when yeh did.

I tried to get there sooner.

Fielding shrugged.

How'd yeh even know where to go?

That tape. Watched it till I nearly wore it out. Then I went to talk to Dee about it. His wife was there and told me you and him went down south together. So I got in the car.

You were there on a hunch?

Yes.

And all them officers?

Hunch.

Good hunch.

Got Price in on it too.

The chief?

Yes. He was all tangled up in it. He was trafficking minors for this Noon guy. Found him dead in his house. Self-inflicted gunshot wound.

Shot himself?

Yeah.

I'll be danged.

Yeah.

How about them three in the cellar? Fielding asked. What was with all that?

Distraction, Wilson said. A game for him.

To throw us off?

No, Wilson said. Just a game. Pure amusement.

Shoulda told yeh about that tape sooner, Fielding said. Sorry about that.

That's okay. I pieced things together. It worked out. That's all that matters now.

Fielding turned his head to the window. Looked out at all the blue sky. He said, Wish I could unsee it all. Every little piece of it. Just wipe it clean. But yeh can't do that, can yeh?

No you can't.

Fielding turned back and Wilson held out his hand and Fielding shook it.

For the sake of the world, Wilson said, I hope this is goodbye.

Yeah, Fielding said. Let's stay strangers for a while.

Wilson nodded and left the room and Fielding knew he would never see him again. The nurse came back in. She said, Friend of yours?

Yeah, Fielding said. Barely even know the guy.

She came over and checked his vitals.

This drip stand have wheels? Fielding asked.

Wheels?

Yeh mind if we go for a little walk?

You feel up to it?

Yeh'll be the second to know if I ain't.

She helped him out of the bed. He put his feet into a cheap pair of hospital slippers. He held the drip stand for balance.

Okay? she asked.

Think so.

They walked slowly out of the room. Down the hall. They passed open doors with patients watching television. Patients asleep. Passed patients in the hall stretching their legs just like him. He was reading the names on the doors. When he got to BATEY he stopped. The door was open a crack. Fielding knocked on it.

It's open, Batey called.

He turned when Fielding entered and just sat there shaking his head. Fielding found a chair near the bed.

I'll give you boys some time, the nurse said.

When she left Batey and Fielding stared at each other for a long time. Then Fielding nodded and shuffled over to the window.

Wilson come to see yeh?

Batey nodded. You?

Yeah.

It's over, isn't it?

Yeah, Fielding said. It's over.

I don't remember any of it, Batey said.

Wilson said yeh wouldn't.

He started to tell me, Batey said, but I stopped him. Told him so long as the girl was okay and healthy and nothing happened to her then I don't want to know.

Fielding nodded.

How are you? Batey asked.

Fielding shrugged.

I feel like I've just woken up from a dream. Like all the rain and darkness and all of it was just a dream.

He looked out the window.

Has the sun ever looked this bright to yeh? he asked.

Mighty bright.

What do yeh think is over those mountains there? Fielding said.

I suspect the Pacific Ocean.

And what's after that?

After the Pacific?

Yeah.

I suppose it's Asia.

And then what?

After Asia?

Yeah.

Is this a geography lesson?

What's after Asia?

Europe, I guess.

And then the Atlantic, Fielding said.

Then the Atlantic.

Then yeh hit America again.

The Big Apple, Batey said.

Yeah, Fielding said. And past New York is Pennsylvania and Ohio and then Indiana and Illinois. And then yer back to Iowa.

You can see all that out that window?

I came out here because all I could see back there was Sara. All I wanted to do was run away from it all. Sara's memory. That whole life. But that's just it, partner. There's too much of her back there. There's too much I left behind. I left because everything I saw or heard or did reminded me of her and to be reminded like that, that intensely, every second of every day felt like too much. But now I realize that's not a thing. Being reminded too much. If it's a toss-up between being constantly reminded or forgettin her altogether, I'll take the misery of rememberin. The memory of her might as well be that sun. Shines that bright.

Fielding pointed a weary finger. He squinted one eye. Tapped the tip of his finger against the plate glass several times.

And without the sun, he said, yeh ain't got a thing.

We'd hate to see you go, Batey said. If that's what you're getting at.

I ain't goin, Fielding said. Not really. No one is ever really gone.

Batey watched Fielding's back. Out beyond the window seagulls were cast about. Watercolor images of the birds on a stretched blue sheet of cotton.

EPILOGUE

(1994)

THE AIR AT THAT HOUR WAS WARM AND HUMID AND THERE
were a few goldfinches on the feeders. It was Saturday night in
Oscar, Iowa, and stock cars could be heard faintly in the distance. Through the elms and the darker green oaks the lime-
stone bluffs flashed the last of the day's purple light. The fireflies
had come out early and were winking on and off.

Fielding walked out of the house and onto the porch. The
screen door snapped shut behind him. He could hear the crick-
ets out in the tall grass and the cicadas like sirens in the trees.
The air was robust and he had forgotten how sweet it smelled.
Out past the yard the horses were feeding on the good grass in
the pasture. Fielding clicked his tongue and both Snake and
Buckshot raised up. They tossed their tails.

Fielding stepped off the porch. The cut grass was going wet
with dew. He crossed the yard to the fence and the animals came
to meet him. Buckshot trailed Snake and then got distracted
by something and dropped his head and began to eat again.
Through the bluestem Snake walked toward him. His wild
pattern and his wild mane looked not like a horse but like the
idea of a horse that a child imagines when told a story. Snake

dropped his face over the top fence board and allowed Fielding to rub his nose.

Yeh seem in good spirits tonight, Fielding said. I told yeh you'd like it here.

And then Fielding looked to his right and the young face of Sara was looking back at him.

ACKNOWLEDGMENTS

This book is for Harry Kirchner, and for good reason. A writer of fiction endures more rejection than any sane person should, but he said yes and then went to battle for me. Had he said no, I'd be someone different. I've said it before, but he changed my life, and I'm not sure how other writers share their gratitude for their editor, so I'll simply say: I love the hell out of you, Harry. Till the bitter end, my friend.

Dan Smetanka needs to be thanked profusely. He is tough and cutting and quick and wickedly smart and deftly observant and wields tough love like no other. I'm certain he could make most of the guys in the shipyard cry if he wanted. Every word of criticism and insight was precise, and when he finally passed along his compliments I teared up. I'm humbled by you, Dan. Thanks for not giving up on me.

I need to thank Glen Chamberlain yet again. Without her my life would be a very lonely thing. I love you, I love you, I love you. Tom Barrett has to be included in that love. He shared his wisdom of horses with me, taught me how to rope (finally), showed me how to tie a hackamore. There are few men like him in the world.

Thanks to my mother and father, who still read every word I write. Thanks to Jenny Schumacher for her grace. Thanks to DB and Little Red, for clouting me on Broadway—you two make life better. For Andrew and Rialin, two people who make me better. For Abe and Abbie and their early reads and encouragement (and read aloud on rainy Northwest nights, I might add).

And for Don Mancini, and one hell of a good elk-hunting story. I'd be a lousy person without you all.

I want to thank everyone at Counterpoint who worked hard on every aspect of this book. To: Laura Berry, Olenka Burgess, Barrett Briske, Wah-Ming Chang, Andrea Córdova, tracy danes, Rachel Fershleiser, Megan Fishmann, Vanessa Genao, Madelyn Lindquist, Yukiko Tominaga, and Kira Weiner. When I was on book tour for *The Houseboat* and my boys got COVID, everyone working on that book wrote to me and expressed their concerns and sympathies. I'll never forget that.

A huge debt of gratitude goes to Al Heathcock. He's a hero of mine and has been for a long time, and it's more than a little surreal to have his appreciation for this book. Next time I'm in town, dinner and drinks on me, pal.

If my heart could be halved, one piece would go to Tøren, the other to Anders. There aren't enough words in the world to tell you how much I love you. You boys are the best.

And ultimately, as it seems to be time and time again, for Madeline. You have the ability to arrest time and let us slow together. I've seen the stars swirl in your wake. The world has never looked brighter than after you've passed through it.